The Lady of the Lake

The Lady of the Lake

JEAN MENZIES

MICHAEL  JOSEPH

PENGUIN MICHAEL JOSEPH

UK | USA | Canada | Ireland | Australia
India | New Zealand | South Africa

Penguin Michael Joseph is part of the Penguin Random House group of companies
whose addresses can be found at global.penguinrandomhouse.com

Penguin Random House UK
One Embassy Gardens, 8 Viaduct Gardens, London SW11 7BW

penguin.co.uk

First published 2025

002

Set in 13.4/16pt Garamond MT
Typeset by Falcon Oast Graphic Art Ltd
Printed and bound in Great Britain by Clays Ltd, Elcograf S.p.A.

The authorized representative in the EEA is Penguin Random House Ireland,
Morrison Chambers, 32 Nassau Street, Dublin D02 YH68

A CIP catalogue record for this book is available from the British Library

HARDBACK ISBN: 978–0–241–67569–4
TRADE PAPERBACK ISBN: 978–0–241–67570–0

Penguin Random House is committed to a sustainable future
for our business, our readers and our planet. This book is made from
Forest Stewardship Council® certified paper

This book is for Chris, my real-life love story.

Content warnings: Death in childbirth, death of parental figures, grief, sexual harassment.

A Reading Playlist

'Road to Camelot' – Enaid & Diane Arkenstone
'Maid o' the Loch' – Eddi Reader
'labour' – Paris Paloma
'Castles' – Freya Ridings
'A Fairy's Love Song' – Jean Luc Lenoir
'Under a Violet Moon' – Blackmore's Night
'Witch's Rune' – S. J. Tucker
'Savage Daughter' – Sarah Hester Ross
'Landscape with a Fairy' – aspidistrafly
'I'd Like to Walk Around in Your Mind' – Vashti Bunyan
'Runaway' – AURORA
'Would That I' – Hozier
'Far Across the Land' – Eurielle & Ryan Louder
'Graceland Too' – Phoebe Bridgers
'Same Old Energy' – Kiki Rockwell
'Heartbeats' – José González
'Corals Under the Sun' – Yehezkel Raz & Sivan Talmor
'Ragged Wood' – Fleet Foxes
'Weaver' – Heather Dale
'Mud' – Dune Moss
'Butterfly Water' – Pastelle & My City Glory

Cast of Characters

Principal Characters

Viviane – Princess of Dál Riada, fostered at Camelot
Morgan – Princess of Camelot, half-sister of Arthur
Arthur – Prince of Camelot, half-brother of Morgan
Guinevere – Princess of Cameliard, fostered at Camelot
Merlin – Sorcerer in the service of King Uther

Kings and Queens

Queen Igraine – Queen of Camelot, mother of Arthur, stepmother of Morgan
King Uther – King of Camelot, father of Arthur and Morgan
Queen Breage – Queen of Cameliard, mother of Guinevere
King Leodegrance – King of Cameliard, father of Guinevere
King Bagdemagus – King of Gorre, father of Maleagant
Queen Malinda – Queen of Dál Riada, stepmother of Viviane
Queen Elaine – Queen of Benoic
King Ban – King of Benoic
King Nentres – King of Garlot

Queen Anna – Queen of Orkney
King Lott – King of Orkney

Named Knights

Pelleas
Kay
Accolon
Lancelot
Gawain
Constantine
Meliadus

Everyone Else

Mistress Mae – Viviane, Morgan and Guinevere's tutor
Maleagant – Prince of Gorre
Diana – Roman goddess of the hunt
Faunus – Roman god of dreams
Adhan – an ordinary woman
Alrec – a somewhat hopeless guard
Beatrice – Guinevere's lady's maid
Clarine – a servant at Camelot
Fodor – a fairy and flautist
Galahad – a baby
Luar – a horse
Wellefed – a dog

The Lady of the Lake

Prologue

One step further, then another, and I could feel the water lapping at my waist. This was the point where the silt bed dropped off, where, were I to walk any deeper, my feet would lose purchase and I would be forced to swim, or sink. My toes curled possessively around the tiny rocks that littered the ground as I paused to look out across the loch, taking in its great expanse. When I glanced down, the dim haze of dawn lit my path just enough that I could make out the shadow of countless tadpoles scurrying away from my intrusion. Meanwhile, two lone swans floated by, barely registering my presence, so used to it by now were they. This was what I would miss the most.

And then I sank.

I dove from the precipice and let the loch swallow me, sinking deeper and deeper beneath its surface before finally, I began to swim. Twisting and turning in its arms, I revelled in the water's cool embrace. I was home. As I reeled, I watched a shoal of pike meander past before deciding to tag along behind them. Together we swam through the watery depths, kelp occasionally tickling at my feet as I passed by. Down here I was free. Free from austere fathers and absent stepmothers. Down here I was my own lord and master. I could go wherever and do whatever I wanted. Down here I was not alone. I had the fish and tadpoles as my friends. Down here I could still feel the memory of my mother in the water's embrace. And down here I could pretend that the time had not come to say goodbye.

ONE

Camelot: nothing could have been more in contrast with the loch I had left behind than the looming structure laid out before me. Even from the confines of our carriage it was an imposing sight. While I had heard stories of the castle built wholly from stone by the Britons, I had never in my wildest imagination pictured anything quite like this. Bricks stacked upon bricks to create walls that not even a giant could scale. Colossal turrets ran along the outer walls, with two spiralling higher than any others from its centre. Even the rolling hills and wide expanse of green that surrounded the structure could not take away from its severity.

'Viviane, inside,' snapped my chaperone, tugging at my shoulder so that I was forced to sit back in my seat. Evidently lolling from carriage windows was not the kind of ladylike behaviour she expected of me. Certainly not today at least.

For today was the day. The day of my fifteenth birthday and the day I would be sent far away from the place I had always called home. Although perhaps it was wrong to call it that now. For as long as I could remember I had known this day would come. I had been informed by each nurse or lady's maid in turn that this place was only temporary, that I was intended for the court of King Uther. My presence at his court would foster a bond of kinship between my own father's kingdom and the Pendragons. I would be raised alongside the young princess and her brother, the future king of the Britons. I would be educated in the manner of the noblest of ladies. I would receive introductions to the bravest lords and knights from Dál Riada to Cameliard. I would be a useful tool in their game of courts and kings.

'You must be on your best behaviour from now on,' my chaperone hectored.

A tiny part of me was tempted to snap back; I was always on my best behaviour, wasn't I? Quiet and obedient, rarely speaking unless I was spoken to.

'That means no wandering off or disappearing for hours on end.' Oh right, that. 'You're a guest here and you mustn't do anything to embarrass your father's house.'

A guest. There it was. The reminder that Camelot was not, in fact, my home. Nor would it ever be, unless I married its future king.

Thankfully, I was saved from any more kind words of advice by our driver, who chose that moment to bring the horses to a halt. As the door to the carriage swung open and I was pushed forward by my companion, I was confronted by the reality of my arrival.

A not insignificant crowd milled around outside the front of the castle, presumably having gathered at the sound or sight of our approach. Some were clearly guards and servants but among them I thought I could make out three well-dressed youths close to my own age. Two girls and a boy. Before I could fully absorb their appearances, however, I was forced down the steps of the carriage, an armour-clad arm outstretched to assist my descent. Somewhere in the distance I thought I heard a voice announce my name, but I was too focused on not tumbling inelegantly on to the cobblestones in front of me to identify its owner.

The next thing I knew there was a grey-haired woman in front of me, speaking rapidly, a wide smile of welcome on her handsome face. Maura, had she said her name was? My ears were abuzz and her exact words passed me by. Before I could find my own tongue, however, the older woman – Mae, that was it – proceeded to usher forth the two girls I had seen from the carriage.

'Allow me to introduce Princess Morgan of house Pendragon and Princess Guinevere of Cameliard. And this,' she gestured forward a red-headed boy, 'of course, is Prince Arthur.'

Prince Arthur: future king of the Britons. He was of a height with myself, his shoulders pushed back and his head held high: a young man entirely aware of his own import-ance. As I stared into his green eyes, I wondered what I was supposed to be feeling. Because I didn't imagine I was feel-ing any of it. This boy might be my husband one day, yet I experienced nary a flutter of the stomach nor a quickening of my pulse, only a residual queasiness from the carriage ride.

'Princess,' Arthur gave a curt nod of greeting that snapped me out of my reverie, his expression unimpressed. Was my mouth open? Belatedly, I dipped low in the deep curtsy I had been taught, hoping the extent to which my legs were trembling was disguised by my long skirts.

'I do hope you will be a more interesting classmate than Guinevere – she is such a bore.'

My head turned to look at the figure on Arthur's right. Princess Morgan was the taller of the two girls, dark hair hanging loose about her face in contrast with her companion's tightly braided crown. Meanwhile her piercing green eyes, the same as her brother's, seemed to burrow into me, and I had to resist patting my own golden locks to check their travel braid was still in place.

'Your Highness, please,' squeaked Mae.

'Well, it's true,' muttered Morgan, rolling her eyes. 'Although I suppose you'll be just as busy competing for my brother's hand.' She raised an eyebrow, testing me, figuring out if she could bait me.

Shifting my gaze, I glanced behind the older woman, at Guinevere who had remained standing a few steps back from the others. The younger girl seemed unperturbed by Morgan's words, or she was at least doing an excellent job of hiding her reaction. In fact, I couldn't make out any particular emotion on her features at all. She simply stood straight-backed, hands clasped at her front, watching demurely as the taller girl disparaged her.

'Perhaps Lady Guinevere reserves her most interesting topics of discussion for those she finds more engaging conversationalists.' The first words out of my mouth and they were sharp and goading. This was why I usually kept my mouth shut, especially when I was both travel-weary and more than a little nervous, a deadly combination. I had hoped that I might make friends at Camelot, but maybe there was a reason I had spent so much of my life thus far alone.

While it might not have been the smartest thing to say, the look of surprise it elicited from Morgan was gratifying.

'Well, so far you're certainly more entertaining at least.' She cast her eyes across my face, paying more attention this time, measuring me up with her gaze. I wondered how I had fared. After a moment she seemed to come to some sort of decision and, moving to my side, she threaded her long arm through my stiff one. 'Let me show you around.'

This didn't feel like friendship, not that I was an expert, but for the time being I would have to take what I could get. I had not failed to notice that the king and queen were absent from my welcoming committee, but I sensed there were still more eyes on me than just those I could meet. Unnerved, I let my gaze roam the towering walls of Camelot until finally they alighted on a shadowy face peering down from above. Although their features were obscured by the limitations of my vantage point, I thought they might belong to a man.

'Who is that?' I asked Morgan, pointing towards the window in question.

'Who's who?'

And sure enough, when I looked back from Morgan's face, the figure, whoever he had been, was gone.

TWO

The towering stone walls of Camelot were not the only thing differentiating it from my father's home. Within three weeks at the castle I had already spent more time in the company of others than I might have done in six months at Dál Riada. My new home was both bigger and busier than I was used to, with servants and lords seemingly constantly coming and going for one reason or another. Meanwhile, I spent most days in lessons with Mistress Mae, occupied by tasks suitable for both my station and sex.

There was weaving, and sewing, and scripture, followed the next day by more weaving, and sewing, and scripture. Morgan and Guinevere were my fellow pupils while Arthur was off doing whatever young princes were trained to do. Since the first day I had only seen my potential husband during evening meals where we were typically separated by numerous bodies, or Sunday services in the castle chapel where we sat in silence while the priest sermoned in Latin. I should probably have been disappointed there were not more opportunities to spend time with Arthur. Yet, every time I dug deep for the emotions I imagined my father and stepmother would have liked me to have, I only found apprehension instead.

It was all, I hated to admit, rather dull. In Dál Riada I had been free to roam the grounds and pass my hours swimming in the loch to my heart's desire. Well, free in that no one had paid much attention to me. A laxity that wasn't entirely absent from Camelot either. Despite being tasked with our education, Mistress Mae often disappeared for hours on end, leaving us to our own devices. Only, now I had classmates, and I wasn't sure how either of them would react to my wandering off.

'This is insufferable,' groaned Morgan, throwing her embroidery to the ground. I could feel Guinevere flinch on my other side. 'I am tired of wielding needles while Arthur learns to brandish a sword.'

'You wouldn't survive a day in a monastery, Princess.' I looked up, surprised to hear these words from Guinevere who I had noticed generally preferred to ignore Morgan's not infrequent outbursts.

'You speak as though you have experience?'

'That's where she was before she came here,' Morgan interjected.

'You were?'

'Yes.' Guinevere nodded, not taking her eyes from her wool. 'Until I was thirteen.'

'God, I shudder to think,' said Morgan, making an unpleasant face in Guinevere's direction.

'You shouldn't take the Lord's name in vain,' Guinevere murmured, although she didn't look particularly perturbed. I supposed she had two more years' experience with the daughter of Camelot than I.

'What about you?' Morgan transferred her attention to me. 'Are not the northern kingdoms all overrun by pagans?'

'My father is a Christian, if that's what you mean.' I shrugged. 'But yes, there are still those who worship the old gods among our people.'

'My mother was pagan.' Morgan's tone changed to one of pride, and I thought I detected a straightening in her spine as she made this declaration.

The princess was almost two years older than Arthur and Guinevere, who I had learnt were both of an age with myself. She was also taller, louder, bolder, and just more of everything than anyone I had ever met; and part of me was delighted by it. 'Queen Igraine is pagan?' I asked.

'The queen is a follower of the true faith like the king.' It was Guinevere's turn to answer on behalf of her school-mate. 'Our gracious princess's mother was King Uther's first wife.'

Morgan's title did not sound entirely reverential coming from Guinevere's mouth. It was clear Morgan heard it too, for the next thing I knew she had kicked the younger girl's chair before rising from her own. Guinevere, however, ignored her and simply spoke her next words to me in a quieter tone. 'The previous queen died when Morgan was a babe.'

I shifted in my seat so I could look at Morgan directly and thought I caught an unfamiliar expression on her face: like a lost child, her usual confidence temporarily faltered. 'I didn't realize.' I was uncomfortable with the fact that it was Guinevere who had shared such a personal piece of information with me rather than Morgan herself, and a part of me wanted to make up for my possessing it. 'I also lost my mother before I could know her.'

It was and wasn't true. My mother had died before I turned four years old, yet I had a few hazy memories of warm afternoons spent submerged in the nearby loch. There she wore a smile I only remembered from beneath the water, where rather than swim she seemed to dance in its embrace.

'Yes, well.' The brief flash of sadness that I thought I had seen on Morgan's face disappeared quicker than I could snap my fingers. 'In that case, we should make the most of having no mothers to scold us for not behaving like proper young ladies.' I couldn't decide whether the way her eyes seemed to light up as she spoke terrified or excited me in that moment. 'I for one would like to know what Arthur gets up to when we're stuck in here weaving and citing psalms.'

'You mean, abandon the schoolroom? What if Mistress Mae comes back?' I was torn between my desperation to escape the confines of our classroom and recognizing how delicate my new position at court could yet prove to be.

'You can't be serious, Morgan,' Guinevere protested.

Morgan, however, was already halfway to the door, only pausing to cast a withering look over her shoulder. 'Well, if she returns you two can explain why the young princess of the house has disappeared, and why her companions are here without her.'

It was weak blackmail material. Mistress Mae was well aware of Morgan's temperamental nature – I'd witnessed enough of their altercations in the past few weeks – and I doubted our tutor would hold her absence against us. But then maybe I wasn't worried enough because Guinevere's expression had certainly paled at Morgan's threat. And maybe it didn't matter. Maybe this was just the excuse I needed. Straightening my shoulders, I rose from my seat, discarding my spool, and met Morgan's eyes. 'Where are we going?'

Together, we fled the room, Morgan taking the lead while Guinevere and I had to practically gallop to keep up.

'Arthur usually takes his morning lessons up here,' Morgan explained as she led us both to a small staircase tucked inside one of the stone turrets.

'Won't his tutor be angry if we interrupt Arthur's lessons?' whispered Guinevere.

'Not if we have good reason.' Morgan's eyes gleamed in the dim light of the stairwell. 'One of us just needs to tell him that Mistress Mae sent us, something about being called away on an emergency and needing someone else to take over our lessons for the day.' She looked at Guinevere.

'I'm not going to lie for you!'

'It's not for me, it's for all of us!'

'I'll do it,' I found myself offering before Guinevere could respond. What possessed me I wasn't certain, but it might have had something to do with the resulting grin that spread across Morgan's face. Maybe, just maybe, I wanted to prove myself?

Moving to the front of our small band, I took the lead as we climbed the remaining stairs to the top of the tower. There I was met by a tall wooden door with iron fixtures. For a split second I considered turning on my heel and running straight back to my tapestry, but then I thought of the two girls standing eagerly behind me. A quick look over my shoulder and I caught Guinevere's attempts to smooth her skirt, all of a sudden more concerned with her appearance than her rule-breaking. Morgan, meanwhile, simply raised an eyebrow, and I wondered which royal sibling I was more interested in impressing. Either way, I knew what I had to do. Straightening my spine, I raised a fist and brought it down firmly on the oak panel before me.

'Come in,' came a voice that sounded a lot younger than I had expected. Cautiously pushing the door open, I peered inside the large circular chamber, expecting to find Arthur's tutor staring back at me. To my surprise, however, there was only Arthur.

'Lady Viviane,' Arthur frowned, craning his neck to see beyond my shoulder, 'Guin, Mog, what are you doing here?'

Morgan pushed to the front when she heard her name. 'Where is your tutor?'

'How should I know? He disappears once or twice a week and leaves me here to get on with whatever history book he's got me reading.' Arthur shrugged. 'That still doesn't answer my question though.'

'We're here to learn like boys for the day.' Morgan grinned.

'I can't imagine this is much more interesting than whatever Mistress Mae has you doing.' Arthur waved his book in the air.

'No swords or daggers we could take for a spin?' Morgan tried, making Guinevere go pale.

'This isn't the armoury, Mog,' Arthur rolled his eyes.

While the two siblings continued to squabble, I moved towards the narrow window on the opposite side of the room from the door. Gazing out, I was struck by just how high up we were, and I felt a flurry of nerves in my stomach. The sight was breathtaking.

The castle grounds sprawled beneath me, countless courtyards teeming with ant-size figures, all scurrying around occupied by their various activities. I could see two men practising their swordsmanship in faux battle while spectators cheered from the sidelines. Servants moved swanlike through the throngs of people, minds set on their next task, while others paused to chat awhile with friends or family whom they spotted along the way. Guards milled around on top of the fortification walls, occasionally shouting at one another or adjusting their armour. Beyond the fortifications roamed flocks of sheep and the occasional horse attended to by the king's groomsmen. And further afield still, densely packed trees stretched out against the horizon as the landscape rose towards the skies. One thing in particular caught my attention, though, and my heart thumped harder in my chest at the sight.

'Is that a loch?' I asked, interrupting the others' conversation.

'A lake,' Guinevere corrected, but nodded all the same. Meanwhile, I was aware of Morgan's curious gaze studying me from across the room.

'So back to my point,' Arthur insisted, raising his voice to be heard over our conversation. 'What are you going to do now?'

'Why, we're going to the lake, of course.' Morgan smiled. 'Want to come?'

THREE

Arthur, it turned out, was not difficult to convince. And once the young prince was on board, Guinevere's earlier objections to adventure seemed to disappear. So down the stairs and along the corridors we ran, a newfound exhilaration coursing through my veins. It seemed it was about as easy for noble children to go where they pleased at Camelot as it was in Dál Riada. Without our tutors watching over us, simply proceeding with confidence ensured no one else wanted to be the one to question our purpose.

We were well on our way to the outer walls when Guinevere stopped in her tracks. For a moment I thought she was backing out, as it seemed did Morgan, whose expression immediately grew angry. Before Morgan could rebuke her, however, Guinevere held a finger up to her lips and gestured for us to listen. Sure enough, without the steady beat of our footfall I could hear a stream of soft squeaks coming from behind the nearest doorway.

'What is that?' Arthur whispered to Guinevere, who simply shrugged.

'Well, one of us better take a look. Somebody might need our help!' Morgan declared before turning to me.

Great. She was testing me. I had volunteered once

before, but would I do it again? Before I could lay my hand on the door handle, however, Guinevere had laid her hand on mine.

'My turn.' She smiled softly and allowed me to step back.

Guinevere opened the door the tiniest of cracks, not enough that any of us could see beyond her shoulder, and let it close almost as quickly.

'Well, what is it?' Morgan pressed.

'It's Mistress Mae,' Guinevere's cheeks had turned red, 'and she's fine.'

The rest of our journey was a short one. A few ducked heads and hurried footsteps through the bustling court-yards later and we finally reached an unattended stretch of wall where Morgan held up a hand for us to pause. I frowned but said nothing. Did Morgan expect us to scale the wall? There was no way we were getting to the lake if so. To my surprise, however, Morgan pulled from the folds of her dress a strip of metal and held it aloft for us all to see. It was, I realized, an iron door handle. Fascinated, I watched as Morgan lowered her hand and brought the handle to the wall as if there was a door before her. And suddenly there was. What had previously been uninterrupted rows of bricks now had a small wooden door just like those inside the castle.

'You used magic!' I exclaimed.

'She stole magic, you mean,' Arthur frowned. 'That belongs to Merlin.'

'Well, he's not using it.' Morgan shrugged, pulling open the door and ushering us through.

'Who's Merlin?' I asked as we walked, glancing back in

disbelief to the spot where the door had now vanished and been replaced with stone once more.

'My father's sorcerer,' answered Arthur. 'He's away from court at the moment, on some sort of errand I believe, but he's my father's closest advisor.' Turning to Morgan he added, 'And I don't think he will appreciate having his possessions looted while he's away.'

'He shouldn't have made it so easy then, should he?' Morgan laughed before breaking into a run.

As I watched Morgan sprint ahead, that was when I heard it – the gentle murmur of water disturbed only by the tiniest of animals and birds. It wasn't a rushing river or babbling burn, but the mild hum of a lake confined on all sides – a sound I had always been surprised no one else could hear. Then I saw it. Behind a cluster of trees that had obscured its presence, a lake spread out, covering a vast area of land that exceeded even the size of the loch in Dál Riada. As soon as I laid eyes on the sparkling surface, something within me began to loosen that I hadn't even realized needed to be unwound. It was in that moment I felt, for the first time, as if Camelot could really be home.

Resting on the shore of the lake, letting the water slide between my toes, it was as though I could finally breathe, for the first time since I'd taken my seat in the carriage at Dál Riada.

'How strange,' murmured Guin, leaning over my shoulder, 'it's like the water is rising up to meet the grass.'

She was right. It was subtle, but the water was indeed lapping at the ground, occasionally tickling my ankles, slow ripples rolling across the surface from the centre to the very spot where I sat. Instinctively I withdrew my feet, splashing myself in my haste and bringing my knees up to my chest.

'Maybe there are fish down there.' I made a face, pretending to be momentarily disgusted at the thought.

'Hmm, maybe.' Guin nodded slowly but she didn't immediately take her eyes from the spot where my feet had been.

'Ugh, I wish I'd pinned my hair back this morning,' I moaned, pretending to be annoyed by the straggling tresses that fell in front of my face.

'Oh, here.' Guinevere finally turned away from the lake and pulled a finely wrought pin from her own hair. 'I always have spares.' She gave me a small smile as she pushed the pin into my hands. 'Keep it. A belated welcome gift.'

'Thank you.' I smiled back, a tiny twinge of guilt marring the pleasure I felt at Guinevere's words.

'I'm bored!' Morgan groaned, throwing the flower she had been twirling between her fingers at Guin, and I found myself relieved when Guin diverted her gaze from me to her.

'I'm shocked.' The dry tone of Arthur's sarcasm made me chuckle aloud, earning me a grin from the prince and a glare from Morgan respectively.

'Well, perhaps if you were more entertaining company, brother, I wouldn't be so bored all the time.'

'You could argue that finding oneself bored so often might be more of a reflection on the person who is bored.' Guin's response turned my chuckle into a splutter. Those were fighting words.

'We've not been here long.' I didn't mean to side with

anyone; I was merely hoping to spend a little longer lazing by the lake. I realized I could hardly strip off my clothes and take a dip with Arthur here, but it was enough for now to simply be by the water. Morgan, however, did not take my response as such.

'Well, Lady Viviane, you're Arthur's latest companion – surely the future queen of Camelot could suggest some way to pass the time?'

I avoided both Guin and Arthur's glares and kept my gaze focused on Morgan. The princess had chosen her words carefully – perfectly picked to remind me of my place – and my first instinct was to tell Morgan to entertain herself. I bit my tongue, however; I still had hopes of fitting in at Camelot after all. I just wasn't sure how.

'We could play a game?' I finally suggested, hoping I wasn't giving away my social inexperience. Morgan raised an eyebrow at me.

'I'm not a child.' Arthur's tone was now one of indignation.

'Adults play games too,' Guin pointed out and I gave her a grateful smile.

'What, like a game of dice?' Arthur looked horrified at the thought. 'Because I don't exactly think you three would make very good wrestling partners.'

'I like the idea,' Morgan interjected. I was starting to realize that as sure as a cat will try to swipe a bird, Morgan would, without fail, always choose to do the thing her brother wouldn't. 'But instead of an ordinary game, it should be a contest.'

'We don't even know what the game is yet.' Arthur rolled his eyes.

'What kind of contest?' Guin looked worried.

Morgan meanwhile just looked back to me, as if I was meant to miraculously have the answer. *Well*, I thought, *may as well give it a try*. 'A scavenger hunt?' I offered. Morgan clapped her hands together, a look of glee spreading across her face. I was already regretting my suggestion.

'A scavenger hunt! It's perfect. We shall split into teams of two and the first team to find everything on the list shall be declared the winner.'

'And what exactly will we be scavenging for?' Arthur looked sceptical but his question told me his interest was piqued.

Morgan stared back at all three of us thoughtfully for a brief moment before answering. 'A guard's helmet, a jug of ale, and . . . and a surprise. But it has to be interesting. Nothing boring.' She narrowed her eyes at Guin, clearly still bitter about her earlier jibe. 'First team to bring all three items to my chambers wins.' Morgan turned to look back at me, a smile I couldn't quite read dancing across her face. Before she could add anything else, however, Arthur spoke up.

'In that case, Viviane will be on my team.' The prince didn't even glance my way.

But Guinevere did, confusion and then hurt flitting across her features.

It didn't take a genius to understand what was happening, and it had nothing to do with me. Not really. Not in anything more than that I was new and sparkly. Nevertheless, I knew what my stepmother would have told me: this is an opportunity. Arthur's interest could be fleeting, or it could be something more long-term, if only I were to hold it.

The thing was, I wasn't sure I wanted Arthur's attention, no matter why my father had sent me here. Guin, however, was enraptured by the prince, or at least more committed to her family's intentions than I. So, while Arthur's declaration seemed innocent enough on the surface, I knew exactly why he wanted to have me on his team: to test Guin and torment Morgan. Like she had said herself, I was *his* companion. She was merely his sister.

Neither Morgan nor I objected, however. She, I imagined, so as not to give the impression that Arthur had taken something she had wanted. Me because I wasn't ready to swear any allegiances – not yet, anyway.

FOUR

'Right.' Arthur rubbed his hands together and cast a glance around the chamber to ensure no one was listening in on our conversation.

Once our teams had been decided, the four of us had split up and made our way to the castle to begin the competition. Arthur and I were now ensconced in an alcove of the otherwise empty chapel discussing our plans. Or at least Arthur was discussing them. 'There's a side room off the armoury where the guards keep spare armour. I should be able to get a helmet from there easily enough. Morgan probably doesn't even realize, she's never been allowed in there.' He chuckled at his own cunning. 'And I already have a jug of ale in my rooms.' I couldn't help but notice how his posture changed, his spine straightening.

'You do?' I asked, a little surprised. 'What for?' The prince blushed ever so slightly and I realized, belatedly, I was meant to be impressed by this, not question it.

'Never mind that, what are we going to fetch for our third item?' If he had been any taller I might have imagined Arthur was trying to peer down at me, the way his chin tilted into the air, and he raised his eyebrows in a paltry approximation of the expression Morgan often wore. Unfortunately for him, we were the same height.

'It's going to have to be really good for Morgan not to find a way to disqualify it.' I grinned. 'You know she'll want to.' Arthur grinned back, his stature softening, maybe even relaxing a little. I liked him better this way.

'You already understand my sister pretty well, I see. We could maybe take a sword while we're in the armoury without anyone noticing?'

I mulled it over. 'I don't think any old sword is going to cut it.' Craning my neck around the corner of our alcove, I peered around the chapel, looking for something I had noticed during the first Sunday service I had sat through in Camelot. 'What about that?'

I directed Arthur's attention to the gleaming sword, its point buried in a decoratively carved anvil, which in turn sat atop an imposing hunk of rock. When I glanced back at him, however, the prince was staring back at me as if I had suggested we cut off our own feet and present them to Morgan and Guinevere.

'We can't take that! Only the one true king might draw the sword from the stone.' The words sounded well worn, as though they had been oft repeated to and by Arthur over the years. I, on the other hand, had no idea what he was talking about.

'Well, aren't you the future king?' I pointed out.

Arthur didn't like that.

'My father is still king right now if you hadn't noticed.' He bristled and I wondered, too late, if he had tried to draw the sword before. 'What about you – surely you brought something from home that might be of interest? Something unique from the North?'

Arthur couldn't know how much those words truly stung. I had nothing. Nothing that might mean anything, anyway. Dresses and hairnets, but nothing personal or unique. No gifts or heirlooms of value beyond what any noblewoman was expected to have. I wasn't sure the notion had even crossed my father or stepmother's minds.

I shook my head. 'I imagine it will have to be something we're not supposed to have if it's to compete with whatever the other two find.' Arthur looked thoughtfully at me for a moment, as though this statement had prompted something in his mind.

'You're right, any old sword won't do. That doesn't mean a sword's an altogether terrible idea though.' He paused dramatically and, caught up in the moment, I took the bait.

'Yes?'

'My father keeps the sword with which he defeated Hengist on permanent display. A reminder of glory past and future, he says.'

Arthur didn't need to say any more. Everyone knew of Uther's defeat of the Saxon leader Hengist. The same man who had killed the last king of the Britons and Uther's brother, Aurelius. That meant it must also be the sword with which he had knighted the first men to sit at his Round Table. All of which had taken place long before I could possibly comprehend its significance, but the story was a popular one. Not least because Hengist's son Octa still threatened our isles.

A grin blossomed across Arthur's face. 'Nothing could compete with that.'

I grinned back. 'Where do we find it?'

Just as Arthur had predicted, the first two items on our list were easy enough to come by; even the guard's helmet, which Arthur was able to acquire by simply striding into the armoury with confidence. While the attendant on duty had given me an odd look, he made no move to get in our way, allowing Arthur to liberate our quarry from exactly the spot he said it would be. It was certainly useful to be the future king.

Now, however, came the time to acquire the third and most challenging item on our list: King Uther's sword. The now purely ornamental weapon was, according to Arthur, stored in the king and queen's private solar within the castle keep. I had not had cause to visit these chambers in the time I had lived in Camelot; nor would I unless I were to marry Arthur one day and become queen myself. Meanwhile, there was something quite exhilarating about being somewhere I wasn't supposed to be. I found myself laughing aloud as Arthur and I ran up the stairs together, determined to be faster than Morgan and Guin.

As expected, the guard stationed at the entrance to the keep let us past without question. Once inside, there did not appear to be another soul around. Finally, we came to a decorated archway that led into a small but opulent room with a closed door on either side: one to the king's bedchambers, one to the queen's.

'There it is,' Arthur whispered, pointing at a shining silver blade that hung from the stone wall with iron brackets.

We both ran forward but Arthur reached the wall first, grabbing the sword with two hands and heaving it over his head like the prize it was.

'We did it!' I cried a little too loudly, the excitement overtaking me.

'Shhh,' Arthur whispered, covering my mouth with his hand while fighting back his own laughter, 'we've still got to get it to Mog's room if we're to win.'

I smiled as I gently pulled his hand away from my face. 'Don't worry, there's no way they've managed to complete the list as quickly as us. And it's all thanks to you, Your Majesty.'

I thought Arthur might preen a little, or even offer me a mock bow in response to my praise. What I was not prepared for, however, was for the young prince to awkwardly grab at my arm with the hand that I had only just released and pull me to him. Before I knew what was happening, he had leaned across our oddly tangled limbs and planted his lips on mine.

I had never been kissed before, but I knew immediately this was not the kind of kiss I wanted. His mouth was dry and hard against mine, while his eyes were screwed tightly shut: an expression that made him look as uncomfortable as I felt. Yet he was the one to have initiated the encounter. Before I could pull away, however, the kiss was already over and Arthur was staring at me as if trying to figure out my reaction.

'What was that for?' I spluttered, whipping the back of my hand across my lips before I could think better of how it might look.

'I thought you might like it if I kissed you?' It sounded more like a question than a statement.

'Why in God's name would you think that?' I was annoyed now.

'I'm the prince,' he responded matter-of-factly. 'Aren't you here to compete for my hand?' He took a step back, tilting his head to one side and looking me up and down, trying to figure me out.

'I'm here because my father sent me,' I scoffed. 'I would appreciate it if you refrained from doing that again.'

To my relief, Arthur nodded his assent. He didn't seem angry with me, just slightly confused. I realized too late that this could have gone very differently. I was grateful it had not.

'Arthur? Is that you?'

I swivelled on the spot, heart thumping in my chest, to see who had spoken. It was, to my absolute horror, Arthur's mother, Queen Igraine.

In the weeks I had spent at Camelot I had never been in such intimate company with the queen before. It was well known that Queen Igraine had been sickly for more than a year, with no sign of improvement, and was generally confined to her private rooms. Knowing and seeing were two very different things, however. The queen was clearly a beautiful woman, but the life had been drained out of her. Her appearance was wan, her face gaunt, and her sunken eyes were made all the more alarming by the dark circles that surrounded them. Her dull brown hair hung lank around her shoulders and the dress she wore looked as if it had been made for a much larger woman.

'Mother.' Arthur gave a polite bow, which I followed with my own much deeper curtsy. 'I didn't know you were up today; I would have kept you company.'

'Oh no, dear, I wasn't, I just . . . I thought I heard . . .' She trailed off, looking around us as though searching for the reason she had risen from bed.

'That was just me and Lady Viviane, Mother.' Arthur walked over and took the older woman's hands. 'We didn't mean to disturb you.'

'The Lady Viviane, yes, it is a pleasure to meet you in person.' She nodded, her eyes settling on me. 'You are just as beautiful as your mother was.'

I should have simply offered her my thanks, but the mention of my mother made my pulse quicken. 'You knew my mother?'

'Just once, I met her once, at a feast in my husband's honour, but was it my first husband, or . . .' She trailed off, looking down instead to the hand clasped in Arthur's.

'Let me take you back to bed, Mother,' Arthur offered, making her smile.

'Mothers,' she gave a reedy laugh. 'Not exactly the kind of company two young lovers desire.'

'Oh no, ma'am,' I started to object, but Arthur shot me a look that made me fall silent.

'We were just playing a game, Mother, nothing to worry about.'

'I see,' she nodded, although I couldn't tell if she meant it. 'Be careful though, this castle has eyes. You're never really as alone as you think you are.'

This I didn't know how to respond to. I remained silent

as Arthur led her back through the door that led to the queen's bedchambers.

Our journey to Morgan's chamber was more subdued than our earlier adventure around the castle had been. Arthur was silent, a serious expression on his face I hadn't seen there before. I didn't get the feeling that any attempt at comfort from me would be much appreciated. What was there to say anyway? While I felt the loss of my own mother, it had more to do with the absence of her in my life growing up; I had no idea what it was like to watch a parent slowly deteriorate before you. I kept my mouth shut, for better or worse.

I was prepared for more awkward silence while we awaited the others' return, but just as we crossed the threshold to Morgan's chambers I heard pounding footsteps approaching behind us.

'We're here!' cried Morgan, skidding to a halt in the doorway. She held the guard's helmet aloft, a wide grin painted across her face.

Guinevere meanwhile was bent at the waist, panting, clearly out of breath but sporting an equally bright smile. 'We got them,' she choked out and Morgan cast an appreciative glance back at her.

'That's all very well, but we finished first.' Arthur had already taken a seat on Morgan's bed, our spoils scattered around him on the mattress. I, on the other hand, couldn't stop myself from laughing at the picture they made, framed in the open doorway.

'Why are you so out of breath?' I asked between giggles.

'You should have seen us,' Morgan responded. 'We found

a guard in training and Guin actually flirted his helmet off, distracting him just long enough for me to grab it and run.'

'You did?' Arthur looked surprised, and possibly a tiny bit perturbed.

'It was easy.' Guinevere stood up straight, regaining her usual composure, all the while refusing to look directly at Arthur. Perhaps the division of our teams had stirred up more trouble than I realized.

'She's a natural.' Morgan laughed, setting down the helmet, followed by a ceramic jug.

'What about your mystery object?' I asked, raising one eyebrow in the hopes of mirroring some of Morgan's usual airs.

'Oh ho, just you wait.' Morgan wafted a hand in the direction of Guinevere, who proceeded to pull from her skirts a thick volume with an ornate gilded binding.

'Is that the Abbot's bible?' Arthur strode forward and took the book from Guinevere's hands without pause.

'It is indeed.' Morgan's chest was practically jutting out in front of her from her evident pride. 'He was eating his lunch in the vestry and left it on the altar.'

'We'll have to get it back to the chapel soon, though, before anyone notices.' Guinevere was looking distinctly more nervous than she had done moments before.

'Yes, well, so will we.' I beamed as I gestured at the heavy sword Arthur had abandoned on Morgan's bed.

'That's not Father's Round Table sword, is it?' Morgan looked between Arthur and me. 'You didn't?'

'We did.' Arthur stood, gripping the sword tightly in both hands.

'Give it here.' Morgan lunged for the object.

'Uh, uh.' Arthur shook his head and moved the sword behind his back. 'Swords are not for princesses. But now we're officially the winners, I believe Viviane is right, we better be getting this back.' He turned from Morgan. 'Guinevere, you will escort me. We can return the bible while we're at it.'

'Who said you're the winner?' Morgan objected, but Arthur wasn't listening. He had moved to Guinevere's side and, offering her his free arm, escorted her and the sword from the room, leaving Morgan and me alone. It didn't take a genius to figure out I had failed his test. I might have won the sword, but Guinevere had won the prince.

FIVE

That day would not be our only game together, but it was the first and last time I would meet Her Majesty, the Queen. For, within the month, Mistress Mae had sat all four of us together one morning, in the room where we girls usually worked. We were not there to learn, however.

'I regret to inform you all that last night, Her Majesty, Queen Igraine passed peacefully in her sleep.' Mae sniffed and it was only then I noticed how red her own eyes were. 'I understand this will be a difficult time for you both, Your Highnesses –'

'Why is our father not telling us this?' Morgan slammed her fist down on the table in front of her, causing me to flinch and glance around at my companions.

Morgan looked furious, whether at the news or the king's absence was unclear, while Guin had turned a shade of ghostly white. It was Arthur's demeanour that made the starkest difference, however. The young prince had curled up on himself in his chair, beetlelike, his back arched, his shoulders drooped, his eyes glassy as they stared at the wooden tabletop.

'Your father has a great number of arrangements to deal with in the wake of your mother's death. I'm sure he would be here if he could.' Mae's voice was soft, consoling, but not entirely convincing.

Our tutor turned her gaze to Guinevere and me, glancing between us, almost pleadingly. She didn't need to say it aloud for her expectation to be clear; we were the prince and princess's companions after all. Except that, who was I to counsel another in their grief? What comfort could I possibly offer? As ill as she had seemed, the news was nevertheless a shock to me, and I could not even begin to conceive of how Arthur must be feeling, having seen first-hand the care with which he had handled his mother. While I panicked, Guinevere, to her credit, was at Arthur's side within minutes, her hand clasped tightly around his arm as the colour drained from his face. A role I surely should have vied to fill if I were to compete for Arthur's hand, but had there ever really been a competition? I turned to Morgan, ready to offer my condolences, but to my surprise she was already on her feet, the fury in her eyes fading to something else. In that moment I saw something of myself: a mother-less daughter, confused and overwhelmed. We expressed ourselves differently, but perhaps that in itself meant we had something to offer each other.

Before I could say or do anything, however, she had marched from the room. My eyes flitted between the figures of Arthur and Guin and the doorway through which Morgan had departed, trying to figure out what it was I was meant to do. I had to make a choice, and as I watched Guin leaning on Arthur, whispering words of comfort in his ear, I knew exactly which one it would be. Rising from my seat, I nodded to our tutor, who somehow looked even more uncomfortable than I felt, and followed in Morgan's footsteps.

'Morgan,' I kept my voice low as I pushed open the door to Morgan's chambers, 'are you all right?'

'Of course. It's not my mother who has died,' came a voice from the furthest corner of the room.

Deciding to take Morgan's lack of dismissal as a tentative invitation, I entered the room and closed the door behind me before continuing to speak. 'But she was your stepmother.'

'A pale imitation of the real thing.' She sniffed, her voice catching on the words. 'Do you know that my father married her not a handful of months after my own mother's passing? He swapped them as though it was nothing and never mentioned my mother again.'

My heart ached at how familiar this story was. The timing varied by a couple of years, but I knew all too well how it felt to have your mother's memory erased by the man who had claimed to love her. I didn't blame my stepmother, however, regardless of how distant our relationship was, and I didn't think Morgan had blamed hers either.

'You can mourn them both, you know.'

'I know that,' Morgan replied, but there was no bite to her words. 'It's not her fault anyway. Igraine's first husband died mysteriously and there was Uther the very next day to offer for her hand.'

'What was so mysterious about it?' I asked, lowering myself to the floor where Morgan sat, happy to let her lead the conversation.

'At the same time her first husband was dying of a fatal wound miles from home, he was also in bed with Igraine.' She pulled at a loose thread on her gown. 'And they weren't sleeping, if you know what I mean.' Morgan didn't look me in the eye but continued to stare at the tapestry which hung on the opposite wall. I was silent for a moment while I processed what she was saying. Did Morgan mean that Uther . . . ? Disguised as Igraine's husband? It was possible, if magic was at play. 'Nine months later my baby brother was born.'

'How do you know all this? You were only a child.'

'Igraine told me, last year when her illness had worsened and kept her confined to bed most days.'

'I see,' I replied, not sure I did see at all. My first thought was what a horrible story that was to share with a child, especially about her own father. But then I considered the queen's words during our one and only conversation. Her warning, rather. Perhaps in Igraine's deteriorating state that had been exactly what she'd also tried to pass on to Morgan.

'Do you ever wonder, Viv,' Morgan turned her gaze to mine for the first time since I'd entered the room, 'if that is the fate of us all?'

'For whom?'

'Women. To have each day of our lives decided by the most powerful man around us, only to die alone and unloved when we have outlived our use.'

'I don't think the queen was unloved,' I offered while considering her words. 'Arthur loved her a great deal. I think you might even have loved her too, though you have not said it.'

'I hated her,' Morgan hissed. 'I hated that she wasn't my mother. I hated that she bore Uther a son when my mother could not. I hate that her child will always be more powerful and more loved than me because he is a boy. I hate that she still tried to be my mother even though she knew all of that.'

Despite the darkness of the room, I could still make out the glistening of silent tears as they streamed down Morgan's cheeks. Each one made my heart twist painfully in my chest and I leaned further over to take her hand in my own. Shimmying across the ground on my knees, I pulled her forward and encouraged her to rest her head on my shoulder, which she did easily enough. I ran my free hand through her hair.

'If anyone is the mistress of her own fate, Morgan, it is you. But if you're worried, then know that I will not let anyone decide your future for you.'

Neither of us acknowledged how futile a promise this was. As a guest, I held less sway at court than Morgan, and hers wasn't much, but I felt in that moment that I truly would try to do exactly that.

'You're a lot kinder than me, you know,' Morgan said. 'I've not exactly been the most welcoming host.'

I shrugged. 'I've never felt unwelcome.' Morgan gave me a look. But it was true, I hadn't. Morgan, Arthur and Guinevere didn't actively avoid me like my stepmother and her lady's maids had done. Had I felt challenged? Yes. Goaded? Sometimes. But unwelcome? Never. If anything, rightly or wrongly I'd taken Morgan's demeanour as something of a test. A test to ensure I was worthy of her friendship. That I was more than just a girl vying for her brother's hand.

Morgan wiped at her face with the back of her sleeve, mopping up the lingering tears. 'What about your step-mother? Do you miss her?'

I held back the derisive laugh that threatened to break free at her words; now was not the time. 'We were, we are, not so close as you and the queen were, I think.'

It was an understatement, of course. My father's second wife had barely acknowledged my presence. I could count the number of times we'd been alone in the same room on one hand. The longest conversation we'd ever had was on the night of my departure, when she had taken me aside to remind me of what she and my father expected from my fostership.

'If anything, Lady Malinda actively avoided me when I was there.'

For a while, I thought perhaps it was because I looked so much like her, my father's first wife, that it made my step-mother uncomfortable. I was a constant reminder that she had not been his first choice, for she had grown up in his court, a distant cousin who had been fostered by my grandparents just as I was now. But over time I had realized it was more than that. Especially after my half-brother was born. She had kept us apart as much as she could, and when that was impossible she had never taken her eyes from me. It was not disdain or apathy I'd seen in them, however; rather, something akin to fear. She watched me like a hawk protecting its young, but I was the threat.

'What about your own mother?' Morgan's voice startled me from my reverie, making me flinch.

'She was from the islands to the north. I'm not sure exactly how she came to marry my father, no one talked about her much after my father remarried, but I know she loved me. She used to take me swimming in the loch. She could swim all day. I overheard a few of the servants referring to her as the selkie queen, but I never saw any seal skins.' I forced out a laugh, brushing off the memories and attempting to distract from the tears that had welled in my eyes.

'I'm sorry.'

'No, I'm sorry. I'm supposed to be comforting you, remember.' I gave her a friendly nudge.

'You know, Viv, I'm glad you came here.' She nudged me back, wiping her cheeks with the back of her hand.

'You know, Morgan, so am I.'

Smoke rose from the enormous funeral pyre to sear my eyes. Tears of sadness mixed with pain fell all around me. My nostrils filled with the acrid scent of burning wood and flesh; the crackling of the fire interrupted only by intermittent sighs and sobs from the gathered crowd. On my left stood Morgan, her hand gripped tightly in mine, wet tracks streaked across her cheeks, while to my right were Arthur and Guinevere, arms interlocked, the latter watching her companion as he stared unblinkingly at the flames that slowly consumed his mother's body.

The queen's funeral had been a sombre affair. While Igraine had been ill for a number of years, she was still relatively young, only just approaching her fifth decade. Her loss was clearly felt by all of Camelot. The entire castle had come together to witness her final moments on this earth – young and old, servant and noble, all had gathered in one place, King Uther included. The king himself stood to Arthur's right but not close enough to touch. Beside him were his knights of the Round Table, each man dressed in full ceremonial armour apart from one. The individual in question occupied the position to Uther's right, his face and body hidden beneath a long brown hooded cloak not unlike those I had seen worn by monks. Based on his position, this man, however, did not appear to be a monk, and as I watched he leaned in to whisper in the king's ear, providing me with a flash of dark hair but no more.

'It's Merlin,' came Morgan's murmur from beside me. 'The man beside my father.' She had evidently caught me staring.

The sorcerer, I thought. Not sure what I was supposed to say, I simply nodded and forced my gaze back to the funeral pyre. Within seconds, however, I felt the previously still figures to my right begin to stir. A quick glance back told me that the king had made known his intention to leave and the knights around him had fallen into step behind, the cloaked figure of Merlin remaining at his side.

Morgan made a scornful noise that I hoped the small group were too far away to hear. 'Of course he'd be the first to leave – what use is a dead wife after all?'

'Shut up, Morgan.' This time it was Arthur who spoke, although it came out more like a bark. 'That is not only our father you speak of, but your king.'

'And Igraine was my queen, one deserving of more respect than Uther has shown her.'

'Bite your tongue. She was my mother, not yours,' Arthur growled, making me wince.

'Perhaps now is not the time to argue; everyone is upset,' I murmured, disappointed by how much it sounded like a plea. The thought of a full-blown argument breaking out between the two of them, in front of the burning pyre and gathered mourners, made me sweat uncomfortably.

'Viv is right.' Guin stroked Arthur's arm, though I wasn't sure he noticed. He only stared back at Morgan, whose eyes had narrowed, her mouth set in a hard line.

'Upset, yes,' Morgan responded, her voice expressionless.

'Some rest before the feast tonight,' I suggested, squeezing her hand.

'An excellent idea,' Guinevere nodded.

When we sat down to dine that evening in the late queen's honour, I was surprised by the number of empty seats. In particular, those positioned at the head table, where the knights of the realm usually sat with their king, the queen not having attended many public meals since my arrival. Of course, there were always those who missed a feast or two but the difference this evening was stark, especially given the occasion.

'Where is everyone?' I asked Morgan, who had taken the seat on my right. She simply shrugged in response, letting out an embarrassingly loud snort when her eyes locked on the king's unoccupied chair.

'Preparing for battle,' came a voice from my left. It was Pelleas, a courtier a couple of years my senior who had taken to sitting beside me at evening meals over the past few weeks. Surprised by his words, I turned to look at him, my shock clearly etched on my face. 'I heard the sorcerer had a vision,' he continued, 'that Saxons were approaching from the east, headed for one of our neighbouring kingdoms.'

'Surely not?' I frowned. 'Not with King Uther's presence in the region.' I was not completely naive about the Saxon threat. Their mercenaries had been visiting our isles for longer than I had lived, often employed by the Romans who had occupied the South until recent years, but their numbers were small, or so at least I thought, and surely no threat to the powerful Britons who ruled these lands.

Pelleas shook his head at me, sporting a pitying smile I found I did not appreciate one bit. 'They are arrogant, and their arrogance makes them bold.' He leaned in closer and whispered conspiratorially in my ear. 'There's no need to worry yourself though, I will make sure you don't come to any harm.'

This elicited a guffaw from Morgan, who had evidently been listening in. 'And what exactly are you going to do, Pelleas – get your mummy to send them away? I saw you last week crying on her shoulder when you thought no one was there.'

'Just because you don't understand the bond between mother and child, Princess, doesn't mean –'

Morgan didn't let him finish. 'Why, you arrogant little prick.' I thought she might be about to throw the goblet in her hand at Pelleas' face when Arthur called out.

'Morgan. That is enough. Go to your chambers until you are capable of being around company.'

I winced at the sharpness in Arthur's tone and water

sloshed from my untouched cup. Thankfully, no one was paying me any attention, all eyes on the prince and princess.

'Since when did you tell me what to do?' Her words came out as a snarl but she was already standing. 'Never mind, I wouldn't want you to tell on me to Daddy.'

Pelleas meanwhile had paled. 'I'm sorry,' he muttered, but I didn't think Morgan heard him as she stormed from the room. The great hall had otherwise fallen silent, the unfolding scene having drawn the attention of all those gathered. It made me angry, I realized – the gaping mouths and knowing looks between neighbours, not an ounce of sympathy among them. Morgan's grief might be loud, it might be furious, or even ugly, all things we women had been taught to circumvent, but at least she was honest about how she felt. She wore her heart on her sleeve. I wished I could be a little bit more like her in that.

'I think I might retire too; it's been a long day.' I rose from my chair and offered both Pelleas and Arthur a small curtsy in turn. Arthur narrowed his eyes but said nothing, while Guinevere watched on in horror. Would my decision to follow Morgan be considered a criticism of Arthur? I suspected my stepmother would have told me to sit back down, to drink my wine and smile at my companion. But I couldn't. Something in my very bones compelled me to leave at that moment. An irresponsible move perhaps, but right then, I found it hard to care.

SIX

'Well, you know, there is one way to settle this.' Morgan's eyes gleamed; it was a gleam I had quickly come to distrust in the three years I'd spent at Camelot.

'What?' I asked, suspicious. I had found suspicion the best way to approach most of Morgan's suggestions.

'There's a whole library specializing in the magical arts right here in the castle.'

'Morgan, be serious – you can't just break into Merlin's chambers whenever you like.'

'Why not?' Morgan grinned. 'I've done it before.'

'And I let Pelleas kiss me behind the stables last week, but it doesn't mean I'll do it again.'

Morgan scrunched her nose. 'Not all ideas are made equal, Viv,' she scoffed, her smile quickly returning. 'Plus, aren't you desperate to prove me wrong once and for all?' Her eyebrows wiggled teasingly. If I had thought it could have prevented her from goading me into doing exactly what she wanted in the future, I would have plucked them out hair by hair, but she would likely have found another way easily enough. Life as Morgan's friend and companion had proved infinitely more exciting than my life had ever been before, and if I was honest with myself, I was more than happy to go along with most of her hare-brained schemes.

'Fine! But let's be quick about it.'

Although it was common knowledge which tower housed Merlin during his stays at Camelot, I had never been to his chambers myself. Morgan, on the other hand, was a not infrequent visitor to the magician's sanctum – only her visits were exclusively reserved for when Merlin himself was elsewhere.

'I don't know why I let you talk me into these things,' I huffed as I climbed the winding staircase behind her.

'Because,' Morgan laughed, prancing ahead, 'it's more fun than you'd ever have with Severe Guinevere.'

'Why exactly do you hate Guin so much?' I asked, not for the first time.

'Why don't you? She's your competition for Arthur's hand in marriage, after all. Not that you're faring very well in that regard. Sorry, darling. They're all but engaged.'

I rolled my eyes. 'I've no interest in marrying Arthur.'

'None at all? Arthur's wife will also be queen, remember?' Morgan pushed.

'None at all,' I reaffirmed. And I meant it. Arthur was . . . fine, I supposed, but I struggled to picture a future in which we were husband and wife. He was everything a nobleman should be, but that was also the problem. Nothing about the prim and proper prince excited me, not even the title he could give me.

Uther entertained me as a prospective match for his son in order to retain my father's support in the North, just as Guinevere's presence ensured him the same in the South. Yet, one day, the pretence would be over. Arthur would be married and I was certain it would not be to me. The purpose of my being here would be gone, with nothing left in its place to replace it. So, while losing Arthur's hand to Guinevere didn't frighten me, every now and then the issue of where that left me as a guest in Camelot did.

'Here we are!'

Hovering at the top of the stairwell, I watched as Morgan brought a hand up to the solid wooden door before her. Surely it wouldn't open; Merlin was a great magician after all. But it did, as easily as turning the next page in a book. Smirking, Morgan disappeared into the room, leaving me to follow after her. Which of course I did.

Whatever I had expected from the personal chambers of the king's closest advisor and distinguished spell caster, it was not this. This was a pigsty. Perhaps that was unfair, I reprimanded myself; pigs were merely as messy as their keepers, whereas only the occupant could be to blame for the chaos before me. Sheaves of parchment were stacked precariously across every surface. Bunches of herbs and flowers hung drying from the rafters without rhyme or reason. Heaps of clothing lay strewn across the floor, of which there was barely an available spot to step on. And there was Morgan in the middle of it all, a delighted grin spread across her face like she was welcoming me to the most marvellous place in all of Camelot.

Regretting our plan already, I took a few tentative steps into the room itself. 'Ugh, this place is such a mess.' I grimaced as my dress snagged on an open drawer, causing me to stumble.

'If I'd known to expect guests, I would have tidied up.'

My stomach dropped. Despite my reservations, I hadn't really expected to be discovered. How many times had Morgan come up here by herself, after all? And not once had she reported running into the elusive magician himself, always away tending to more serious business than teenage trespassers. If it wasn't for the handful of times I had glimpsed him in conversation at the king's side, I might have thought Merlin more myth than man. Yet here he was before us both – a long, narrow face in keeping with his willowy height and sharp features made all the more arresting by bright blue eyes the colour of the sky on a summer's day. He leaned casually against the open doorframe, the satisfied smile of someone who had caught the guilty party red-handed playing on his face.

'Master Merlin,' I stammered, dropping into a low curtsy.

The magician ignored me, instead stepping into the room itself and feigning interest in the detritus on the floor. 'I suppose it could be neater, but I prefer to keep my private rooms just that – private, from maids and noble ladies alike.' His comment made me frown. Why had it been so easy for us to enter uninvited, then? 'This is not your first time visiting in my absence though, is it, Princess?' He turned to meet Morgan's glare.

'Perhaps you should consider investing in a lock if you're so concerned with privacy?' she responded, making me wince. De-escalation was not Morgan's strong suit.

'But then I would be denied the pleasure of catching arrogant thieves in the act.' Merlin was still smiling, but there was something else in his eyes that suggested he was not entirely relaxed about our intrusion.

'We weren't here to steal from you, sir, only to see if we could find the answer to a question in your books,' I offered.

'Ah, I see, a pair of scholars then.' Merlin glanced my way briefly before returning his gaze to Morgan. 'Was it for the same scholarly pursuits that you took the tome on garden plants? Or the jar of wormwood? Or the iron door handle?'

I groaned internally. It was clear that Morgan had stolen much more from Merlin than I had previously realized. Nor had her frequent visits gone unnoticed. I had not spent three years as Morgan's companion to expect her to express contrition now, however. Still, that didn't mean I could have anticipated what she said next.

'Teach me.' It was hard to tell if Morgan's words were intended as a command or a request, but they were shocking nonetheless. All the times she had snuck away and returned with grains of magic, it had never occurred to me that this was her end goal. Grasping it now left me torn between feelings of stupidity that I hadn't realized it sooner, and bitterness that three years' worth of friendship hadn't made me worthy enough to share this with.

'Teach me to wield magic as you do, and you will never have to fear me breaking in again.' She took two steps closer to Merlin, back straight and eyes locked with his.

'Fear you, little girl?' Merlin scoffed. 'I could simply inform your father of your criminal propensities and let him discipline you. Why would I dedicate my time to teaching you my craft?'

'Because I'm no fool. There might not be a physical lock on your door, but you do not leave your room unguarded. I've spoken to the servants. None of them can pass that

threshold. There is magic of some sort to keep them out.'
This was news to me, but clearly not to Merlin, who chuckled for the first time since he'd joined us.

'Not so silly after all. You are correct, of course. My
rooms are locked against ordinary intruders, but I found I
was curious who at court might not be so ordinary.'

'So you would allow any unknown spell caster access to
your things?' I asked, truly baffled by his words.

Merlin's eyes twinkled as they finally met mine. 'Not to
everything.' Unease climbed up my spine and the hairs on
the back of my neck stood on end as he stared at me without blinking. I couldn't move beneath his gaze although
whether it was magic or fear that had me rooted to the
spot it was impossible to tell. Finally, after what felt like an
age, the magician raised a hand and brought his thumb and
middle finger together. With a single snap I felt the room
around me fall away.

My stomach plummeted once more as darkness flooded
my vision and the floor vanished from beneath my feet.
Before I could scream, however, it was over. Once again,
I was standing with Morgan and Merlin in what according
to shape and size was the same room as before, but those
were the only similarities. All the clutter and disorder had
disappeared, leaving behind a chamber completely unrecog-
nizable from the one we had entered. Bookshelves lined one
wall, their contents neatly arranged, while a glass cabinet full
of jars and crystals stood on the opposite side. The room was
mostly occupied by a large four-poster bed hung with rich red
fabric that had replaced its much smaller counterpart from
before. There was also a secondary door to the right of the

cabinet, which should logically have led to thin air. I was not, however, about to make any more assumptions when it came to Merlin's abode. Gazing around the now spotless chamber, I caught Morgan's eye; she looked back at me with an equal amount of astonishment etched on her face.

'As I mentioned, I prefer my privacy.' Merlin turned back to Morgan but not before giving me the smallest hint of a smile. 'I am not ignorant of what happens in this castle, Princess, nor of your natural abilities. If you can swear your obedience to me better than you have to your hapless tutor, then I will take you as my apprentice.'

'You have my word,' Morgan responded without pause, her excitement plain to see.

'We shall see what that is worth.' Merlin nodded in Morgan's direction before retraining his gaze on me. 'And what about you, Lady Viviane?'

'What about me?'

'Would you like to become my pupil along with your friend? She is not the only one to have passed over the threshold to these chambers after all.'

A sharp intake of breath from Morgan indicated that I was not the only one surprised by this offer, but Merlin held up a hand before she could say whatever it was that was on her mind.

Never in my wildest dreams. Merlin was asking me if I would like to learn magic, to become a spell caster like him? His was a kind of power not even kings or lords could wield. Was I, daughter of a king, bred for marriage and to build alliances, even allowed to take the new path that had appeared before me?

Then I remembered my mother. My mysterious, beautiful mother from lands unknown. There was something of the fey about her. That's what everyone had said. She who had swum each day in the same loch I had once called home – trapped by a marriage I didn't even know if she had ever wanted. And then I thought of Morgan, who stood so confident and proud beside me, determined to choose her own fate rather than leave it up to anybody else.

Two different kinds of strength, but strength nonetheless. I had hoped for something more when I came to Camelot than a life of meaningless isolation. Although I hadn't been sure what that would look like, maybe this was it? Magic. More than just unnatural waves and hours beneath water. Magic that could grant me an independence I'd only experienced glimpses of. If Morgan could say yes, then why couldn't I? Better yet, we could do it together. I had nothing to lose.

'Yes,' I finally whispered. 'I would.'

'Morgan, wait! Slow down.'

I was forced to sprint to keep up with Morgan's longer stride as she rushed down the stairs and into the small courtyard at the foot of the tower. So, when she finally stopped one foot in front of me, I almost slammed into her with my whole body.

'How could you!' she bellowed.

'How could I what?' I took a step back, shocked by her ire.

'*I* was meant to be Merlin's apprentice.'

'You are,' I stuttered, 'we can both –'

'This was my way out!' Morgan was practically screaming

now, and I flinched. Out of the corner of my eye I was aware of a busy maid turning on her heel and scurrying back down the corridor she had been exiting. 'This was how I showed everyone my worth, my power – not my father's, not Arthur's: mine. Merlin was meant to be mine!'

Now it was my turn to get angry. 'You think you're the only one who wants to live for herself? Who wants to be free of the shadow of men? I was sent here as a pawn by a father who barely registered my existence. I had no home or family, or at least I thought I didn't. But then I met you, and Guin and Arthur, and despite how you provoke me and infuriate me, Morgan, I thought we were in this together. I thought you were my friend. It could be me and you against it all, but no, you'd rather do everything alone. You have to be the only one!'

I was pleased when Morgan was silent for a moment, clearly too stunned by my outburst to immediately respond. Of course, it was still Morgan, and the last thing she would ever do was concede to another as quickly as this. Her expression warred between shock and fury, her cheeks growing steadily redder until the second emotion finally won out. 'I have never been the only one, I have never been the one. I am always second. I was born first but I still come second. Second to Arthur, my little brother. Second to Guinevere, the future queen. Now second to you who . . . who . . .'

'Not second, equal.' I ground my teeth together. 'But don't worry, Your Highness, I would not wish the burden of sharing upon you. I will return to inform Merlin that I refuse his offer.'

And with that I stormed from the courtyard, refusing to hear what else Morgan might have to say.

SEVEN

I did not, in fact, go immediately to Merlin's chambers. No, instead I stormed through the halls of Camelot in search of my own. In my anger it took me longer than it should have done, with a series of distracted wrong turns, and aimless pacing while I muttered to myself beneath my breath. It was a rare day when I couldn't outwardly control my own emotions; this was further evidenced by the number of servants who hastened their pace when we passed in the corridors. Thankfully, before I could lose all decorum and punch a wall, I reached my destination. Finally, alone to stomp and rage, throw whatever I pleased, my ire was suddenly gone. Sapped from my body. It was disappointment that lay beneath my initial outburst. Disappointment in Morgan. Disappointment that our growing friendship had crumbled so easily. And with disappointment came sorrow. Without the burning rage I had felt during our argument to sustain me, I slumped on to my bed and buried my face in the sheets, my tears only stopping once I had fallen fast asleep.

'Viv, Viviane, wake up.'

I became aware of a hand gently shaking my shoulder. I had barely moved from the position in which I had originally collapsed, fully dressed; my entire body felt stiff as a board. My eyes were sore and swollen, and I groaned as I tried to open them.

'I think it's very rude of you to lie there making such ghoulish noises when I've come all this way to apologize.' *Morgan?* Sure enough, when I eventually rolled over on to my back and looked up at the face of my intruder, it was Morgan's gaze that met mine. 'You look awful,' she added.

'What do you want?' I scowled, pulling myself up to a seated position.

'Didn't you hear me the first time? I'm here to apologize.' Her voice was light, almost dismissive, but her expression was less nonchalant – her eyes darting back and forth while her bottom lip fell victim to the repeated scraping of her teeth. If I hadn't known better, I would have read her demeanour in that moment as one of anxiety. But Morgan didn't worry about what other people thought of her. At least, I'd never seen her show signs of such concerns before. Yet, here she was, in my chambers, in the dead of night judging by the dwindling embers in the fireplace, trying to tell me she was sorry for . . .

'And what exactly are you apologizing for?' I asked, finding my words.

Morgan grimaced. 'For being selfish. For trying to stop you from learning magic. But most of all, I'm sorry for talking down to you, for treating you like you're lesser.' I made to interrupt but she ploughed on before I could say anything in response. 'Because you're not less than anyone, Viv, least of all me. You're clever and insightful and I think you might just be the only person I genuinely want to be around.'

'Except for Arthur.' I didn't bother mentioning Guin.

'Arthur, it depends on the day.'

I choked on a groggy bark of laughter, which started Morgan cackling. It was a cathartic laugh that had nothing really to do with Morgan's dig at Arthur. We both lay flat on our backs, shoulders trembling as we let it all out – each of us as relieved as the other. I hadn't wanted to fall out with Morgan. Her declaration had made me realize just how much her company had come to mean to me since arriving at Camelot. I wanted to be friends, companions, partners even, but it couldn't be on her terms only. We had to be equals.

'Can I stay here tonight?' Morgan sighed after we had laughed ourselves out.

'For what's left of it.' I nodded and shifted so there was enough room for us both to get comfortable.

Morgan repositioned herself so she lay beside me, face turned to stare at mine, eyes wide in eager anticipation. 'What do you think he'll teach us?' I knew she was speaking about Merlin.

'I don't know,' I whispered back. 'But I can't wait to find out.'

Thankfully for everyone involved – for I don't think I could have coped with an impatient Morgan when my own nerves were so on edge – we didn't have long to wait. When the sun had finally risen, Morgan and I made our way to the expanse of land towards the back of Camelot's stronghold where Merlin had promised to meet us that morning. Although it was early, the castle and its inhabitants were wide awake.

Men sparred with one another, sweat dripping down their necks as though they had been at it for hours already. The sounds of their clashing swords were joined by the slapping of heavy fabrics being beaten by household servants, while young children screamed joyfully as they chased each other around the grounds.

Merlin meanwhile stood amid it all. He could have passed for a man coming towards the end of his fourth decade, but surely he was older than he looked. I hadn't heard much about him that didn't reek of rumour and speculation, yet everyone was certain he had served at Uther's side for two decades at least. Before that he had already been considered an accomplished sorcerer. He wasn't handsome, not like the young courtiers and knights who passed through Camelot vying for the king's (or, as was becoming more common these days, Arthur's) attention. But he was certainly striking.

'Welcome.' He greeted us with a short bow of the head that from anyone else would have been deemed an act of impertinence.

'Good morning, Merlin.' Morgan offered a nod of the head in return while I dipped into a shallow curtsy.

'You are both to be my pupils from this day on; therefore you will refer to me as Master Merlin or simply Master.'

It was obvious from Morgan's expression that she wanted desperately to fight him on this point but presumably understood that doing so would only get her further from her goal rather than closer. I couldn't help but smile and look between her and the magician, who if I wasn't mistaken was giving me a small smirk in return – perfectly aware of how his words tested Morgan. The possibility made me bolder.

'What do you have planned for us today,' I grinned before adding, 'Master Merlin?' Morgan gave me a friendly elbow jab while we listened to what the magician was to teach us.

'Magic is order in the chaos. No matter what is happening around you, you must be able to harness that order to do your bidding. That is why I've brought you here this morning.' He gestured around us with both arms. 'It is a useless test of your potential to have you practise spells in the library where no one would dare disturb us. For me to be sure you are worthy of my time, I must see how you handle simple distractions such as these.'

Morgan looked disconcerted. 'But you already said yourself we both have an affinity with magic. You know we are capable.'

Merlin shook his head. 'I know you have the capacity to be excellent sneak thieves.' Morgan looked like she might argue this point but Merlin held out his hand to stop her. 'I am here by my own will, Princess. If you wish to be my student you will accept my methods, or I will find some nursemaid who brews a half-decent chamomile sleeping draught and teach her instead.'

This particular comment made me bristle. Not because of the comparison with a nursemaid, but the suggestion that we had shown no more affinity with magic than the ability to mix a common herbal blend. I doubted very much that Merlin would have agreed to even talk to us about his craft if he did not think we were capable of more. Still, this didn't feel like the moment to argue the point.

'As I was saying,' Merlin continued, 'you must be able to shut out whatever is happening around you in order to seize that one thread with which you will begin to weave your intention. The magic is already there; the question is whether you can harness it.' At these words he reached into the folds of his robes and withdrew two clay cups, both filled with what looked to be dry soil. 'Inside these pots there are two seeds. Your task this morning is to make them grow.'

'You want us to take up gardening?' Morgan huffed.

I thought Merlin might have actually rolled his eyes. 'I want you to use magic.'

'But h—'

'If you don't manage the task today, I want you to come back tomorrow and the next day until you have.' He held both clay cups out to us and I gingerly accepted the one nearest to me. There was seemingly nothing but dry soil inside, the seed buried deep within. 'Now, ladies, I am a busy man, so I will leave you to your lesson. I trust you can be relied on to follow my instructions and remain within the courtyard walls?' He peered pointedly at Morgan. 'I will know if you don't.'

Both Morgan and I silently acquiesced. What else was there to do? We had been given the strangest of tasks — impossible by any reasonable standard — yet here we were, tiny cups cradled in our hands, exchanging bewildered looks as Merlin strode back towards the main building. I had to believe there was a point to this. Squaring my shoulders, I held my cup aloft and gestured for Morgan to do the same.

'To becoming sorceresses.' I grinned, clinking our cups together, and making Morgan laugh.

'I think I shall be a sorcerer, like Merlin.'

'Then we shall be the greatest sorcerer and sorceress this land has ever known.' I looped my arm in hers. 'Come on!'

Together we wove our way through the growing crowds of busy courtiers and servants and found a small space for ourselves atop a short stone wall where I sat myself cross-legged. *Now what?* I stared at my cup, the arid soil within making my mouth dry just to look at it. How was anything supposed to grow under such inhospitable conditions? Yet there was a reason I sat here, a myriad of competing noises fighting to be heard above one another, each one briefly grasping at my attention before I forced myself to return my focus to my charge. What had I screamed and stormed at Morgan for if it was not to embrace this opportunity?

So I stared, narrowing my eyes at the soil in search of any signs of seeds or tiny shoots. No matter how hard I stared, however, I experienced nothing akin to what I thought magic must feel like; there was no tingling in my fingers, no warmth spread down my spine, and my mind refused to be transported to some ethereal other place. Instead, I heard the squawks of birds and clashing of steel, the laughter of playing children and calls of men above the crowd. I felt the soft breeze as it played with loose tendrils of my hair, occasionally obstructing my vision, and the twitching of Morgan's knee that was almost but not quite touching mine.

Occasionally my eyes would flicker in her direction, wondering whether Morgan was faring any better than I, only to see her soil was equally barren; a fact I couldn't help but find a tiny bit reassuring. Maybe it was mean-spirited of me, but now we were here I found I was terrified she might leave me behind. A thought I might have scolded myself for if it had not been interrupted by the sound of laughter from three young knights who had pointed us out on their way past our wall.

'Hmph, they won't be laughing when we can tie their tongues in knots,' Morgan grumbled beside me.

So I continued to stare, and stare some more, until there was no time left in the day to stare at all.

EIGHT

The staring did not end after day one either. The next day came, and I continued to stare, as I did on the following day, and the one after that. If anything, I grew more frustrated and less in tune with the world around me with every day that passed. I had always considered myself a patient person, happy to take my time and observe. This task, however, forced me to face up to the fact that I was perhaps not exactly who I had always thought I was – not in this at least. By the fourth day, I was no longer focused on my own 'work', and instead spent large chunks of the morning leaning over Morgan's shoulder, peering into her cup, wondering if she knew something I didn't.

'Is that a shoot?' I asked in dismay as I studied the other girl's seed. It had now been five days of the same monotonous task with no word from Merlin.

'I think it might be,' nodded Morgan, holding the cup up so we could both examine the tiny fleck of green more closely.

'How did you manage that?' I asked, a little perturbed.

'I'm not sure I did.' She frowned. 'I think it might just be growing of its own accord, it's been so long since we started.'

'Ugh,' I groaned, placing my own cup down beside me. 'This is impossible. How does he expect us to do anything with this lump of dirt if he doesn't teach us any magic?'

'I don't.'

I would have fallen head first from the wall we sat upon if Morgan hadn't grabbed my arm at that moment. Both of us were so focused on each other that we had failed to notice the sorcerer's approach, even when he stood before us.

'You are quite correct, Viviane.' The look he gave me was one of amusement. 'I never expected you to do anything with those "lumps of dirt", as you call them. What I wanted to see was whether you could commit yourself to a seemingly impossible task without giving up after only a few hours.'

I didn't know whether I wanted to laugh or scream at his words. Morgan, on the other hand, looked unequivocally furious. 'It's been a lot more than a few hours,' she practically growled.

'Hours, days,' Merlin shrugged. 'Magic sometimes takes months or years to enact or perfect.'

'And did we pass your little test?'

'For now.' He held out a hand, which I realized after a split second he was offering to me. Cautiously, I took it, and allowed the sorcerer to pull me gently to my feet. 'Shall we return to the castle, ladies? There is a large stack of books and parchments I expect you'll want to get started on waiting in my chambers.'

I hadn't had a chance to fully absorb the contents of Merlin's chambers when we had last visited, what with the breaking and entering. There was the initial room, set up for both sleep and study, which looked much the same as it had the first time I had been there. But there was also a second room which, just as I had noted on the previous occasion, should surely not have been there at all. Each of the castle's towers appeared the same from the ground, and based on the two others I had visited, there was barely room for one chamber in the spiralling turret top. Yet a second room there was, evidenced by both my eyes and feet as I stood and gazed around myself.

This room, unlike the mixed purpose of the first, appeared to be a dedicated workshop for the magical arts. The rows of bookshelves we had already passed were nothing compared to the staggering number that obscured these walls. There were either no windows or those too were hidden behind the bookcases, and the scrolls and sheaves of parchment that had been bullied out by larger tomes were piled high on the floor. More herbs and flowers hung drying from the ceiling, and in the centre of the room stood a sturdy-looking wooden table which bore a well-worn iron cauldron.

I could see the hungry way in which Morgan eyed the flora and fauna scattered across Merlin's tabletop, her fingers twitching at the prospect of digging into the practical side of things. I was more interested in the books themselves, however. What knowledge they might contain, what subjects they might cover. While I hadn't long dreamed of sorcery as Morgan had, now that the opportunity had been offered to me I was no less eager to learn what Merlin had to teach. These rooms, their contents, teased at a freedom I had always craved, a freedom I'd only ever experienced beneath the surface of the water; hoping for that same feeling in my everyday life had always seemed futile, until now.

'The first principle of magic is simple. You must learn to focus and shut out all distractions. But that alone is not enough. There is no bending the world around you to your will without first understanding what it is you wield.'

Morgan and I exchanged bemused glances. Leave it to a man of Merlin's station to talk in intellectual riddles. He carried on.

'You must understand the purpose of a thing. Take the door handle I know Princess Morgan has used so extensively in the past.' If I hadn't known her better, I might have thought the faint pink tingeing Morgan's cheeks signalled her embarrassment at Merlin's words. 'It is enchanted, yes, but to do what? Transform your guise? Heal a wound? Kill a man? No, with it the wielder can simply open doors, because that is what a door handle is for.'

'I bet you could kill someone with a door handle if you tried hard enough,' Morgan muttered, scuffing one foot along the floor.

Merlin let out a surprising bark of laughter at Morgan's words. 'Perhaps you could. It is wrong to limit the possibilities of any one object, but I can guarantee you will find it easier to manipulate once you understand its own goal.'

It was my turn to frown. *Goal?* What goal could an inanimate object possess that was not defined by its creator?

'You look sceptical, Viviane?'

'I . . .' I didn't want to seem as though I couldn't comprehend his meaning.

'Knowledge is everything. You can have all the raw talent for magic, but without understanding your materials and tools, you will never learn to build a castle,' he raised an arched brow, 'or bring one down. That is what you must focus on.'

What Merlin's words translated to, it turned out, was a *lot* of reading. There was no treatise or manuscript too esoteric, no obscure subject deemed useless or irrelevant. I read ancient medical documents on human anatomy, much of which I hoped must since have been proven wrong; I read obscure manuals on beekeeping that had me considering honey in a whole new light; and even Merlin's own botanical notes on the local flora and fauna passed beneath my nose, with the clear instruction not to damage the pages if I wished to return.

Not that there were no practical lessons to be learnt. Morgan and I were expected to begin each day in a state of silent contemplation that had me wondering if I would not be just as well living in a convent. At first. Over the subsequent weeks I slowly began to appreciate these moments. I grew better able to shut out the sound of Morgan clicking her tongue beside me or the fractured memory of last night's dream, and simply exist. Merlin warned us time and time again that the smallest distraction could be the difference between life and death when it came to magic.

'Let your mind wander to the pain in your temple while brewing a potion to summon sleep, and the drinker will experience only a restless, distressing slumber. Allow a shout to pull your attention while you calm an agitated animal, and the beast attacks you tenfold instead. You open up a passage between yourself and your subject when practising the craft, and that passage must always remain clear.'

Then there were the tests. What is the name of this particular plant? During which seasons will you find it grows? What uses does it have in spell-craft and potion-making? These were the only moments when I felt as if Morgan and I were truly in competition, but then again it might just have been my own growing desire to impress Merlin with the knowledge I was acquiring. Either way, I relished the opportunity to show off what I was learning and I allowed the glow of Merlin's praise to sustain me for days after it was given.

Still there were days when we were left to our own devices. Merlin was a busy man after all – advising the king, strategizing with his knights, disappearing to whatever far-off places sorcerers disappeared to for days at a time. When we were not in Merlin's company, Morgan and I spent our time comparing notes, drilling each other on magical theory, and speculating about what else our mentor might have in store for us. Just as before, we also exchanged dreams for our futures, except that now we were bolder with our predictions.

Morgan was determined to become a valuable enough magician that not even her father could force her to marry.

'I'll travel the length and breadth of this island, maybe even cross the seas with no one else telling me what to do.'

'Maybe you'll discover an entirely new species of plant and write a treatise of your own?' I offered one lazy afternoon when Merlin was otherwise occupied with Arthur's education.

'Of course I will.' Morgan nodded, allowing her day-dream to spiral up and outwards. 'And I'll build a community of like-minded women, free from husbands and fathers.'

'Am I your first follower then?'

'You won't be able to bring Pelleas, you know,' she teased.

'Ew, Morgan, I've already told you I'm not interested in him like that.'

'Good. You're too pretty for him anyway.' I felt my cheeks redden at Morgan's surprise compliment before her tone grew more serious. 'You'll have to swear off marriage altogether, like I've done.'

Swear off marriage? I thought. Morgan made it sound like something in which I had a choice. I had long given up any illusion of competing for Arthur's hand; he and Guinevere were bonded by a shared sense of duty that I could never hope to match. Still, I could hardly imagine never marrying at all. If not the future King of the Britons, then surely my father or King Uther would choose someone else on my behalf. It wasn't that it was what I desired, but what I'd always been told was my future. Although sometimes, just sometimes, Morgan made me wonder if it truly had to be.

Never one to allow a silence to linger, Morgan changed subjects when I didn't immediately answer. 'What do you think Merlin and Arthur talk about besides battle plans and political alliances? Arthur's not exactly the magical type.'

I laughed. 'Table plans?' And this set Morgan off too.

We both knew Arthur's time with Merlin was dedicated to strategy and warfare – the sorcerer's skills well known to go beyond magic. It was impossible to be envious, however, when our lessons seemed exceedingly more exciting, and when Arthur did nothing but bemoan his own tutorials. Once or twice, however, I did experience a brief pang of guilt that in some ways we had all left behind Guinevere, the only one of us whose life had barely changed in the three years or so since I'd arrived. But then I watched Merlin compel a bird to sing him a tune, or an apple to fall from an otherwise wizened tree, and I forgot all about Guin and her scriptures.

NINE

'Bring me back something nice.'

'Like what? A husband?' Morgan snorted at her own joke.

'You know what I mean.' I gave her a small shove, aware that Uther could turn his gaze from his driver at any moment.

The king was readying to depart for a diplomatic visit to the kingdom of Garlot, a visit which apparently required the whole family, as Morgan and Arthur would be travelling with him.

'I wish you weren't leaving for so long,' I grumbled, disappointed by my own neediness. To my surprise Morgan didn't chastise me for it; instead she leaned in and gave me a tight squeeze before stepping closer to the carriage.

'The month will fly by, you'll see. And in the meantime I need you to take thorough notes in Merlin's lessons, so I don't miss anything!'

I grinned, imagining Morgan saying the same thing about Mistress Mae's tapestry tutorials, and nodded. 'You can count on me.'

'I know. I just . . .' She chewed her bottom lip. 'I don't want to fall behind.'

While Morgan and I grew closer every day, these moments

of vulnerability were still few and far between, and part of me was still surprised to hear the confident princess of Camelot express any doubts at all.

'I don't need to see the future to know you're destined to be a great sorcerer one day, Morgan.' My words elicited a small smile, but any response was intercepted by a look from Uther indicating it was time to go.

As I watched the royal carriage depart I pondered what came next. Morgan's trip had been relatively last-minute, so at first I had assumed Merlin would pause our lessons while she was gone. Merlin, however, had presumably anticipated my reaction, as that same morning I had received a sternly worded letter informing me that Morgan's absence would not be an excuse to take a holiday.

I was torn. Part of me was glad our lessons would continue, desperate to hone my craft, even a little thrilled at the prospect of one-on-one attention. The other part, however, was wracked with anxiety at the very same prospect. One-on-one lessons meant one-on-one critique. No Morgan to split the sorcerer's attentions. Perhaps, alone, Merlin would realize how unsuitable a pupil I was. The tag-along, the spare who just so happened to be there. Still, I had to try.

Before I could get as far as the castle halls, I was interrupted by a call from somewhere close behind me.

'Viviane.' At the sound of my name, I stopped and turned around; it was Guinevere, presumably returning from wishing Arthur farewell.

'Guin,' I smiled, genuinely pleased to see her.

'Where are you off to in such a hurry?' She smiled back. 'I thought perhaps we could take a walk together.'

I winced, sorry to disappoint the other girl. 'I'm sorry, Guin, I have a lesson with Merlin.'

'I see.' Her crestfallen expression made me momentarily waver. Maybe I could tell Merlin that something came up. Until she spoke again. 'Do you really think those are a good idea?'

My lessons? 'Why not?'

'Well, it might hurt your marriage prospects. I'm not sure how many men are in the market for sorceresses as wives. They might find it kind of . . . threatening.' She scrunched up her nose and I wondered if she spoke not only of potential suitors' feelings, but of her own.

My guilt immediately vanished. 'Maybe I'm not in the market for someone who prefers their women weak and obedient. Maybe I don't want to be on the market in the first place.' We were the ones for sale after all.

Guinevere gave me an infuriating shrug. 'You might feel differently when you are the only one of us left without a husband. I will be Arthur's wife one day and, who knows, Morgan might even return from Garlot engaged.'

My frown deepened. 'What do you mean?'

'Well, Morgan is there to be introduced to King Nentres, of course. The king hopes to make a match between them, to help solidify Nentres' support against the Saxons. Arthur told me.'

I had no idea how to respond to this revelation, nor did I wish Guin to bear witness to my growing discomfort. 'I think I better get going.'

I wove past the other girl without another word, ignoring the look of hurt on her face. Now there was something more to weigh on my thoughts than just impressing Merlin.

75

I wasn't allowed to wallow in my own emotions for long, however. As I ascended the stairs to Merlin's chambers a loud crash echoed from above. Hiking up my skirts, I took the final few steps in pairs and pushed the door at the top open without waiting to knock.

Everything was as it usually was. Everything, except for Merlin. The dark-haired man was bent over on his hands and knees, his entire body shaking as his fingers clung on to the solid wooden floorboards.

For a split second I was too shocked to do anything. I simply stood there, staring, horrified by the sight of my mentor fallen before me. Then the spell broke. 'Merlin!' I cried, scrambling to the ground beside him.

'Quick, hand me some parchment and a quill.' Although his eyes remained tightly closed, his voice was even if clipped.

Galvanized by his words, I grabbed the tools he had asked for, loading the quill with ink on his behalf before handing it over. As I watched on, tongue-tied, he began scratching words on to the sheet of parchment in front of him. His movements were jerky and awkward, the handwriting I glimpsed over his arm unlike his usual flowing script. I knew I had not been invited to look, nor were the words intended for me, but I was mesmerized, and as he wrote I couldn't help but make out sporadic words: *king*, *battle*, *river*, *Octa*, and, although I only glimpsed it briefly, *poison*. Before I had a chance to fully digest the text I had seen, however, Merlin had dropped the quill and whisked the parchment from my sight.

'Here, help me up.' I took the sorcerer's arm and allowed him to put his weight on me long enough to get to his feet.

'Are you all right?' I finally spluttered.

'I will be.' Merlin grimaced before attempting what I assumed was meant to be a reassuring smile. 'Some are more difficult than others.'

'You had a vision?' It didn't take a genius to guess what had just happened. Merlin's gift for prophecy was common knowledge, although I had never seen the onset of a vision before.

Merlin gently lowered himself into the nearby armchair while I hovered over him, unsure what else I could do. 'I did,' he finally replied.

I waited but it didn't seem as though he was about to expand, and, based on experience, there was no reason to expect he would if I prodded further. So, instead, I asked, 'How did you learn to see the future?'

'I didn't,' he sighed. 'It was a gift from my father.' When I looked blankly back at him, he continued. 'As you know, magic is a part of the natural world. Some, with the patience and aptitude to study, can learn to wield that which already exists.' He raised a pointed eyebrow in a way that forced a smile from my lips. 'Some, however, have a little of that magic within them already. Like the ancient fair folk who once wandered this island freely. When a powerful magical being such as that mates with a mortal, some of that magic might be passed down to their child.'

'Your father was one of the fair folk?' I whispered.

'Not as I imagine your mother was, no. There are many forces in this world.'

'My mother?' The words came out louder than I had intended and I grimaced, embarrassed at how childish I must sound. Yes, I had heard the rumours before, I had pondered my own sparse memories of my mother. Merlin, on the other hand, was not a gossiping courtier; his word meant something more.

'Your affinity with water. Don't think I haven't noticed.' Merlin nodded to the water clock on the nearby shelf, a contraption not unlike an hourglass which he had called a clepsydra when I had asked about it a week or so ago. Curious, I stared intently at the glass container for a moment before it hit me. The water was not pooled in the lower portion of the device as you would expect; instead, it had warped unnaturally, curving up the rounded walls and pushing up against one side. The side closest to me.

'By all logic it should fall from top to bottom and remain there, but instead it gravitates towards you. The same is true no matter where in the room you are. Only when you leave does it return to normal.'

Slowly I walked around the table in the centre of the room, towards the wall on the right-hand side. Just as Merlin had indicated, the water in the clepsydra moved too. It rippled and caressed the glass, following mc as best it could.

'Surely you are not surprised?' There was a note of barely concealed amusement in the sorcerer's voice.

'I . . .' What was I supposed to say?

I knew well the way that water reacted to me. I felt the way the water in the lake wrapped around me as though greeting a friend. The connection had been more reliable than any other relationship in my life thus far. But as firmly as I recognized this, I also knew never to talk about it. Wasn't this the exact same reason the other youths in Dál Riada had avoided me, the reason my stepmother had always eyed me with suspicion? I, in my natural state, was considered entirely unnatural by those around me, so I had done my best to avoid the subject since arriving at Camelot. Except, that was, with Morgan. That grief-filled afternoon where I had talked about my mother's gifts and found only acceptance in her eyes. Maybe I did Merlin a disservice by refusing him the same openness. He was my mentor after all.

Still, I tilted my head. 'But how do you know it was my mother?'

'I have met your father,' Merlin shrugged. 'A more mundane man than most. Even the most ordinary of men might steal themselves a seal wife, however.' His words were like the twist of a knife to my gut.

'Any natural ability you have will only grow as you learn the particulars, little sorceress,' he continued. 'What you must work on if you are to make full use of your mother's gift, however, is control. The water is a tool. You simply need to learn how to wield it.'

Maybe, maybe not, I thought.

The previous day had left me with much to think about. Too much. I had not forgotten the scribbled words of Merlin's vision, their ominous if unclear meaning. Yet the discussion of my mother and the gifts she may have handed down to me had eclipsed everything else. My dreams that night had been of the nearby lake where I had spent less and less of my time in recent months, the gentle caress of the water still detectable on my skin when I awoke.

Spurred on by the memory of my dream and Merlin's

words from the previous afternoon, I decided to use my day to myself to do something I might have been too embarrassed to try for the first time with company. And that meant returning to the lake.

I didn't even stop to eat breakfast before I was dressed and on my way, striding through the castle corridors like a woman on a mission. Which, I suppose, I was.

It was a mild day and when I reached the lakeside I immediately discarded my shoes so I could enjoy the feeling of the crisp grass between my toes for a few silent, blissful moments. I needed to let go, I told myself. Set everything else aside and focus only on this. Once I felt my chest loosen and my breathing steady, I turned my attention on the lake. Now it was time to test my theory. All my life I had felt at home in the water, felt drawn to its embrace. But if I could draw the water to me, what else might be possible?

I began my experiment tentatively, approaching the lake so I stood within a whisker of the glittering surface. My bare feet flexed against the grassy soil. There was nothing between me and the water but earth and air.

Focus.

The leaves of the trees rustled in the wind and the nesting birds called out to one another through their branches. Instead of listening in, however, I closed my eyes and let the sounds around me disappear. Inhaling deeply, I concentrated on the body of water in front of me. It was in the air: the atmosphere felt different from that inside the castle, richer, causing the tiny hairs on my arms to stand to attention. I could almost feel it brushing up against my skin – no, I *could* feel it against my skin, against my feet. Opening my eyes, I glanced down. Sure enough, the lake had reached out, spilling over its shore, beyond the boundaries imposed on it by nature, and was now lapping pleasantly at my toes.

The laughter burst out of me without preamble, my body bending, doubling over as my chest vibrated and tears fell down my cheeks. It was a release. Not just of the pent-up nerves that had been building since that morning but of all the magic I had been trying so hard to conjure for weeks and months. I could feel it. The path between myself and the water was filled with an eagerness and joy I knew wasn't purely my own.

'It's good to meet you.' I laughed harder, falling to my knees to caress the water with my open palms. I didn't even have to submerge my hands; the liquid spiralled up my skin, wrapping around me from the tips of my fingers to the bottoms of my wrists.

Show me what you can do.

I didn't have to speak the words out loud for the lake to respond. The water receded from my hands and I watched as the individual droplets shot upwards, criss-crossing through the air in a mesmerizing display of aquatic acrobatics. I whooped and clapped as my eyes followed their dazzling tracks through the air. Still, I wanted more. After a few moments of watching passively, I reached out across the connection we shared and asked the water to mimic the image I was picturing in my mind. There was no hesitation and I grinned even more widely as I watched the droplets coalesce to take the shape of a transparent rose before me, stem reaching up from the surface of the lake. Next I imagined a crow and let out an audible gasp when the shape conjured flapped its glistening wings. This was followed by a sword, double the size of any that I had ever seen in person. Despite the blurry shades of green and brown visible through its watery body, I couldn't help but be amazed by how real it looked. Hypnotized, I stretched out a hand and made to wrap my fingers around its pommel, only for them to close on themselves, as empty as they had been before.

I should probably have ended my efforts there, but instead I carried on playing with the water, conjuring shapes and patterns in the air until the sun was little more than a pinkish blur fading fast behind the treeline. I was so wrapped up in what I was doing that I barely registered the passage of time, or the steady depletion of my energy. I knew magic was an exertion, just like any physical or mental activity, but in that moment I felt so alive, kept afloat by giddy excitement alone. Still, eventually the exhaustion came for me, pulling me under until I could only feel the grass that tickled at the back of my neck and blackness overwhelmed my vision.

At some point during the night, I was roused from my slumber just long enough to feel two surprisingly strong arms slide beneath my body and haul me from the ground. My eyelids refused to open fully, my entire body still too heavy to heed my command, but I thought I could just make out two piercing blue eyes looking down at me.

'It's all right, little sorceress, let's get you to bed,' murmured Merlin close to my ear. Reassured, I let my eyelids flutter closed once more and fell back into a deep slumber. When I finally awoke, dawn was approaching and I was alone in my bed, a familiar quilt wrapped around me. Another day I might have thought the whole adventure a dream, except that my feet were bare and my brown suede slippers were nowhere to be found.

TEN

'I'd like to show you something, Viviane.' I sat up straighter, my curiosity piqued. 'It will take us almost a day to travel there, however, so you would have to be willing to spend the night outside. Perhaps sleep beneath the stars,' – a small smile tugged at the corner of Merlin's mouth –, 'not that you're any stranger to that.'

I blushed. What could Merlin have to share with me that would take us so far from Camelot? What magical lesson might I be privy to? The possibilities were both intimidating and exhilarating. Part of me wanted to jump to my feet and demand that we leave that instant, but another part forced me to pause.

'What about Morgan?'

'Morgan is not here,' he shrugged, turning from me as though his words didn't matter. 'I will be leaving in an hour regardless; it is up to you whether you join me or not.'

How could I say no?

Just as Merlin had promised, our horses were saddled and our journey commenced within the hour. I hadn't had much cause to ride in my three years at Camelot, so I was glad to discover that my own steed, a beautiful dappled grey mare who went by the name of Luar, was of a calm and amiable temperament, unperturbed by my unpractised riding. Together, we followed alongside Merlin and his dove-white stallion at a steady pace for the better part of the day.

At no point did I ask where we were headed. If the sorcerer had wanted to tell me he would have done so already, that much I knew of his character from the months I had spent as his student. That did not prevent me pondering the possibilities to myself, however. Another castle? I was not aware of any that could be reached on horseback in less than a day from Camelot. An entrance to the otherworld? I wasn't sure I relished such a prospect based on the stories I had heard. Merlin's private residence? For surely there was somewhere he called his own outside the fortress walls, somewhere he spent his time when he disappeared for days.

Yet no building or structure appeared upon the horizon as the hours ticked by. We passed through woodlands and open pastures, past small farmsteads and winding rivers, none of it worthy of comment as far as I could tell. The sun reached its peak in the sky and started to descend once more, as if overcome by the same exhaustion I myself was beginning to experience atop my steed. My thighs burned from riding and my cheeks smarted from the open air, but I was reluctant to complain, knowing it would likely lead nowhere but would make me seem impatient and immature. The temptation was becoming almost too much to bear when finally, thankfully, we crested our final foothill and Merlin slowed his pace to a trot.

'We're here,' he called over to me and gestured to the valley below.

My first instinct was to ask, *where?* Where was here? But upon further inspection I noticed there was an interruption in the otherwise unscathed landscape, one that surely could not be natural. A wide circle of impossibly tall stones stood sentry over the open grass, with what could only have been a man-made firepit nestled at its centre.

'What is that?' I asked as we rode forward together.

'This is where I come to . . . recharge, shall we say. These stones, they were all once a part of the land. One hewn from a cliff face shaped by the sea, another chipped away from the depths of a quarry.' He waved a hand almost nonchalantly in their direction. 'Each one a connection to the ancient magic of these isles.'

When we reached the monument itself, Merlin came to a halt and gracefully dismounted his steed, offering out a hand to help me from my own. I was grateful for the assistance, not entirely sure of the effectiveness of my legs after so long in the saddle, and made no objection when he lifted me by the waist and placed me gently on the grass.

Now that my feet were planted firmly on the ground once more, I was at last able to fully absorb the scale of what I was seeing. There were fourteen stones in total, each of them towering over me, more than three times my height and too wide to reach the edges with my arms fully extended. As Merlin had indicated, no two were made of the same stone, subtle differences in their texture and colour now visible up close. As I walked between them, the final vestiges of sunlight were blocked intermittently from my view and their outlines glowed fiery orange against the horizon. It was breathtaking.

'But how did you get them here?' I finally asked. Nothing about this monument could be natural.

'Well, that would be telling, now wouldn't it?' the sorcerer grinned down at me. *Insufferable.* Yet I couldn't help grinning back.

'Here, touch one.' Merlin approached me from behind and took one of my hands in his, pressing its palm against the rough stone before me. 'Can you feel it?'

My initial reaction was to ask, *feel what?* But before the question could pass my lips I already had my answer. Beyond the cold, hard surface of the monument was something else. Something far less stiff and unyielding. Something vital. It was almost as though a heart beat beneath my hand. The stone had a pulse, a slow, rhythmic ache that was anything but human, yet still undeniable.

'Is it alive?' I whispered, as much to myself as to Merlin.

'That depends on your definition of what it means to be alive.'

'But that's not a heartbeat?' I asked, unable to pull my hand away.

'It is the thrum of magic. The kind of magic that only comes with age. A magic imbibed through the centuries. More powerful than anything one person has ever been able to wield.'

'But you can channel this magic?'

'Some of it. Some.' He had let go of my hand and now traced his own fingers across the surface of the rock.

'Can you show me how?'

This made Merlin chuckle. 'There's no need, little sorceress. You already have your own conduit.' His smile only widened when I frowned back at him, nonplussed. 'The lake you are so fond of?'

I blinked. 'I don't . . .' Or did I?

Merlin laughed again. 'There is something I would like to share with you though.' He held out his right hand in the direction of my left and instinctively I took it. 'Keep your palm on the stone.' He nodded at the arm I had been about to drop and placed his own free one down next to it so we created a sort of dance circle with the imposing monument as our third.

A moment passed in silence. I stared between our joined hands and the two that lay a hair's breadth away from one another on the stony surface. Then the visions hit me.

A woman who looked a lot like me but was not, swimming in the loch at Dál Riada. My mother? My father striding past without sparing me a glance. A frog hopping across my leg as I lay in the grass – the texture of its rubbery limbs lingering on my skin even after the scene had passed. An awkward kiss from Arthur in his parents' private solar. A young man, a few years older than I was now, with black hair and dark skin, clasping my hands, a pleading expression on his face. Morgan grinning down at me, unfamiliar fine lines marking all the smiles she'd yet to smile. Unfamiliar waves crashing against a rocky cliff. Merlin's hands on my shoulders as magic crackled between us. And finally, Morgan's hands, smeared with blood, anguish and determination warring across her features.

My eyes were forced closed as images danced across the backs of my eyelids and my head spun. The scenes and faces seemed almost endless, each one blending into the next, with no apparent rhyme or reason to their order. Some I recognized while others were a mystery, and many slipped from the grasp of my memory as quickly as they came.

It felt like a lifetime and just a few seconds had passed all at once. I stumbled backwards, almost tumbling to the ground. Both arms wrapped around my stomach, the circle now broken, I took deep, desperate breaths as though I'd almost been suffocated a moment before. Merlin watched me, waiting, and saying nothing. After a few minutes I was finally able to compose myself, even though the dizziness had not entirely dissipated, and meet Merlin's gaze.

'What was that?' I gasped.

'A vision.'

'You told me you couldn't teach the art of prophecy?' My voice was too high, sounding shrill to my own ears.

'I can't. But I was able to share my own gift with you, if just for a moment, with the help of these stones.'

'Another conduit?'

Merlin smiled. 'Exactly. I'm glad to see your grasp of the magical principles strengthens with each passing day.'

After another moment of loaded silence, I finally found the courage to ask what I really wanted to know, now that I understood what I had seen. 'Did you see what I saw?'

Merlin shrugged. 'Some of it.'

I didn't know how to feel about that.

It was an eerie place, this valley. As Merlin had warned me, we were to set up camp for the night by the stones themselves. The sorcerer had come prepared with two bed-rolls and some provisions for our dinner, including a small wineskin. For a while we simply sat there idly, or rather I sat idly while Merlin positioned himself beside the now lit firepit and stared into the flames, meditating. He never asked me to join him or instructed me on how to spend my time. My lesson had begun and ended with the visions I'd received and since then I'd been left to ponder. When the sun had set, Merlin finally moved from the fireside and took a seat beside me on the soft grass, taking a long swig from the wineskin I had discarded.

'Why did you offer to teach Morgan and me?' The question was one I had turned over in my mind for the past few weeks but been unable to speak aloud. In this quiet, mystical place, however, where Camelot and reality seemed so far away, the idea that I should keep my curiosity to myself seemed equally remote.

'Why did you agree to become my student?'

I snorted. I should have seen that coming. It was typical Merlin, answering a question with a question that wasn't really an answer at all. Nor did he rush me to respond, but eventually I replied: 'It was the first time anyone had ever asked me if I wanted to do something or not. Something besides choosing between green and blue embroidery thread, at least.'

'Still. You chose to learn when you didn't have to. You could equally have chosen to refuse.'

I hesitated before elaborating, worried I might sound like a silly child to the revered magician who sat before me. 'It was a chance to determine my own destiny. If I had said no, things would have remained as they were, my path set out for me by others. I would have been a fool to turn you down.'

'Some have before you.' Merlin chuckled, his eyes no longer meeting mine but instead focused on the middle distance as though recalling a memory.

I pondered this. It made sense, I supposed, that Merlin had taught others the craft. He was an advisor to kings and lords, after all. Not to mention I had no idea how old the sorcerer actually was. He could have had a dozen, a hundred, students before Morgan and me. Rather than make me envious, however, the thought made me braver. If I was one of many, what did I gain from holding back?

'How do you know when to stop them?'

'Stop them?'

'The prophecies, what you see in them.'

'I see.' He nodded. 'Sometimes it is not about stopping them, but ensuring they come to pass.' When I frowned he chuckled. 'It's not all bad, Viviane. These visions I have, that you experienced today, are but a glimpse at possible futures, moments that might be. As their custodians we must also learn to be their judge. To have this information, however uncertain, is a good thing. It is power.'

I thought of the last image I had seen. Morgan's hands smeared with blood, no context for who it belonged to or why it was there. I didn't know if I wanted to be the custodian or judge of this information, but here I was. When I didn't say anything else for a few minutes, too wrapped up in my own thoughts, Merlin eventually said something I wasn't expecting.

'Shall I tell you a story?'

I bristled. 'I'm not a child.' Although I thought I might have sounded like one in that moment.

'Of course not. Nor is this a story for children.'

Slowly, I nodded, accepting the wineskin when he passed it back to me.

'When the Romans landed on these shores they brought with them their gods and goddesses, one of whom was the huntress Diana. A goddess of young women, like yourself. Diana was accompanied by Faunus, an ancient being, part man, part beast, whose dreams revealed the future. Faunus had loved Diana since their first meeting, but the goddess had sworn a vow of chastity and so they lived together as friends and friends alone.

'Faunus still desired the closeness of another body and so he found himself a mortal lover. Her name was Adhan. At first Diana didn't seem to care what Faunus did outside of their time together, but things changed when Adhan fell pregnant. Diana became jealous of the mortal woman and wished to punish Faunus.

'Faunus, however, had seen his demise in a dream. Diana couldn't kill him but she could trap him, forever, in stone. He believed his fate impossible to escape, but that didn't mean he couldn't change Diana's, to prevent her hurting Adhan and the baby.

'So, instead of fighting Diana, Faunus channelled his magic into his followers, those who had come with him from Rome and those who had joined him since. He gave them his rage, his strength and his divine protection. This magic fuelled them, and even as Diana trapped Faunus' earthly body, his followers swarmed her, tearing her limb from limb. They discarded her body in the nearby lake, but it was still too late to save Faunus from his fate.'

Merlin's eyes were no longer on me but were instead trained on the same pillar through which he had channelled his magic only hours before.

'You mean, that is Faunus?' I set the wineskin aside, suddenly queasy.

Merlin nodded. 'I believe so.'

'What about Adhan, and the baby?'

'They survived,' was Merlin's only response.

It was certainly not the kind of story you told a child. It was a sad and violent tale with no apparent happy ending that I could ascertain. Yet Merlin must have shared it with me for a reason.

'His vision of the future allowed him to protect others?' It was meant to be a statement but it came out more like a question.

'I suppose it did.' Merlin nodded, leaning back on to his bedroll. 'Although I'm not sure I would have given in so easily.' He smiled at me before lying down completely. 'Now, little sorceress, I think it's time we got some rest – we have a long day's travel ahead of us tomorrow.'

ELEVEN

'Excellent work, Viviane!' Merlin held my pot up to the light. The iris inside was in full bloom, with its tall green stem reaching towards the ceiling, and pinkish purple petals curling outward from their centre. I had been pleased with my results before, but I couldn't help my chest swelling a little with pride under the sorcerer's acknowledgement. 'Morgan, you will have to do better,' he added, barely glancing at the stub of greenery protruding from Morgan's pot.

'I've been away,' she responded indignantly.

'And yet you have to find a way. You might have been born a princess but you must choose to be a sorcerer.' Morgan's expression appeared to be at war between anger and embarrassment. 'Anyway, that is all I have time for today,' Merlin continued. 'I expect you both to continue your studies between now and the next time I see you.' He looked pointedly at Morgan.

'Yes, of course, Master Merlin,' I agreed for both of us, taking Morgan's arm in my own. Merlin simply nodded in response, turning to his own work without another word. We had been dismissed.

Morgan was silent during our walk between the tower and my chambers. After four long weeks, she and Arthur had returned from their trip to Garlot the previous day, while Uther had gone on to join his troops, and this was the first time we had been alone since. I wanted to ask her how it had gone but I didn't know where to start. Guinevere's words still rang in my ears. Had Morgan spent time with the young king? His family? Had he been handsome? Kind? What exactly had been discussed?

'I don't know what he expects from me!' Morgan's exclamation came just as I was pushing open the door to my rooms. With every ounce of drama in her body, she proceeded to stomp past me and throw herself upon the emerald settle.

'I think he just wants our commitment,' I sighed, pushing in beside her.

Morgan rolled her eyes. 'Not Merlin, my father.'

'Ah right,' I nodded, chewing my bottom lip. 'Your visit to Nentres' court didn't go well then, I suppose?'

'The man is a decade older than me.'

I grinned, experiencing a tiny spark of joy at Morgan's obvious distaste for the match. 'Successful marriages have begun with much larger age gaps,' I still felt obligated to point out.

'Well, if my behaviour was anything to go by, this one certainly won't be.' Her eyes twinkled.

'What did you do?'

'I refused to bathe or let my maid douse me in scented oils the entire time we were there.' Her eyes gleamed and I chuckled. 'I stank so badly of the road and stale wine after a while that my prospective husband refused to sit next to me.'

My nose wrinkled simply listening to Morgan describe it. 'You were gone almost a month – how did you not scratch yourself raw?' Perhaps I was the strange one, but I couldn't imagine not soaking my skin for so long without wanting to turn myself inside out.

'It's all in the herbs you use.' Morgan arched an eyebrow. 'I might not be Merlin's favourite student but I have learnt a thing or two from all that reading he's had us doing.'

I cringed a little at the implication of Morgan's use of the word 'favourite'; I was still all too aware of the fight that had erupted the last time Morgan had felt threatened by my presence. That was then, I had to remind myself, this was now, for Morgan didn't linger on the subject. Instead, she cooried a little closer and leaned her head against my shoulder.

'So, what did you get up to while I was gone? Was Merlin a demanding master?'

Quite the opposite, I thought. If anything, a new level of respect had arisen between Merlin and myself; he took me more seriously as a sorceress every day we spent alone together. The past four weeks had left me with a new sense of pride; that pride, however, was tinged with guilt now that Morgan sat before me.

I hadn't yet had a chance to tell her about Merlin's and my visit to the standing stones, and now that the opportunity had arisen I was suddenly reluctant to do so. I wasn't sure why exactly, only that it had felt personal, more intimate than our typical lessons, something that had been just for me. Nor had Merlin raised the topic. I didn't want to arouse Morgan's envy, I told myself; we were simply on different paths. Despite Merlin's criticisms, Morgan was showing an aptitude with plants and healing magic way beyond anything I could manage. This was the same, wasn't it? We were both developing our craft but we didn't always have to do it in tandem, surely?

'The same old thing.' I shrugged, searching for something else to share beside my excursion. Only when my eyes alighted on the tapestry that adorned my wall, a scene of knights atop their horses, their ladies waving them farewell, did I remember what had happened that first day. 'Merlin did have a premonition the day you left. I'd never seen one before. I didn't know they would be so . . .' I wracked my brain for the appropriate word, but Morgan saved me from having to find it.

'Visceral? I remember him having a vision during a feast when I was younger. It was kind of terrifying; I had no idea what was going on. But it turned out that was the vision that predicted my father would become king. News of Aurelius' death came the next day. What was this one about?'

'I don't know.' I frowned. 'A battle, maybe?'

'Aren't they all?'

The lie slipped out before I could second-guess it. Although lie was perhaps too strong a word. A simplification, for I had read the word *battle*. But so too had I read the words *poison* and *king*. Except I hadn't been supposed to, and I had no idea what they meant. Morgan was my closest companion, yet to share Merlin's scribbled words felt like a betrayal of my mentor. Surely Merlin would have shared whatever he'd seen with Uther, that was his job. It wasn't for me to speculate on something I couldn't understand, nor to worry Morgan unnecessarily. At least, that's what I told myself.

Not sure what else to say and ready to move away from

the topic of what had happened while Morgan was away, I decided to change the subject. 'So, there's been no betrothal?' I wanted to sound casual, but I wasn't sure I pulled it off; my cheeks certainly felt a little more flushed than they had a moment before.

Morgan gave me a small smile that did not quite reach her eyes. 'No, and I can only hope it remains that way . . . indefinitely.'

Buoyed by this news, I decided to make a proposition. 'Well, I can't do much about your father, but Merlin, there I think I can help.' I grinned at Morgan, pushing any thoughts of marriage to one side. 'If you'll come with me?'

'Always.' Morgan grinned back.

Although I never told Morgan where we were going out loud, it soon became evident that the lake was our destination. Together we snuck from the castle grounds, Morgan clasping her tiny pot to her chest while I led the way. I'd been sneaking out to the waterside often enough lately that I shouldn't have been nervous, but there was something about Morgan's company that renewed the illicit thrill of the escape. We were in this together.

When we came to the clearing I settled myself down on the grass beside the lake and patted the ground in front of me so she would do the same. 'It's just you and me out here, no one else besides the birds and frogs.'

'And the fairies.' Morgan wiggled her eyebrows at me as she crossed her legs beneath her.

I laughed. 'If there were any fairies lurking around these parts, I think we would have heard from them by now.'

'Hmm, always so certain.'

Ignoring Morgan's teasing, I waved my hand to shush her and carried on. 'Pay attention. You need to let the rest of the world slip away. Focus on what's right in front of you.'

Morgan placed the clay pot on the ground between us and stared at me as if awaiting further instruction. When I didn't say anything else, however, she refocused her attention on the seedling, frowning down at it as if it had personally murdered her grandmother.

'Stop trying to control it,' I finally said when I thought I could hear the sound of grinding teeth.

'If I'm not trying to control it, what am I trying to do?' Morgan's tone was petulant and I had to resist laughing aloud. I thought back to the first evening I had come here alone, when I had asked the water to do my bidding. Except it hadn't been my bidding, not entirely. The water had been a willing dance partner, just as eager as I to demonstrate its capabilities. I knew that now. All it needed was a helping hand.

'What do you want from the plant?' I nudged.

'I want it to grow.' Morgan rolled her eyes; I rolled mine exaggeratedly back.

'No, it has to be more than that. What kind of seed is it?' I decided to start with the basics.

'It's a lavender plant.'

'All right. Tell me about lavender. What is it used for? I know you know, all that reading up on herbs you do. So, tell me.'

'Well, it's an all-purpose healing plant really. The scent can ease headaches and it's especially potent when used in steaming. A lavender tea can help the drinker sleep, or if it's ground down into a poultice it can be used to treat burns and shallow cuts.' Morgan's face transformed as she spoke, frustration ceding to passion. The sight and sound brought a smile to my own lips. 'One of the maids even told me she hides it in the laundry to keep the moths away,' Morgan chuckled.

'That's it, then. That's what you want from the seed, and it wants it too. You just have to set it free.'

'Set it free, you say,' Morgan laughed and grabbed the plant from between us.

Before I could guess what she was about to do, Morgan had brought the pot down hard, shattering the clay and letting earth spill out on to the ground. With equal ferocity she stretched out her fingers and dug her hands into the soil, a feral grin spreading across her face. Rather than flinch, I leaned in further, watching as tendrils of green began to rise from the chaos. They stretched and writhed, either reaching for the sun or for Morgan herself, I wasn't sure which. Then, one by one, the buds atop their stems began to bloom, each tiny petal a brilliantly vibrant shade of purple, unfurling before my eyes. The spectacle only ceased when Morgan withdrew her hands, soil falling from between her fingers as she met my gaze over the flower bed that had sprouted between us.

'You've cut yourself,' I gasped. Without thinking I grasped her hand and lifted her fingers closer to my face to examine them. Blood was beading at the site of the wound before trickling down to trace a pathway to her palm. And for a split second I remembered another image of Morgan, blood staining her hands, before I shook it away again.

'Just a little.' Morgan smiled and pushed her hand forward so her fingers entwined with mine, trapping the mixture of blood and dirt between them. 'I think it was worth it though.'

I looked at the lavender plant and grinned back. 'I think you might be right.'

TWELVE

'So, if I succeed, will you give me another kiss?'

'Pelleas, if you draw that sword from the stone I'll marry you.' I rolled my eyes, content in the knowledge that there was no way Pelleas would manage such a feat.

In contrast with the warmth of the past few weeks, a storm had fallen upon Camelot during the previous night and rain continued to pelt the ground well into the morning. It was no weather for being outside. At least, that was everyone's excuse. Guin and I were lounging on the pews in the chapel, resigned spectators to the lordlings and princes as they tested their strength on the famously immovable sword.

'I'd be king and you my queen.' Pelleas puffed up his chest and I had to stifle a snort.

No one seriously expected any of the young men gathered there to draw the sword. Not even Arthur. *Only the one true king might draw the sword from the stone.* Those had been Arthur's words more than three years earlier. Words that I had heard repeated many times since. The only reason we were even here was a quarrel that had begun with Arthur and his cousin Sir Kay an hour or so before.

'I bet it's not even enchanted. It's probably just a rumour Uncle Uther made up to deter his challengers.'

'Sounds exactly like something someone who will never be king would say,' Arthur had retorted.

Youthful posturing or not, we had all taken the bait, and I found myself watching as Kay marched up to the stone. No one knew its origin, only that Merlin had brought it to Camelot – when I had asked him about it, the sorcerer only smirked and tapped his nose – but it didn't take months of sorcery lessons to sense there was something magical about both sword and casing.

'I swear I felt it shift,' Kay protested as the other men jeered him from the pew.

'You don't think anyone other than Arthur would really be able to draw the sword, do you?' Guin whispered from my other side.

I shrugged. 'I've no idea.'

'But can't you tell, with magic?' she persisted.

I slapped my palm against my temple and closed my eyes. 'You're right, I see it now, the sword shall be drawn by . . .' – pause for dramatic effect – 'Wellefed.' Wellefed was the sword master's retired hound who liked to hang around in the kitchens.

'All right,' Guin nudged me with her elbow, 'no need to tease.' She cast a quick smile my way before returning her gaze to Arthur.

Although the youngest of the gathered men, really still a boy, Arthur had begun to gain popularity among his peers in the past year. In particular, he was proving to be an expert swordsman, often disarming even the most experienced of the king's knights, which in turn was all it took to win him their respect. And he was revelling in it.

'Did I miss all the fun?'

I turned from Guin and Pelleas, a wide grin spreading across my face as Morgan approached. She had spent the morning playing catch-up with Merlin, determined to make up for the time she had been away, and I was eager to hear how she had fared.

'Ah, the night to your day, Lady Viviane.' Pelleas winked at me. He and Morgan never had quite learnt to get along. 'Right, I'm next up after Accolon – wish me luck.' Without waiting for my response, he rose from the pew and strode over to his friends, allowing Morgan to take his empty seat.

Accolon, meanwhile, jogged up to the dais to the cheers of his comrades. As he readied himself, he glanced our way, his eyes lingering a split second longer on Morgan than on anyone else, finally offering her an almost imperceptible nod before returning to his task. Morgan, I was surprised to see when I turned to look, was smiling back at him, her hand raised in the briefest of waves. This was new, I thought, a niggling feeling developing in the centre of my chest. It felt an awful lot like jealousy, but over what I wasn't quite sure.

'How was your lesson with Merlin?' I whispered, hoping to regain her attention.

'Oh, you know, close but not quite, you need to take the craft seriously, you're too easily distracted.' Morgan imitated Merlin's deeper voice while keeping her eyes trained on the fight unfolding before us. 'You'd think I was away a year and not a measly month based on the way he talks.' She sighed a little too emphatically. 'Tell me again, Viviane, what did you get up to in your sessions while I was away?'

'Nothing special.' I frowned, repeating my answer from the other day, confused as to why she was asking again.

'Nothing at all? Nothing you might like to share with me?'

I felt a curdling sensation in the pit of my stomach. 'Like what?'

'Oh, I don't know, like taking an overnight trip to a sacred stone circle.' Morgan finally turned to look at me, her voice not much more than a low hiss.

'Merlin told you?' I whispered back.

It was not the correct response.

'Obviously. But I'm more interested in why you didn't. What were you trying to hide, exactly?'

'Nothing, Morgan.' That was the truth, wasn't it? 'It was a spur-of-the-moment trip, it was nothing.'

'Right, nothing.' Morgan narrowed her eyes at me. 'Weren't you the one who said we were in this together, Viviane?'

'Morgan –'

'Don't bother,' Morgan snarled, returning her attention to the men.

I needed to say something else, to make amends for my secrecy, because why had I kept it a secret at all? Merlin hadn't told me to; it had been my choice entirely. And for what? So Morgan wouldn't be jealous? So she wouldn't feel excluded? Fat lot of good that had done me. And was I really that selfless? A small part of me had to admit I had enjoyed my time alone with Merlin. Our trip had made me feel . . . special – something I wasn't used to feeling. As I wracked my brain for an appropriate response, an unexpected sound broke through the chatter of those around me.

Steel on stone.

I spun in my seat just in time to witness the very tip of the blade slide free from its prison, the echo of the metal edge against the anvil the only sound in the now silent chapel. For a moment everything Morgan and I had been arguing about fled from my mind and I stared in shock at Arthur, now standing upon the dais, a gleaming sword quivering in his hands.

I felt Guin's hand on my thigh, her fingers digging into my flesh.

'The one true king.' Kay's voice was barely more than a whisper, but in the silence of the chapel it rang out like a sermon. 'All hail King Arthur.' He sank to one knee.

Prompted by Kay, the other men dropped one by one, knees bent, heads bowed, repeating their comrade's words in turn.

'All hail King Arthur.'

Guin was next to fall, squeezing herself between the two pews and dragging me down with her. Morgan meanwhile didn't move. She remained seated, her eyes trained on her brother as he met them across the hall. Neither of them was smiling, which I might have expected from Morgan, frustrated at being constantly overshadowed by her brother, but Arthur should be ecstatic, surely? If anything, Arthur's expression struck me as alarm. And then it hit me, what Morgan and Arthur had already realized: who did Arthur's ascension to the throne mean more to than his sister? Uther.

Before I could catch Morgan's attention, she had risen from her seat and stormed from the room, alerting the rest of its occupants to the fact that all was not as it should be. The young men began to clamber to their feet, moving towards their friend and future king, while Guin glanced between me and Morgan's vanishing hem.

'I'll explain later,' was all I said, turning my back on the unfolding spectacle and running after my friend.

I wasn't fast enough to catch up with Morgan in the corridor outside the chapel but was instead forced to follow the sound of her rapid footsteps as she made her way to the main entrance of the castle. When I stepped outside close behind her, however, I discovered we were not alone.

Everywhere, small groups were amassing, exchanging questions in hushed voices, glancing around curiously, confused as to what might have happened to have brought them out into the rain. Guards, meanwhile, had come together in droves, presumably abandoning their stations across Camelot, and stood in hastily formed rows leading down the hillside.

'The king's retinue approaches!'

Everyone turned towards the guards upon hearing their shout. And for a few moments the atmosphere lightened; excited murmurs passed among the gathered people. Uther had returned. News had already reached us of Octa of Kent's defeat the week before, a defeat that marked a huge victory against those who had killed Uther's brother. Now there would be an opportunity to celebrate. There would surely be feasting and dancing and general revelry. Or at least that's what everyone had thought.

I moved to Morgan's side, ready to beg her forgiveness.

Then another voice broke through the throng.

'The king is wounded!'

This single cry quickly turned into a chorus of shouts – their words indiscernible as people called over one another, trying to ascertain what was going on.

'He's sick!' came another, louder voice, which made me gasp.

'The poison.'

'What?' Morgan spun on her heel to face me. 'What did you say?'

'Merlin's vision,' I stammered, 'it mentioned something about poison but I didn't –'

'You knew about this?' she interrupted.

'No –'

'You said you didn't know what Merlin's vision was about!'

'I didn't, I don't! I only saw a few words of what he wrote down afterwards.'

'Another secret,' Morgan snarled. 'They just keep coming with you, don't they?'

I cringed backwards. 'I just –'

'Just what?' But she didn't pause to let me answer. 'Why are you even here, Viviane? Not here,' she gestured around us at the courtyard, '*here*, Camelot. Why are you still here? There's no one left to foster you. Arthur doesn't want you as a wife. And I certainly don't need you as a friend.'

Her words stung but I was not unfamiliar with the princess's barbed tongue. Unwilling to give up so easily, I pushed on. 'I know I should have told you about my journey with Merlin to the standing stones.'

'Oh, and don't forget the prophecy that might have heralded my father's death,' Morgan spat. 'Don't stand there acting contrite. You should be happy. Everything has worked perfectly, hasn't it? Arthur will be king, Guinevere queen, and you the sorcerer's favourite apprentice. What could you possibly need from me?'

My eyes stung with the strain of holding back my tears, Morgan's words ripping through me as she stared at me with contempt. I didn't know that I could say anything to undo the hurt she was feeling and that was now bubbling inside me, but still I decided to reach out one last time, grabbing hold of her shoulder.

'Morgan, don't do this.' My voice cracked on the words.

'Don't tell me what to do!' Morgan practically shouted, bringing her hand up to my own shoulder and shoving, hard.

Shocked by the vitriol in her tone and the force of her push, I stumbled backwards. Instinctively, I tried to reach out for some purchase but all I found was the hem of another woman's dress, which tore as I fell. I hit the ground with a hard thud, a sharp pain radiating up my spine and forcing a groan from my lips. Meanwhile Morgan simply turned away, no longer even bothering to look my way.

'My dress!' cried the older woman, whose face I hadn't registered.

But I didn't look back. I was humiliated, and so I ran. I ran from the crowd gathered outside the castle, past the figures in the halls whispering to one another of the king's fate. I didn't want to go back to my rooms, I didn't want to be alone, but where else was I supposed to go? It seemed, however, my feet knew better than I what I needed as I automatically found myself climbing the winding stairs of Merlin's tower and pushing open the door to his chambers.

It took me less than a handful of seconds to ascertain that both rooms were empty – Merlin was clearly elsewhere, which shouldn't have come as a surprise given the much larger crisis that was unfolding downstairs. Still, I decided, I was here now. Slumping down on to the floor, I leaned my back against the side of Merlin's bed, and that was when the tears began to fall.

I wasn't sure how long I sat like that, head buried in my arms, tears soaking through the sleeves of my dress. By the time my eyes had dried the sun had set outside, leaving me in total darkness. Just as I was wondering if I should leave, however, I heard the creak of the nearby door.

'Viviane?'

I looked up, squinting through the rawness of my puffy eyelids to see Merlin standing in the open doorway. 'I'm sorry, I didn't know where else to go.' I sniffed.

'Morgan?'

I nodded.

Merlin let the door close behind him and sighed, his long fingers massaging the skin on his forehead. 'It's my fault, really. I should have seen this coming.'

I wiped my eyes with the back of my hand. 'What do you mean?'

'The jealousy. When I offered to teach you both together, I worried this might happen. But I suppose it is only natural; you are both young, ambitious in your own ways.'

'I didn't . . . I wasn't trying to exclude her.' Should I have refused to go with Merlin in the first place?

As though he could read my mind, Merlin shook his

head at me. 'Sometimes, little sorceress, we must take things for ourselves.' He crouched down so we were eye-to-eye. 'Morgan has asked that if I continue to teach you both I teach you separately, and I have agreed.'

I should have expected it, but it had all happened so quickly, his words were like a punch to my gut. There was no point in arguing, even if I had wanted to, which I wasn't sure I did.

Merlin didn't resent my grief. He didn't chide me for crying or reprimand me for disturbing his chambers. Instead, the older man took a seat on the floor beside me, his much longer legs stretching out next to mine. He didn't say anything or make to touch me, to rub my back or brush my tears away; he simply sat there in silence providing me with the comfort of his presence as long as I needed.

Later that night, as I lay in my bed staring up at the ceiling, I half hoped, half expected that Morgan might knock at the door or simply stroll in – an apology dancing on her lips just like the last time we had seriously argued. This was not like the last time, though, and Morgan did not barge into my chambers forgiving our fight. Nor could I entirely blame her. I had chosen to keep my time with Merlin secret knowing exactly how she felt. And why? Because of some deep-rooted need to feel special? I didn't feel special now. I felt spurned, and lonely, like I'd lost more than I could explain.

THIRTEEN

In the name of our Lord Jesus Christ, I now proclaim you, Arthur Pendragon, King of the Britons. Long live the king!

'Long live the king!' The chorus of voices filled the chapel, my own among them.

The bishop stepped back from the dais as the crowd broke into applause and King Arthur rose to his feet.

'My queen.' He offered his hand to the still kneeling Guinevere, who took it, a demure smile the perfect accompaniment to the gleaming circlet that now adorned her head.

After months that had felt more like hours, the day the castle had been preparing for since Uther's death had finally arrived. Arthur and Guin's wedding and coronation all wrapped up in one. An official engagement between Arthur and Guinevere had almost been unnecessary – their union effectively a given from the moment the kingdom knew Uther would not recover, my own candidacy quickly forgotten. Not that I minded. If anything, it was a relief to have officially been superseded, removed from the running. When I thought of Arthur, I felt nothing. And I knew now I was capable of more.

In that moment, as I sat in the chapel pews with the other courtiers and watched Arthur bound to my friend in matrimony, I wondered that anyone could have doubted him. I thought it was the first time I had really seen Arthur for the man he had become. The gangly, laughing teenager I had first met at Camelot seemed to have vanished before my eyes – the weight of expectation and doubt pushing him down, hardening him under the pressure. Once of a height with Guinevere and myself, he now towered at least two heads taller over his bride. Meanwhile his orange hair had become richer, darker, and a fine down had spread across his jaw.

Of course, the appearance of a man was not enough. No, what had ensured Arthur's acceptance despite his age was the gleaming sword that hung from his belt. The story of how Uther's son had drawn the sword from the stone had already travelled far beyond Camelot's walls, taking the shape of a legend that would likely grow and warp beyond all our lives. Only those who had been in the chapel that day truly knew what had happened. All I saw when I looked upon that blade, however, was the moment my own heart was broken.

The entire ceremony seemed to pass by in a matter of minutes, yet by the time we sat down to eat, the sun that had sat high in the sky during the new king and queen's coronation was rapidly retreating behind the horizon. It was a lavish feast; the plates stacked higher and the wine flowing more freely than on a regular day. The conversation was loud and jovial, everyone shouting over their neighbour while musicians played their lyres in the background. And everyone who was anyone was in attendance, Guinevere's parents included.

I was seated between Guinevere's mother Queen Breage and a Lord Constantine, one of Arthur's newly appointed knights and his cousin through some series of relations I hadn't been fully able to follow when he had described them to me. There were plenty of such distant relatives in attendance. While the queen was better occupied with her husband on her other side, I found that Constantine was pleasant enough company. He talked animatedly of his coastal home in Dumnonia where the water crashed against the mighty cliffs and his father's castle looked out across the sea to the shores of Armorica. Still, I missed Morgan who was situated further up the table. Without her there was no one to laugh at Kay and Gawain, who both fought for the attention of a particularly pretty princess from Ulaid whose name I hadn't caught, or comment on which visiting nobles seemed overly curt or friendly with one another; it was really no fun speculating by myself.

'The coast is beautiful. Truly, everyone should visit at least once.'

'I hope one day I might.' I sipped at my wine and glanced further up the table.

Arthur and Guin sat side by side, entertaining those around them. While Guin was doted on by her father, King Leodegrance, to her left, Arthur sat to her right. The young king looked to be regaling his neighbour Queen Anna of Orkney – some cousin multiple times removed, I believed – with the tale of how he had come by his legendary sword; at least that's what I gathered from the way he brandished it over the table like a carving knife. Queen Anna meanwhile hung on his every word, her hand wrapped tightly around

Arthur's forearm, leaning forward so her husband, King Lott, was blocked from their conversation.

And beside him sat Morgan.

This wasn't the first time that evening I found myself watching the princess. It wasn't the first time that week. We may have exchanged little more than a handful of words over the past year or so, but that didn't mean I hadn't noticed her. I noticed how she was almost always alone yet never hid herself away. I noticed how women came to her for advice and she handed out tinctures to them when she thought no one else was looking. I noticed the proud way she carried herself through the corridors of Camelot, shoulders stiff, back straight, taller than any other woman I knew, looking as though she might crush you beneath her shoe if you were to look at her the wrong way. The only way I seemed to look at her. She smiled less in public and I was no longer privy to her private grins. Yet, for all she had dismissed me, calling an end to our friendship with an abruptness that still smarted, she had not continued to persecute me. Her cold words had run dry and instead, I was pretty sure, she was trying to avoid me at all costs. I wasn't sure which hurt more. Part of me thought I should hate her for how she'd rejected and scorned me over something that, as the months passed, seemed increasingly small. But no matter how deep I dug, hate was nowhere to be found.

That evening I watched her in conversation with her neighbour Accolon, even, I was shocked to see, demonstrating a minor magic trick by lighting the extinguished candle in front of him with just her little finger. It was . . . irritating how wrapped up in each other's company they were, and still more irritating how I kept finding my gaze trailing back to them like an uninvited voyeur.

I felt the lightest tap on my upper arm, snapping me out of my trance.

'What?' I flushed at the unintended rudeness of my response.

'Apologies, I didn't mean to startle you. Only, I have just spotted a familiar face I have not seen in quite some time and would like to say hello. I wouldn't want to abandon you without warning though.' Constantine gave me an awkward smile.

'Of course, it was a pleasure talking to you.' I smiled back, letting him go.

When I turned to my right once more to glance along the table, I found for the first time that evening Queen Breage looking back at me. The queen was a beautiful woman who shared her daughter's tight curls and dark complexion. I might have been sitting next to Guinevere twenty years from now.

'Lady Viviane of Dál Riada, am I correct?' I nodded politely, placing my third – or was it fourth – goblet of wine back on the table. 'My daughter has written fondly of you in her letters.'

'She has?' I blinked, surprised that Guinevere would have dedicated any ink to me.

'Yes, and I am glad she has had a friend at court these past five years.' The queen paused to study me a little more closely. 'It is easy for women of our station to find themselves in competition, rather than finding companionship with one another.' I blushed. What was I supposed to say to that? That I would rather have eaten my own big toe than marry Arthur? It hardly seemed appropriate.

'I am glad it did not turn out that way,' I acquiesced, bowing my head ever so slightly.

'It is a shame our son could not attend the festivities,' the queen smiled kindly. 'I'm sure he would have been pleased to make your acquaintance.'

'A shame,' I agreed, because what else was there to say?

Satisfied, she patted my hand lightly before turning back to her husband and leaving me to my own devices.

'A splendid evening, is it not?'

I almost jumped out of my skin at the sound of Merlin's voice. Swivelling in my seat with little grace, I found he now occupied the chair where Constantine had previously sat.

'Sorry, you surprised me there.' I gave a nervous chuckle and reached for my goblet, taking a deep swig of the ruby liquid inside. 'Yes, very nice. Who doesn't enjoy a wedding?'

He chuckled. 'You don't find the occasion a romantic one?'

'I . . .' *Not really*, I thought. 'What is romance? Everyone else is planning my marriage for me, there's nothing particularly romantic about that.'

'Ah, it is a sad thing to hear a young lady so jaded by court already. Although I do agree, you should be able to enjoy your youth without rushing into marriage.'

'I wish my own father felt as you do, Master Merlin.'

'I think it is time we did away with the Master stuff, simply Merlin will do. You are no longer a child, after all.' I turned to smile at the sorcerer, who was grinning back; he looked younger when he smiled, I thought. 'Nor am I sure how I feel about being compared to your father.' This time he laughed. 'Surely I do not seem so old.'

I felt my cheeks flush, but before I could agree aloud Merlin had raised his hand and swept it gently across his face. When I next gazed upon his features unobstructed, the tiniest of gasps escaped my lips.

'You . . . your face.'

My reaction elicited another laugh from Merlin. 'Age is meaningless to those like us.'

I didn't know about age, but in appearance Merlin had transformed from a man of forty to one of twenty-five before my eyes. Glancing around, however, it seemed I was the only one to have spotted the difference.

'To everyone else I look the same,' he whispered, leaning in a little closer.

'How did you do that?' I whispered back.

'Still so much to learn,' he chuckled. 'As I said, you should enjoy your youth. There is much pleasure to be had for a beautiful young woman such as yourself. You simply have to be open to it.' When he said the word *pleasure* I didn't think he meant good food or dancing, and I couldn't help the heat that rose to my cheeks once more.

'Something your colleague clearly understands.' Merlin nodded to the head of the table where my eyes focused on Morgan again. Her hand was placed carelessly on Accolon's arm, and she was laughing behind her goblet as he whispered in her ear. There was something undeniably intimate in the way he brushed the hair from her neck and leaned in a little closer than was entirely necessary. Both of their cheeks were tinged red and they exchanged knowing smiles when he finally pulled away.

When I turned back to Merlin, he wasn't looking at Morgan and Accolon; he was looking straight at me, a gleam in his eyes I didn't recognize. Was he drunk? I was certainly starting to feel the effects of my wine myself, I realized. Rather than making me feel loose and languid, however, I only felt an overwhelming sense of discomfort, like there was too much happening around me right now to fully process how I felt beyond the alcohol.

'Excuse me, it's getting late.' I stood up from my chair abruptly. 'I think it's time I retired.' And with that I was hurrying from the main dining hall, down the corridor towards the stairs that would take me to my room.

Within a few seconds, however, I heard someone calling my name. 'Viviane, wait!'

I turned to ascertain who had followed me and was surprised to find Pelleas striding down the hall. 'What is it, Pelleas? I'm tired.'

'I thought perhaps you might like a goodnight kiss.' He was level with me now and even from a few inches away I could smell the bitter scent of alcohol on his breath.

'Why on earth would you think that?' I demanded, more loudly than I had intended.

'Well, Arthur is married now. There is no point holding out.' He picked up my limp hand and stroked the palm with his thumb. 'I might not be able to make you a queen, Viviane, but I still have a lot to offer.'

What the hell was he talking about? Did Pelleas really

think that now Arthur and Guinevere's match was official, I would throw myself at his feet, or in his bed?

'Get off, Pelleas, you've had one too many cups of wine, and I've no interest in you drunkenly groping me. Or soberly groping me for that matter. How many times do I have to tell you? I'm not interested in being your lover or your wife.' I practically threw his hand from mine. The childish flirtation I had briefly entertained on first arriving at Camelot had slowly soured over the years as Pelleas had pushed harder, his youthful playfulness becoming an almost aggressive insistence despite my lack of response. My words had struck their mark this time, however. In the blink of an eye Pelleas' lecherous expression turned into something far nastier.

'No, you'd rather be Merlin's whore, I suppose.'

His words were a blade to my stomach. 'What the hell do you mean by that?'

He gave a derisive snort. 'Everyone knows it, Viviane. All that time you spend in his chambers. The looks he gives you when you're in public. It's embarrassing, a noblewoman trading her body in exchange for an old man's parlour tricks. I had thought perhaps to save what little of your reputation was left, but I see now I am too late.'

'Get away from me.' I stumbled backwards, trying to put distance between myself and this vitriolic version of the pushy young man I'd thought I knew.

'Gladly, Princess. But don't expect me to save you from ruin when he's done with you,' he sneered. 'Although I might be convinced to take you as a mistress if you're not completely dried up.'

The wine I had been drinking earlier was rising up to burn my throat, threatening to come back out. I had to get away. I turned on my heel, not sparing Pelleas another glance, and practically ran from his presence. When I finally reached my room I sat down on the emerald settle and swiped the abandoned sheet of parchment from my desk, bringing it up to my face so I could scan the words for the second time that day:

Dear Viviane,

News has only recently reached Dál Riada of King Uther's passing and Prince Arthur's impending coronation. Your father was disappointed to learn that after five years at court the Princess of Cameliard was chosen as the young king's wife rather than you, his daughter, especially after the numerous skilled warriors he provided to King Uther in his battles against the Saxons.

Nevertheless, as I reminded your father, you have surely not been idle during your time at Camelot. There are a great number of powerful lords and princes on these isles, many more of whom will be arriving to pay their respects at the castle in the coming months. I do hope you will be making a concerted effort to make their acquaintance if you have not met them already, and present yourself to their liking.

While you may not have won King Arthur's hand, you should not neglect your place in his court. The new queen, for example, could be particularly well placed to make a beneficial match on your father's behalf. If you have conducted yourself appropriately these past years, then you should be in good stead to receive her favour. A wise woman knows not to punish her competitors, but to ensure their own marital success. I am sure Queen Guinevere will understand this.

Your father and I will not be able to attend the wedding or coronation ourselves, but we wish you to pass on our condolences to the new king when the opportunity arises, and remind him Dál Riada remains his ally. We wish him and his bride a long reign and eagerly await news of your own engagement in the coming year.

Yours,

Queen Malinda

My father this, my father that, but perish the thought that his hand might lift a pen. I crushed the offending piece of parchment between my fingers and threw it into the fire. It crackled malevolently as I sat and watched it burn.

FOURTEEN

Pelleas' accusation had weighed heavily on me ever since the coronation. Was that how the other courtiers perceived me – as Merlin's mistress? Was that what Morgan believed? I shouldn't care what Morgan did or did not believe, I told myself, but that was easier said than done. Between this new worry thanks to Pelleas and my stepmother's ominous letter, I was desperate for distractions. Thus I found myself rooting through the pantries of the castle's kitchens one afternoon – with no invitation and no idea where anything was.

Coriander, coriander, where would I be if I were coriander?

'Can I help you find anything, m'lady?'

'Huh.' I withdrew my hand from the cupboard I was currently searching and looked over my shoulder to find a young, red-headed maidservant had approached me without my noticing. 'Oh, sorry, no, I'm fine. Clarine, is it?' I replied, still partially distracted by my quest.

'Yes, m'lady.' She gave a quick curtsy and I smiled.

'Actually, Clarine, you *can* help me – do you have any coriander?'

'Of course,' Clarine nodded. Without another word, she strode across the kitchen to the opposite wall and drew a nondescript clay pot from a shelf that held at least three dozen similar vessels. 'How much would you like, m'lady?'

'Oh, just a spoonful will do.' Clarine moved a small heap of the spice from the larger pot to a small bottle and handed it to me. 'Thank you, Clarine. I appreciate it.' I clasped my spoils to my chest.

'It's no trouble, m'lady.' The maidservant chewed her bottom lip for a moment before adding, 'Perhaps you could pass on my thanks to Princess Morgan for the brew she made me, though. My nausea is almost completely gone.'

'Yes, of course.' I nodded.

And I would tell her, I would. It might just not be today, or tomorrow. But eventually.

If I was being completely honest with myself, I had probably been avoiding Morgan as much as she had been avoiding me. I may have watched her when she was near, but I never set out to find her. I always kept my distance; I turned corners when I saw her coming, and I sat as far away as possible when we dined together in the evenings. Acknowledging this fact, however, made me cringe, so I tried my best not to. I told myself I was respecting her wishes. Had she not made it clear, that afternoon more than a year ago? We were no longer friends. Yet, for someone who was not my friend, I spent an awful lot of time thinking about her.

Of course, I tried to reassure myself, as the new king's sister she was also busy. We likely would have drifted apart regardless; she was expected to entertain the visiting dignitaries at Guinevere's side, and I . . . I had my project. For the past few weeks I had been experimenting with potion-making. All of my potions were water-based, specifically using the water from the nearby lake. I had even squirrelled away countless vials and jars of the liquid in my chamber cabinets, each one waiting to be combined with new ingredients for me to discover the results. Today's trial was coriander: good for inspiring passion and providing clarity.

There wasn't really a grand plan to my research, other than to answer my own curiosity; it was, in reality, only a distraction. Something to occupy my mind so that I didn't have to dwell on the more immediate and personal questions that plagued it. While my understanding of and ability to harness magic had increased exponentially over the preceding years, my emotions remained as complicated, if not more so, than they had seemed when I was sixteen years old. I needed purpose. I had even considered a lover. Pelleas was obviously not an option, but there was Meliadus, new to court since Uther's death, who had thrown some attention my way; when I tried to picture him in my daydreams, however, his dark hair simply made my mind wander back to another raven-headed figure.

It was no use, I told myself.

After thanking Clarine once more, I departed from the kitchens with the intention of heading straight back to my room. It was still early and most of the people I passed on my journey were servants or guards, the rest of the nobility still sleeping off last night's revelries. Revelries I'd failed to attend ever since the night of the coronation. Images of Morgan leaning in to let Accolon whisper in her ear flashed before my eyes. I didn't have any right to be annoyed, I knew that, but the sight had stirred something in me that I realized

I had been trying to suppress for a while, and now I couldn't stop thinking about it. My mind was so occupied by those thoughts that I didn't even notice I had taken a wrong turn until I almost walked into an unexpected suit of armour. Stopping in my tracks, I finally took in my surroundings only to see that I'd reached a dead end.

'Dammit,' I cursed, vexed more by my train of thought than my misdirection.

As I turned to head back down the corridor, however, my ears caught some raised voices coming from somewhere nearby. There was only one door that I could see and, sure enough, when I edged closer it became clear that the owners of said voices were behind it. At first I was inclined to scurry away before anyone could catch me eavesdropping, until I realized who was shouting.

'You can't be serious!'

Morgan? Yes, that was definitely Morgan. Despite everything, my instincts took over. Something was wrong and I had to make sure she was all right. Without further hesitation, I pushed the door open only to be greeted by the sight of three figures standing at the room's centre. As I looked on, Morgan, Arthur and Merlin stared each other down, the animosity almost tangible in the air.

'What you're suggesting is utterly heinous!'

'You put words into my mouth, Princess.' Merlin's eyes were narrowed, his voice distinctly lower than Morgan's had been.

None of them seemed to have noticed my intrusion, evidently too caught up in their argument. 'Morgan? What's going on?' All three of the room's occupants swivelled to face the door.

'Ah, Viviane, come in.' Merlin was the only one to greet me, beckoning me to approach as Morgan continued to glower at him. 'You may as well know, I've had a vision which our colleague here feels I should not have shared with the king.'

Morgan scoffed, but Merlin continued.

'As I was explaining to Arthur, however, what I have seen troubles me, and I could keep it to myself no longer.' He paused, almost as if for dramatic effect. 'There will be a child, born on May Day, who will one day threaten the peace of the crown.'

I looked at Arthur, whose stiff back and clenched jaw did little to hide the worry in his eyes. My heart went out to him. Here I was, bemoaning my relationship status, when he was figuring out how to rule a kingdom. A kingdom that might be under threat if Merlin's prediction was correct.

But a baby? What could the King of Camelot possibly have to fear from one who wasn't even born yet? It would be years, decades even, before this child could pose a threat to Arthur or the crown.

I scanned the three faces before me, all wearing such contrasting expressions that I didn't entirely know how to react. Arthur, uncomfortable despite his position. Morgan, disgust warring with horror on her face. And Merlin, unreadable as ever. That was when the significance of Merlin's words finally hit me. A threat to the crown that could be rooted out before it became a reality. But a baby? I felt sick as the full meaning of Morgan's earlier cry sank in. Horrified, I turned my gaze back to Arthur, but he refused to meet my eye. Gone was the proud, stoic man I'd caught a glimpse of at his coronation. Instead all I could see was a pale young boy trying to fill shoes two sizes too big for him.

'Merlin?' I pleaded when Arthur gave me nothing.

'You are angry with me?' Merlin asked.

Angry? Of course I was angry. Yet for some reason I didn't say that. 'Shocked,' I replied instead.

'Should I have kept my vision to myself? Is not the safety of the king and queen, your childhood friends, my duty at court to protect?'

'No, yes, I . . .' I shook my head, beginning to tremble. 'But there has to be another way. There will always be threats to the crown, jealous kings, dissatisfied lords, invaders from across the sea, but should we slaughter them all as babes?'

'Yes, Merlin, exactly. Where does it end?' Morgan nodded her head, backing up my words, re-articulating how I felt. And although she never looked directly at me, I felt a tiny spark of vindication amidst my distress. It felt good to be on the same side.

'Enough.' Arthur slapped his hand down on the table beside him. 'For now, have a census taken of all the women in Camelot, Merlin. I want to know which ones are currently with child and when they are expected to give birth.'

'Arthur!' Morgan and I spoke his name at the same time, but while my voice came out as a whisper, Morgan's had reached new volumes.

'I said enough,' Arthur rounded on Morgan. 'I will not be told how to run my kingdom by anyone, nor am I making any decisions without more information. You are all dismissed,' his eyes swept around our small group, 'or better yet, I am leaving.' With those words Arthur spun on his heel, head high, shoulders back, and stormed from the room.

Merlin turned back to me, an eyebrow raised as though waiting for me to continue my earlier speech, but I didn't have any words left. What could I possibly say that would hold sway with the king or his sorcerer? Merlin's apparent calm at what he had revealed also left me with an unfamiliar discomfort. I was so used to following his lead, letting him guide the way, that to hear something so horrific fall from his lips was . . . unsettling didn't do it justice. But he hadn't advocated for a violent solution, had he? He had simply relayed his vision. Perhaps my shock at what I'd heard was interfering with my judgement. Either way, I said nothing. Finally, after a few uncomfortable moments, Merlin simply shrugged his shoulders and followed Arthur out of the door, leaving me alone with Morgan for the first time in months.

For a moment I thought she might storm out next but then she turned on me, looking me in the eye for the first time since I had entered the room, a twisted expression on her face. 'Did you know about this?'

'What?' I couldn't believe what I was hearing. 'Merlin's prophecy? You think I've been hiding this kind of thing from everyone? That Merlin told me before you or Arthur?'

'I don't know what you and Merlin get up to in private, that much has always been evident.'

Her words smarted, as though she'd slapped me across the face with them. They also tugged at my earlier anxiety. 'Is that what you think? Is that what everyone thinks?' I slumped into a nearby chair. 'That I'm Merlin's mistress?'

Something about my question, or my tone of voice, must

have made Morgan think twice about her next words as she winced and looked away.

'No, of course not.' But I could tell from the flush on her cheeks and the way she refused to meet my gaze that she had at least entertained the thought before now.

'Well, I'm not!' My tone was emphatic. 'There is nothing like that going on between Merlin and me. Or surely I could accuse you of the same thing?' It wasn't fair, not really. Morgan hadn't said the words out loud, but my anger from the night of the coronation had already been bubbling to the surface, and with Morgan's callous suggestion it had finally boiled over.

An expression of sheer disgust contorted Morgan's features. 'I would never let a man touch me like that.'

I snorted. 'Not even Accolon?' My anger was running away from me now and I knew it, tapping into more than a year's worth of unaddressed emotion.

But rather than bite back, Morgan's brow furrowed. 'Accolon? You think there is something between Accolon and me?' She sounded genuinely surprised.

'You looked awfully cosy at the coronation.' I wasn't exactly sure why I was pursuing this – it was hardly the most pressing issue at hand – but the words just tumbled out.

Morgan looked at me as though I'd lost my mind. 'Accolon's just some randy knight trying to ingratiate himself with Arthur. A distraction.' She momentarily broke eye contact. 'There's nothing between us.'

I felt my cheeks burn scarlet, my anger quickly replaced with embarrassment. 'It didn't look like nothing.'

'You're jealous? Of Accolon and me?'

I didn't know what to say, because of course it was true, so instead I continued to stare at a point on the wall just above Morgan's shoulder.

'Five years, five years we've known each other, and you're still as emotionally repressed as ever. What happened to the girl who shouted me down in the corridor after we broke into Merlin's chambers? Or do you only speak up when it's to criticize others? Do you ever talk about your own feelings?'

My anger flared back to life with a vengeance. 'Five years? Five years? You have barely said a word to me in one! How dare you judge me!' It was Morgan's turn to turn away from my glare. 'You don't need me, remember, I'm nothing. Why should you be privy to anything I'm thinking?'

I had imagined this moment a hundred times since Morgan had turned me away, discarded our friendship thanks to my lies. I had thought I might grovel. Beg for her forgiveness like I had done before. Because I was sorry. I had been sorry from the day I saw the hurt I'd caused, the hurt Morgan hid behind her anger. But apparently something more than sorrow had been brewing within me this past year: resentment. And perhaps as a result of the adrenaline coursing through my veins, it was that emotion that won out in the battle for my tongue.

'You think you're so much better than everyone else. Well, I might not be perfect,' my voice cracked, 'I might have messed up, but at least I don't swan around judging people while making sure it's impossible to meet my standards.'

When Morgan looked back at me I expected to see the same vitriol I had that day when we stood before Camelot's towering walls, while an ailing king was brought home to die. Instead, her eyes were glassy, the first sign of tears glistening in the corners. It took me aback. Morgan didn't cry. Not that I could really say what Morgan did or didn't do these days, but even with so much distance it still felt uncharacteristic. My anger did not immediately dissipate, however. As much as I wanted to brush her pain away, I also wanted Morgan to acknowledge how she'd hurt me. How she'd continued to hurt me every day since.

'I shouldn't have said those things.' Her voice was low, her eyes fixed to the ground, but I was listening too closely to miss a single word. 'You . . . I felt so betrayed. So alone.'

I stepped towards her. Even after so many months I hated to see Morgan so hesitant. Her boldness had always been what drew me to her. Her surety in herself.

'You don't need to tell me what it feels like to be alone.'

'Viviane? Arthur said I might find you in here.'

I swung round to find Guinevere standing in the doorway, her face etched with confusion as she glanced between Morgan and myself.

'I have to go.' Before I could say anything else, Morgan had marched across the room and pushed past Guinevere, disappearing around the corner and leaving the queen looking quite as dumbfounded as I felt.

FIFTEEN

I awoke to the amber light of sunrise filtering through my window and the scent of lavender in my nose. Lavender? Wiping the sleep from my eyes with one fist, I turned to my side and found a small sprig lying on my mattress where there had been none the night before. Tied messily around its stem was an even smaller piece of paper. Still groggy with sleep, I pushed myself up to a seated position and unfolded the note.

Meet me.

As I dressed, I thought of broken pot shards and bloody hands, the scent of lavender and the taste of water in the air. I didn't doubt for even a second who the note was from, nor where she wanted to meet.

My presumption proved correct when I arrived at the lake and found Morgan sitting in the grass. She looked out to the water, her back to me but her hands just visible, a pink dog rose twirling between her fingers. For a split second I wondered if I should turn around, head back to the castle and leave Morgan to her ruminations. I was still unsure where the previous afternoon had left us.

'Viviane!' Too late, Morgan had turned and raised her hand to beckon me over.

'Hi there.' I moved to stand beside her, unsure if I should sit down or not. Now that I was closer, I could see that there were a number of flowers scattered at her feet, variously pulled apart and tied together. 'A spell?' I asked, nodding in their direction.

'Nerves.'

'How long have you been here?' I slid to the grass beside her.

'An hour or so,' Morgan gestured to her discarded handiwork. 'Not long enough to figure out how best to apologize, though.' She blushed, giving an awkward chuckle. There was that shyness I wasn't used to again. Not that it was difficult to ascertain the reason this time. 'You were right. I shouldn't have said those things.

'I wanted to take them back, you know,' she continued. 'It took me a few weeks to calm down, but after my first few solo sessions with Merlin I realized how much things had changed. How much I'd changed them. And I didn't like it. I was too ashamed, though, and still a little angry if I'm honest. I didn't know how to approach you or what I'd even say. So I didn't. And the more time that passed, the further away you felt.' She gave me the tiniest of smiles. 'I had to get all my updates on you from Merlin and Guin, if you'd believe it.'

'That is surprising,' I whispered back.

My mind was all over the place. I was sorry about the secrets I had kept from Morgan, but I'd let go of that guilt a long time ago. Instead I had been battling between resentment of her rejection and desperation to have her back. Now I couldn't help but take a little pleasure in the fact that I hadn't been the only one feeling that way.

'But it wasn't you I should have been angry with.'

My brow furrowed. 'What do you mean?'

'Merlin.' Morgan swivelled her knees so we were face-to-face rather than side by side. 'I don't trust him, Viviane.' She grabbed my hand. 'What he says he saw . . . it's wrong.'

'You know he can't control his visions, Morgan.'

Morgan's jaw tensed. 'That doesn't mean he's honest about them. Maybe,' her eyes flicked to the lake and back to mine, 'maybe if he had told my father about the poison he wouldn't have died so soon.'

I baulked. I knew what it was like to have Morgan's disdain. To have her assume the worst about you. In that moment I felt compelled to defend Merlin. 'We don't know he didn't, Morgan.' I sighed. 'Arthur is the one who has to choose what he does with the information Merlin gives him. He's the king after all.'

Morgan scoffed. 'I love Arthur, but he's a boy in man's armour. He doesn't know what he's doing.' She flung herself backwards so she lay in the grass, staring up at the sky.

'He's the one who's ordered a census,' I pointed out. I knew he was Morgan's younger brother but I thought she dismissed him too easily. He might have been young, but as far as I could see, that only made him all the more desperate to prove himself. Either way we were getting nowhere.

We were both silent while I lowered myself on to my back beside her. After a few minutes, I finally voiced the concern we had both been dancing around. 'Do you think he'll do something to them?' We both knew what I meant; it was just too horrible to verbalize.

Morgan didn't respond immediately, continuing to regard her flower. It was already missing half its petals and those that remained had turned a sickly shade of ochre along their edges. 'I don't know.' Her reply was barely more than a whisper.

I turned to lie on my side, head propped up on one elbow so I could study Morgan's expression more closely. As I considered her, Morgan's eyes narrowed and she slowly curled her fingers until her hand made a tight fist around the pink rose head. Despite the outward aggression of her movement, I didn't flinch. Even now, I knew Morgan well enough to understand the softness that hid beneath her prickly facade. She used her magic only to help and heal. Sure enough, as I watched on, she unfurled her grip to reveal a rose made whole: petals restored to their fullness and gleaming the colour of freshly kissed lips.

Reaching over, I wrapped my hand around the one in which Morgan held her flower, waiting to see if she'd push me away. She didn't.

'We can only control our own actions,' I whispered, and Morgan seemed to ponder something for a few moments.

'Then promise something with me. We will protect those who cannot protect themselves.'

I squeezed her fist more tightly. 'If it is within my power, I swear it.' And in that moment, I thought, maybe, together, we could.

Turning her gaze from our joined hands, Morgan's eyes landed on mine, her face but a hair's breadth from mine. 'And how will you seal your oath?' she murmured.

I took that moment to admire my companion's features.

Unlike my own freckled complexion, Morgan's skin was pale and unblemished besides a few pockmarks that decorated the right side of her jaw. Her round cheeks showed the faintest flush of pink, and her dark lashes fluttered almost nervously against her lower lids. All I'd have to do was lean forward an inch or so and our lips would meet. Once the idea had crossed my mind it consumed me and finally, without allowing myself time to second-guess, I closed the distance between us and pressed my mouth to Morgan's.

I had kissed a couple of men before, but as soon as our lips made contact I felt like this was my first – I was awkward and stiff and unsure if I'd made a terrible mistake. Until Morgan kissed me back.

My heart was beating hard against my chest, and I could have sworn I felt the same rhythm matched by Morgan's as our bodies pressed against each other's. What began as a soft caress of lips on lips changed when Morgan's tongue traced the seam of my mouth. In response, I gently tugged at her bottom lip with my teeth. A small sigh escaped one of our throats – it didn't matter which – and that was when what had begun tentatively quickly became impatient, and our tongues entwined, exploring each other's mouths with enthusiasm.

After what felt like an aeon had passed, we broke apart and, for a moment or two, simply stared at one another.

I was the first to break the silence. 'You know . . . I think I might need a little cooling off, don't you?'

'What are you talking about?' Morgan frowned, looking up at me.

In answer to Morgan's question, I just smiled and began

to unknot the belt at my waist. One by one I removed the brooches that held my overdress in place at the shoulders and let them drop from my hands. Then came the laces at the neck of my underdress, which I untied with a speed that surprised even myself. All the while I kept my eyes locked with Morgan's.

'Come on, the water is waiting.' I threw my last remaining garment in Morgan's lap before sprinting towards the lake.

'I like it when you're bold, Princess Viviane of Dál Riada.' Morgan grinned and got to her feet, hurriedly removing her own layers of clothing, and tossing them to the ground.

'Call me the Lady of the Lake,' I laughed, turning to look over my shoulder as my feet broke the surface of the sparkling water.

Morgan, meanwhile, did not run; instead, she walked slowly towards the lake, her eyes roaming over the dips and curves of my exposed skin. As she dragged her gaze up and down my body, I could almost feel the way her eyes traced the silvery stretch marks across my hips and stom-ach, thanks to the fire that danced in them. Those same eyes narrowed hungrily as they settled on my breasts, and I felt a fluttering sensation in my stomach that threatened to travel lower still.

While Morgan's eyes were focused on my body, I took the opportunity to raise both my hands and reach out to the lake. I didn't need to feel the liquid between my fingers to know the rhythm of its movements. I could feel every drop of water, every bubble of air, every creature and plant that occupied its depths. Two frogs sat half-submerged beneath the shade of the arrowhead leaves. A shoal of carp swam lazily by while several dragonflies buzzed above the water's surface searching for a place to lay their eggs. Life teemed all around us.

Slowly, I raised my left hand and felt the weight of the water come with it. Focusing on my breathing, I lifted my other arm and brought them together, so they made a sweeping arc above my head. As if following my lead, two great columns of water broke through the surface of the lake and vaulted overhead to meet one another. The weight was not insubstantial, but it was lighter than it had been even a month before. Every time I came here, I could feel my power growing, and today the magic engulfed me; the hairs on my body stood on end and my skin tingled from the tips of my fingers to the tops of my toes as I held the pillars aloft. Smiling, I bowed my head to Morgan, indicating she was free to walk through the archway I had created.

Morgan could have been a fairy queen, I thought as I watched her walk towards me, each step causing the water to ripple and stroke against my thighs. In a different time, a different place, we might have been queens together. But I would not be disappointed in what we had. What was happening here, now, was true magic. Not the tricks Merlin taught us, but the fire that raged inside me for Morgan, which I was now certain flared in Morgan too. When, finally, she reached my side, she was beaming, pleasure etched on every feature.

'Show me your realm, lady of the lake,' she whispered close to my ear, sending a tiny shudder down my spine.

Without a moment's hesitation I grabbed Morgan by the hand and practically dragged her deeper into the lake. When our feet no longer touched the bottom, I let go of her and plunged beneath the water's surface, only to reappear a few feet away, a wide grin spread across my face. 'What are you waiting for, then? The exciting part is down below.' I laughed loudly and disappeared once more.

I had never thought a happiness more profound than what I felt when enveloped by the lake's tender embrace was possible – but now I knew I had been wrong. It was so much better when we were together, truly together. The future I hoped we would share spread out before us. I trod water beneath the surface of the lake, brushing away errant tendrils of hair from my face as Morgan swam towards me. When she was a foot away, however, she changed direction and broke back through the surface of the water above. So, I followed.

'How do you hold your breath for so long?' Morgan panted as I swam in tight circles around her.

'Hold my breath?' I paused while Morgan stared thoughtfully back at me.

'You don't hold your breath, do you?' she asked, to which I shrugged. Breathing under water was as natural to me as it was on land. 'You're sure you're not a nymph? A selkie?' Morgan held a hand up to cup my chin.

'You think I'm hiding an entire seal's skin somewhere?' I grinned back at her.

'I wouldn't put it past you. You're full of surprises,' Morgan teased, but I knew from the soft expression on her face that it wasn't a jibe, only a flirtatious quip.

Laughing, I grabbed her hand once more and pulled her back beneath the lake's watery depths. When we were both fully submerged, I released the hand I had been holding and brought both of my own to clasp Morgan's face. Then, slowly, I leaned forward and kissed her gently on the mouth. Prompted by my caress, Morgan responded in kind, parting her lips to allow our tongues to entwine. I was only partly motivated by desire. As I held Morgan to me, I allowed breath to pour from my lungs into Morgan's. After a few moments she pulled away, her eyes wide, and placed a hand to her chest, her question as clear as day on her face. I grinned and nodded. Yes, she was breathing under water.

Together, we swam and played beneath the lake's surface for the rest of the afternoon, continuing to exchange passionate kisses whenever it became clear Morgan's lungs had emptied – not that I was particularly disappointed by this turn of events. A hardship it was not. Even when the sun finally began to dip beneath the horizon and the water grew too dark for us to see each other any more, I wished we didn't have to return to Camelot and leave this day behind.

SIXTEEN

I was slightly embarrassed to admit that there was a new spring in my step the following day, and my cheeks ached from smiling, but I couldn't stop myself. I was happier than I had been in months, years possibly. I could still taste the phantom of Morgan's lips on mine. It was incredibly distracting.

'I wish every day could be like this.'

Morgan's words as we had lain in the grass, letting the sun dry our skin before it settled in for the night, replayed themselves in my mind as I perched on my favourite spot in Merlin's chambers, a worn burgundy armchair that had perhaps seen better days, with a book on lunar phases in my lap. Yet if anyone had asked me about the significance of those cycles, I wouldn't have been able to answer them. My eyes scanned over the words while my mind continually flitted back to the day before, occasionally stifling a laugh as I chewed on my bottom lip. I should have known my mood would not go unnoticed.

'You are in good spirits this morning? I didn't realize the moon was so amusing.'

I glanced up from the page I hadn't been reading and met Merlin's gaze across the room. In the years that had passed since Merlin had invited me to become his student, my lessons had become less structured, more sporadic. I liked to think it was because he had grown to think of himself as my colleague rather than my tutor, albeit a more experienced one. He had taught me the method, he had explained, and was happy to assist me when necessary, but he no longer insisted I schedule our training around his whims. He was simply there if I needed him. When I needed him, I supposed.

I didn't know the last time Morgan had paid the sorcerer a visit – not for a few months at least, I thought. I hated to admit it, but I knew she was right: I was his favourite. We were more similar than I had expected, Merlin and I. Both silent observers of the world while Morgan was loud and brash and open. That was part of what drew me to her, though, that boldness and confidence in her right to take up space. But for Merlin, Morgan's nature seemed to cause only frustration, and vice versa.

So I returned when she did not. And there were the books, of course. I couldn't resist the books, many of which Merlin insisted must remain within his chambers. I would sit in this same seat, flipping their pages and devouring the knowledge they contained. The same seat I occupied that day, my mind a million miles away.

'It is simply a good day, why not smile?' I shrugged, flashing my mentor a grin in the hope of distracting him with a smile of his own.

Merlin, however, raised one eyebrow at me. 'You should be careful who you kiss out in the open like that. You never know who's watching, even in the woods.'

My cheeks flushed.

'You were by the lake yesterday?'

'I was here at my desk.' Something unfamiliar sparked behind his eyes. 'But that doesn't stop me from seeing.'

My stomach plummeted. For a split instance I was fifteen again, out of breath from a scavenger hunt, a gangly teenage Arthur at my side, as his mother warned us that we were never truly alone at Camelot. *This castle has eyes.* Queen Igraine's words rang in my ears.

'You were watching us?' How could he speak so casually when I felt so violated?

'It is part of my role at court to know what's going on at Camelot. You were not exactly hidden.' Merlin shrugged, returning his gaze to his papers. 'As I said though, you should be careful. Many would not look kindly on what you and Morgan were doing.'

'You included?' Anger bubbled within me, threatening to spill over. 'Weren't you the one advocating the exploration of pleasure not so long ago?'

'My only concern is your craft. I would not wish you to be distracted from it.' He paused and let out a sigh, as if considering his next words carefully. 'You have a lot of potential, Viviane, but you mustn't let Morgan lead you astray. Your power could be great, I have seen it.'

'You have had a vision of me? And you didn't tell me!' My voice sounded indignant, even to me, and I cringed at my petulance.

'Some visions are clearer than others.' Merlin spoke slowly, his eyes still fixed on the papers in his hands. 'All I can tell you right now is what I already have.'

I huffed in my seat but knew that if that was all Merlin was willing to say then that was all I would get. I also knew his visions were vague and plentiful, affecting him in more than just his waking hours. So instead I focused on his earlier comment: he knew about Morgan and me. He had seen us together. Whatever his motives, the knowledge made the hairs on my body stand on end. I would have to give that revelation some careful consideration.

Here I was again, standing beside the lake I'd come to love. The one where I'd first felt a sense of peace in this new world; the one where I'd first felt the magic running through my veins; the one where Morgan had first pressed her lips to mine. Nowhere could be safer, could it? But we'd been seen. Observed in the most intimate of moments, by a man I trusted. I trusted Merlin, didn't I? He was my mentor. But I did not like to think of him gazing down at Morgan and me, watching the private touches we had shared from wherever he was. If we could be seen lounging by the side of the lake when no one else was nearby, then nowhere in Camelot was truly private. But, I thought with a sly grin to myself, I was an enchantress, wasn't I?

Slowly, I stripped my dress off, focusing on the ritual of removing my clothes as I did so.

You will not see me. You will not see me. I repeated the words to myself over and over again until I stood bare and unencumbered by heavy fabrics. If my enchantment had worked, I would be temporarily invisible to any observers, here or afar. Now, to set to work.

It was easier than I had expected it to be, to bend the

water to my will. The lake was already a kind of home to me. A sanctuary all my own. Now it would be so for us both. I simply needed to make some . . . alterations.

With each step forward I descended further beneath the watery depths, but I didn't sink: a staircase unravelled underneath my feet, each new step forming just as I needed it. Slowly, my torso and head were submerged and the space around me grew darker as I travelled deeper and deeper. The water rippled around me, but never touching my skin. It lapped up against the surrounding area as though held back by an invisible barrier. Meanwhile I was free to breathe in the crisp air that had accompanied me from above and was now trapped down below.

The water responded to me almost eagerly, sensing my wants, my needs as I walked through its depths. Walls and ceilings formed around me; cavernous chambers shaping themselves as I entered them. These were not like the brick walls of Camelot, however. They were glassy and gleaming, neither entirely sheer nor opaque. From where I stood I could make out the shadowy forms of the fish as they swam by, but their details were indistinct. The same was true of the inner walls. I imagined if Morgan were here with me, standing in another room, I would be unable to make out her features even if I could tell that she was there. It was breathtaking.

As I took it all in, it struck me that, despite the size of my achievement, it had been a relatively easy piece of magic. The exertion on my mind and body had been minor compared to much smaller tasks I had undertaken. My limbs did not ache from the weight of construction. My head was not growing hazy with sleep. If I didn't know any better, I might have suspected the palace had always been there, simply waiting to be revealed. Meanwhile, I expected my footsteps to echo throughout the structure, empty as it was, but they were mysteriously muffled as I trod through the palace I had built. All was silent beneath the water.

'Viviane.'

The sound of my name pricked at my ears, so light and far away I was surprised I even heard it. Now that I had, however, there was no mistaking that voice. Morgan. I hurried back through the halls I had so recently created and up the narrow staircase that led to the surface.

'Viviane?' came Morgan's call once more as I emerged from the water, still as dry as I had been before entering. I smiled wide when her gaze passed my way, but her eyes did not alight on mine, instead staring past me before darting away again. Of course, I chided myself: the enchantment. Closing my eyes, I focused on the physical world and my own existence within it. Sensations that I hadn't even realized had dulled became twice as visceral again.

'Viviane,' Morgan gasped. 'Where did you come from? Where are your clothes?'

I laughed, running forward to greet her. 'I was inside the lake.'

'But . . .' Morgan traced a finger along the skin of my forearm. 'But your skin is . . .'

I laughed again. 'Don't you know, I'm magic?' This made Morgan grin in turn.

'Where were you? You were supposed to meet me after lunch, remember.'

I winced. Between Merlin's words and my determination to do something about them, I had completely forgotten.

'I'm sorry, it's just . . .' I didn't know how to explain what I had done, but then, I didn't need to. 'I have something to show you.' I took her hand in mine and eagerly guided her to the lake, to the point where I knew the entrance was hidden.

'Come on,' I insisted, placing one foot then another beneath the water.

'Shouldn't I take my clothes off?'

I shook my head. 'No need.'

To her credit, Morgan simply shrugged and followed behind me, never questioning where I was going. That trust made me all the more eager to please her. So, for the second time that afternoon, I descended the glimmering steps that spiralled down, down beneath the lake until we stood below the water, the sun that shone through the ceiling the only light we needed.

'What is this?' I watched Morgan as she turned slowly on the same spot once, twice, and a third time just for luck. 'Where are we?' She fixed her gaze back on me. 'Are we really beneath the lake?' I nodded, chewing on my lip while I absorbed her reaction. 'You did this?' she asked, finally.

'I wanted us to have somewhere that was ours alone. Somewhere private.' I wasn't sure why but I didn't mention Merlin's earlier revelation. Their relationship was already strained, I told myself; I didn't want to add fuel to the fire. What I had done would be enough; Morgan need not worry we had been seen.

'It's a palace, Viv.' Morgan laughed, her eyes sparkling. 'An underwater palace and you are its queen.' She strode up to the nearest wall and placed the palm of one hand flat against it, staring intently as shadowy shapes floated by. 'And these must be your subjects, the fish and the frogs.' She laughed again and I joined in.

'Indeed, the burden to rule is mine. Perhaps it would be easier with a companion by my side.' I placed a hand over her own. 'A queen consort, perhaps?' I leaned in to tease a lock of her hair between my fingers.

'It is unfair to make such requests of me when you are in such a seductive state.' Morgan's eyes stroked up my naked body. I blushed beneath her gaze, a hunger stirring deep within me. 'Don't get shy on me now.' She took hold of my hand and brought it to rest against her breast. 'Feel how fast my heart is beating. You did that. Just the sight of you. You're the most beautiful thing I've ever seen, Viviane.'

Unable to hold back any longer, I wrapped Morgan up in my arms, capturing her lips in mine, not letting go until much, much later.

SEVENTEEN

Morgan and I continued to make regular visits to the under-water palace I had built, even decorating and filling the interior together. First we'd needed a bed, as Morgan had not so coyly pointed out. Of course, there was no way we could liberate one from the castle without eliciting some awkward questions, yet, when I had questioned the comfort of creating one out of the same glassy material as the palace walls, Morgan had simply laughed. Without explanation she had practically skipped from the main chamber and up the stairs out of sight. Before I could decide whether to follow her or not, however, she was back, her arms laden with – well – junk.

'What on earth?' I laughed, scurrying after her as she proceeded to the next room. 'What are you doing?'

'Making us a bed.' Morgan grinned as she unceremoniously dumped her treasure upon the floor. I raised my eyebrows as sticks and leaves scattered at my feet, but rather than keep up my questioning I decided I might as well wait and see what happened next.

While I remained standing, Morgan knelt down, her body hunched low to the ground, and stretched out her arms till her fingers were fully immersed in the detritus. And then she began to hum. I'd noticed this about Morgan's craft more and more as we had reconnected. While I preferred silence to work, it was as though she could not focus without some sort of melody, whether she was aware of it or not. As she hummed, I watched on with bated breath, captivated by what was happening before me. Twigs and branches lengthened and intertwined, spiralling up towards the ceiling as they formed a familiar frame. Clumps of greenery crawled up the structure, spreading across the flat surface till it was entirely coated in a thick down of moss, a few tiny buds peeking out here and there. It was the most beautiful bed I'd ever seen.

'What do you think?' Morgan looked up at me, a little shyly I thought.

'I think it looks a lot more comfortable than my current bed.' I gave in to temptation and brushed my fingers through her dark hair. 'Can you make me another?'

This made Morgan laugh, finally clambering to her feet only to collapse atop the mossy mattress. 'Come and test it out before you make any more requests?'

So I did. I let my body fall down next to Morgan's, pleased to discover the twigs did not collapse beneath our combined weight.

'Seems solid to me,' I chuckled, turning on to my side and casually placing a palm on my companion's stomach. I did that a lot, I'd noted. I always wanted to touch her, or be touched by her. It was as though once the wall between us had been broken down I couldn't keep my hands to myself.

'Pfft,' Morgan pushed my hand from her belly, much

to my disappointment, and turned on to her own side. 'Clearly no one has ever taught you how to properly test a bed frame's endurance.'

'Oh no?' I laughed, curious as to what she was planning.

'You're lucky you have me, really.' She grinned and I bit my lip, excitement building.

'Oh yes?'

'Oh yes.'

Morgan rose to her knees and shuffled down to the foot of the bed. I gazed on as she took the hem of my dress in her fingers. Slowly, maintaining eye contact all the while, she pushed the fabric up my legs, revealing my bare skin to the cool air of the palace. My breathing picked up its pace when she let my skirts go, all bunched up at my waist while the lower half of my body was entirely exposed.

'Open your legs for me,' Morgan whispered.

I felt the butterflies in my stomach dance a happy dance as I bent my knees and spread them wide, making enough space for Morgan to settle between them. Her mouth was but a hair's breadth from my slit and I could feel the fanning of her breath across my skin. In a demonstration of remarkable (infuriating) restraint, Morgan did not cross the distance as I'd hoped, however, instead turning her head to trail her lips across the silvery stretch marks on the inside of my right thigh. When lips were replaced by teeth I inhaled sharply, the rhythmic clenching of my inner walls speeding up a pace or two.

'Is this some kind of ancient torture practice? I swear I have no secrets left to reveal.'

Morgan chuckled against my skin. 'Oh, but you do,

Viviane, my love. I have yet to discover all the ways to make you scream.'

My heart was thudding so hard against my chest I thought it might break through my ribs. Before I could respond, however, Morgan had her lips wrapped around my clitoris, sucking the tiny bundle of nerves into her mouth and causing my back to arch up from the bed frame we were supposedly testing. When my legs instinctively clamped together, not through any desire to be rid of her but due to the intensity of the sensations overwhelming my body, Morgan held them apart. She alternated between sucking my apex between her teeth and nibbling around the puffy hood that protected it until my moans echoed throughout the almost empty room.

'Oh, my God, Morgan, I can't . . . don't stop.' I wasn't sure what I was trying to articulate, only that the words clambered to escape. 'Please, please, please.'

At my pleading, Morgan removed one hand from my thigh and placed two fingers at the entrance to my core.

'You're so wet, Viviane,' she murmured in between her ministrations, pushing both fingers inside me with little resistance. 'You taste like magic.'

This was magic, I wanted to tell her. The feeling of her body tangled in mine, her mouth demanding every ounce of my pleasure, her fingers curled up, stroking that hidden spot inside me. But all I could do was moan: a low, guttural moan from the very depths of my soul.

'That's it, my lady, let it out.'

Morgan's movements had picked up their pace and I felt a familiar yet unfamiliar tingling spreading up from the tips of my toes to my thighs. The moment Morgan's teeth grazed against my bud I came undone. Pleasure crashed over me in waves more wild than I had ever experienced before. I did scream then, long and loud, my back arching impossibly before crashing backwards on to the bed once more. As I lay there, drained, I was rewarded with a dazzling smile from Morgan whose head rose from between my legs, her cheeks red and her mouth shining.

'I think it'll do, don't you?'

'What?' I blinked at her, no idea what she was talking about.

'The bed.' And she rolled on to her back, laughing up at the ceiling, my own giggles joining hers as I came down from the high of her touch. This would certainly do.

Merlin made no further comments about Morgan's and my activities. Whether because he was unaware or had decided to no longer interfere, I was grateful either way. On the other hand, I was so wrapped up in my own joy that it took me longer than it should have to recognize that everyone at Camelot was not quite as happy. I was wandering the corridors one afternoon, forced to remain within the castle walls by the furious storm that raged outside, when I heard a sniffling from somewhere nearby.

The sound was coming from the small solar to my right, the person inside likely unaware the door was open a crack. For a few moments I debated if I should interrupt or not and then decided I should at least take a quick look. When I peered round the door I was surprised to find Guinevere seated alone, an embroidery frame in her lap, and a few errant tears trickling down her cheeks. Now I knew who was inside I couldn't leave. Pushing the door entirely open, I padded into the room, alerting Guin to my presence.

'Viviane.' She spoke my name in surprise, quickly brushing a hand across her face.

'Guin,' I approached the sofa on which she sat and placed a hand awkwardly on her shoulder, 'what's wrong?'

'Oh, I just stuck myself, it's nothing.' She waved a finger at me, a drop of blood bubbling at the tip.

'I see.' I paused briefly before deciding to push on. 'It's just . . . that wouldn't usually make you cry.'

'I'm tired.' She shrugged, still refusing to meet my eye.

She did look exhausted, now that I was paying better attention. Her eyes were rimmed with dark circles and her skin had none of its usual golden warmth. Guilt washed over me. This was not the fatigue of a couple of nights of bad sleep but something deeper; the young queen looked as though she was slowly being drained of life.

'I know I haven't been the best friend I could be lately, Guin,' I hesitated, 'but I care about you like a sister. Please, tell me what's wrong. I won't share what you say with anyone else if you don't want me to. You can trust me.'

Guinevere shifted uncomfortably in her seat. 'Arthur and I argued this morning, that's all.'

'What about?' I asked tentatively. 'He hasn't hurt you, has he?' The thought made my blood boil but I was aware of the fate many women faced at the hands of their husbands.

'No, never.' Guin shook her head emphatically before pausing.

I took her hand in mine. 'Tell me, maybe I can help?'

158

'He wants a child.'

I nodded; every king wanted an heir, did they not? 'It'll come. It's only been a few months.'

But Guin shook her head. 'It's just – that's all he wants.' I waited, not sure I understood. 'I thought it would be different when he touched me,' Guin continued, not meeting my eye. 'My mother made it sound like the most wonderful thing to share a bed with your husband, to be held in his arms, to be touched and touch alike. But . . . but there is no tenderness with Arthur. When he comes to my bed it is out of duty.' Guin cast her eyes downwards to her hand in mine. 'I knew there might be some pain the first time; I am not naive. But even now there is no pleasure in the act. He never holds me. Rarely kisses me. Then he is gone and I am all alone. I hate it.' Finally she raised her gaze to mine. 'And I still bleed monthly. I don't know what I'm doing wrong, Viv.'

'Have you spoken to him about it?'

'He said –' a sob broke through Guin's defences, forcing her to take a few deep breaths – he said wives are for heirs. That kings find their pleasure elsewhere.'

I made a choking noise. 'A mistress? But who?'

But Guin just shook her head. 'I won't say. It's humiliating.'

'Guin, please, maybe I can talk to her?' I had no idea what I would say, but surely I could try.

'No. She is married. We both know what happens to married women who sleep with other men. Even kings.' I didn't voice my thoughts aloud, but in that moment an image flashed through my mind, of King Lott's wife, Anna, gripping Arthur's forearm at the coronation while he poured his attention on her.

'Then let me speak to Arthur,' I insisted.

'No, it's not right.' She turned away from me, pulling her hand from mine. 'He's a good king, you know. He listens to their troubles. He only taxes the wealthiest. He has already defeated the army that killed his father, and pushed the Saxons back from the territory they'd gained since. He protects his people.' Guin spoke with an air of finality, refocusing her attention on the needlework in her lap.

He's not just a king, though. He's also your husband, I thought. But I didn't say the words out loud; I didn't push her. I simply sat by her side while she worked on her embroidery and pondered what she had said.

EIGHTEEN

I knew Guin didn't want me to interfere, but I couldn't just let it rest. She was my friend and I could not bear to stand by while she carried so much hurt and pain upon her shoulders. And maybe a tiny part of me felt guilty; once upon a time I might have filled Guin's shoes, but instead I was free from a marriage I didn't want, falling for a woman I did. So I spent the rest of that day and the next pondering how I could possibly help. Of course, the answer was obvious.

I had been given a power, and there had to be more point to it than pretty water shows and private palaces. If I might be able to use my magic to help my friend, then surely I had to try? I also knew Guin's feelings about magic. But what the queen didn't know surely couldn't hurt her. I was good at keeping secrets, after all.

Among my things there was a book of charms I'd found in Merlin's library a few months earlier, which I'd been flicking through sporadically in my free time. They were all relatively small, domestic pieces of magic that included suggestions of how to repurpose everyday items to ease the labours of working life. None of it had held much relevance to me thus far, this much I recognized, but it was one of the few books in Merlin's collection written by a woman and for that reason I'd felt I had to know what was inside. Now, however, might be exactly the time to test its applications.

Returning to my rooms, I flicked through the little book, searching for the spell I needed. One paper cut and a few stubborn pages later I'd found it:

A Charm to Stay an Adulterous Husband

Take a piece each of the husband's and the wife's clothing and sew them together with pale blue thread. Place the scraps beneath the marital bed and no longer will he seek pleasure from another.

And so I set about crafting my charm.

The fabric was easy enough to come by. No one noticed as I snuck into the laundry rooms, where dried garments were waiting to be returned to their owners, and snipped myself two small squares of material: one from Guin's dress and the other from Arthur's shirt. The blue thread was also a simple ask, with my personal basket of embroidery supplies to hand. Once I had sewn the pieces of fabric together, however, I was faced with the more challenging half of my plan: I needed to hide them in Guinevere and Arthur's chambers, which were now inconveniently situated in the castle keep.

I could, of course, have used my camouflaging spell. It didn't make me truly invisible but simply obscured me from a casual gaze. Yet somehow I didn't exactly relish the thought of wandering through the castle naked, enchanted or not. No, I needed to convince the guards on duty that I was meant to be in the keep, not pretend I wasn't. I remembered

the defiant confidence of Arthur at fifteen years old, as he
barged past the men stationed outside to steal away from
his father. I could do that, couldn't I?

So it was that twenty minutes or so later I found myself
at the entrance to Camelot's keep, a vaguely suspicious guard
eyeing me up.

'What is your business here, m'lady?'

'The king has instructed me to wait for him in his chambers.' I straightened my shoulders and placed a hand on my
hip, trying my best to look both important and perhaps a
little bit seductive. It was common knowledge that I had
been fostered by King Uther as a potential wife for the
then prince, and it was an established practice for lords and
kings to take paramours from among the nobility. These
two pieces of information I was hoping would work in my
favour. 'I wouldn't want to disappoint him.' I actually fluttered my eyelashes, cringing inwardly. Thankfully the gesture
had its intended effect, however, and the guard gifted me
with a lecherous grin.

'Of course, m'lady.' And with a nod of his head that
didn't quite dip low enough, he pushed open the door and
let me through.

Before he could change his mind, I was up the stairs and
through the door that led to Arthur's private chambers. I
did a quick scan of the room but I also knew I didn't have
long. So, with very little dignity, I lowered myself to the floor
and crawled beneath the bed until my upper body was in
darkness. I then proceeded to take the piece of fabric from
where I had stashed it against my breast and tuck it between
the wooden slats, reminding myself of my intentions all the

while. When the material seemed secure, I withdrew from the uncomfortable position and made to stand up. As I did, however, I heard a tearing sound and felt a tug on my left shoulder. God damn it. My dress had caught on a rough piece of wood and ripped along the seam to reveal my bare skin. Well, there was nothing I could do about it now. At least I had completed my task.

'What are you doing in here?'

My stomach plummeted. I knew that voice. Sure enough, when I looked up from my torn sleeve I was face to face with the one person I didn't want to see right now: Arthur. I had been so wrapped up in my plans that I hadn't even heard him coming.

'I . . . I . . .' I stammered inanely, unsure what to say. Unconsciously my hand went to my shoulder and I tried to right my dress, but it would no longer stay put over my shoulder. Unfortunately, I realized too late, this had also drawn Arthur's attention to my bare skin.

'I suppose that explains the wink Alrec gave me downstairs.' Arthur's lips curled. That must have been the guard I had misled. 'Well, I'm sorry to disappoint you, but I have no interest in a mistress, Lady Viviane.'

Not another one, at least, I added silently. I had to bite my tongue to stop myself from contradicting him, however; it was what I had implied to Alrec after all. In that moment I was just grateful that Arthur seemed disinclined to take me up on my supposed offer, or else I would have had to come up with some new excuse.

'I'm sorry,' I finally murmured.

'I understand you are your father's tool, Lady Viviane – he

has written to me of his disappointment that we did not wed – but I thought better of you than this.'

Arthur's words made me bristle. 'I am no one's tool.' My words were angrier than was probably wise but I found I could not contain them. To my further annoyance, Arthur merely smirked.

'Tell your father I will find him a suitably powerful match; there is no need for his daughter to raise her skirts.'

I practically ran past the young king and down the stairs of the keep again, overwhelmed by a burning desire to slap him that I was rational enough to know I had to resist. Anger and humiliation coursed through my veins, but underneath it all was the knowledge that, despite Arthur's words, my visit to his chambers had been successful, and that was what I held on to as I hurried to my room.

NINETEEN

I was having the most pleasant dream. Morgan and I were chasing each other through a lake three times the size of the one that bordered Camelot, the sun shining down on our bare skin, the only sounds the splashing of water and our raucous laughter as we narrowly escaped each other's lunging embraces. It was bliss. That was, up until the banging started. At first, I tried to ignore it, but the thuds were growing increasingly frantic with each second that passed. Was it a horse? Was someone riding towards the lake? Except I wasn't in the lake any more, I was sprawled across a mattress, one arm flung across my head, while my companion clumsily extracted herself from the other one around her waist.

'Who the hell is that at this time of night?' Morgan groaned, grabbing her underdress from the floor and pulling it over her head. I followed suit while she marched over to the door, just managing to cover myself in time for it to swing open and reveal the figure behind.

'My lady, I didn't know where else to go.'

Into the room stumbled Clarine, the maid who had helped me in the kitchen a few months before. Even in the dim candlelight, she looked awful. She was sweating profusely and clutching at her stomach, shoulders slumped forward like she wanted nothing more than to collapse in on herself. Horrified, I lurched towards her, arms outstretched to take her weight before she fell over entirely. Morgan, clearly having thought the same, was at her other side in a flash and together we led her to the crumpled sheets we had moments before vacated. Sitting did very little for the woman's comfort, however. She continued to hunch over, shoulders shaking.

'Clarine, what is it? What's the matter?' Morgan pleaded, kneeling at the maid's feet and taking one of her hands in her own. My eyes meanwhile were drawn to the hem of Clarine's dress, visibly wet and bunched up above her ankles by her stomach clutching. Her exposed ankles were equally damp, but it was more than water. Dripping down her leg and on to the stone floor was a steady stream of scarlet blood.

'Morgan,' I stammered, directing her gaze towards Clarine's feet.

She immediately paled. 'Clarine, are you with child?' The young woman nodded. 'We need to get you to the midwife; this is beyond my expertise.'

Clarine let out a pitiful wail. 'No, no midwife, May Day . . .' Her words trailed off into a loud groan as she doubled over again.

She didn't need to say anything else, however. Those simple words were enough. May Day. The day which Merlin had warned Arthur against. The day upon which a babe would be born who would threaten Arthur's reign. This baby? There was no way to know, but Clarine was right. We couldn't let anyone else know this child was about to come into the world, lest they tell the king. Clarine had risked a lot simply by coming here, to Morgan. But it was clear she had little choice: this birth was already proving to be a difficult one based on the state the mother was in.

Without any further hesitation, we had Clarine on the bed. Morgan, as the one with the most medical experience, was at the foot while I held the whimpering woman's hand and stroked her now sodden brow. It was quick as far as I had come to understand the process of childbirth. Clarine didn't even scream, only letting out a series of low keening sounds whenever she was able to muster the energy to push. It seemed that whatever drive had brought her here had since diminished and, as time passed, she responded less and less to our words of encouragement. Nevertheless, I squeezed her hand.

'Everything's going to be all right,' I promised her while Morgan did her best to ease the child's passage into this world.

And then Clarine's final strangled cry of pain was joined by another sound, the distinctive screams of a newborn baby.

'It's a boy,' Morgan declared, holding up the wailing, bloody bundle of flesh for us both to see.

'Galahad . . .' Clarine's voice was as light as a feather. I don't think I would have heard her if I wasn't already so close.

'It's all right, Clarine. You've done it,' I tried to reassure her.

'His name . . .' she tried again, 'Galahad.' Her eyes had fluttered shut yet I nodded all the same.

'It's a beautiful name,' I told her, but it was already too late. The icy-cold hand in mine had gone limp.

'Viviane?' came Morgan's questioning voice, but I couldn't speak. I turned to her, tears welling in my eyes, and shook my head, grateful when this proved enough for her to understand.

'Oh God,' she stammered, glancing down at the baby in her arms who had already started to fuss, as though he knew all was not right in the world in that moment. 'Oh God, Viv, what do we do?' She held the child away from her body as though it was something terrifying in itself. She had cut the cord that bound him to his mother already, but her sense of grim determination was waning now that the immediacy of birth was behind them.

'Here. Give him to me.' I took the now mewling bundle from her hands, feeling the front of my dress grow wet at the contact with his slick skin.

'We have to hide him, Viv. He's not safe here.'

I nodded, trying to soothe him by rocking my arms back and forth, but to no avail. 'The palace.' It was the only place that made sense. 'But he'll need blankets, and milk, and whatever other things babies need. There's nothing for him there.'

This seemed to reignite Morgan's spark: a task, some-thing she could do. 'I'll get them, you stay here.' And before I could respond she was out of the door, leaving me alone in her rooms with a newborn child and his now dead mother.

Cradling him to my chest, I gazed down at the babe, taking in the reality of our situation. While his mouth gaped in distress, his eyes remained firmly shut, making him appear little more than a scrunched-up ball dotted with blood and other fluids. The longer I looked at him, however, the more real he became. His skin was a few shades darker than my own although his hands were almost blue. Instinctively, I found myself rubbing his cold fingers between my own, stunned by just how tiny they were in comparison. This at least seemed to dull his cries to whimpers and it fully settled upon me that, in that moment, I was all he had.

We couldn't just stand there forever, however, so I set about using the time alone to wipe him down with what water and cloths Morgan had to hand. This seemed to further distract him from his turmoil and allow me to fully process our situation. What had we started? Because I already knew a silent agreement had been exchanged between Morgan and me the moment we brought Clarine into the room. We were going to hide this child's birth, or at least we were going to try. But that also meant hiding his mother's death. It would be clear to anyone who saw her body how she had died.

'I'm so sorry,' I murmured – to Clarine or her child I wasn't sure.

'Viviane.'

I'd been so deep in thought that I hadn't even noticed the door to Morgan's chambers opening and closing to let her in. 'Did you get everything?'

'Everything I could think of.' She held up a bulging bag before helping me to sling it across my body while still holding the babe. 'Now you need to get him out of here.'

'What about Clarine?' I asked, trying to stop my voice from cracking when I looked back at her empty eyes.

'I'll take care of her.' Morgan placed a hand on my back and pushed me towards the door. 'Just focus on him and I'll come and find you when I'm done.'

My heart was pounding in my chest as I hastened to the lakeside, my bundle held tightly in my arms. It was pitch-black, with only the stars to light my path, but I knew the way well, and I knew how to tread unnoticed. I was lucky, I quickly realized, that the baby didn't begin to wail once we had left the castle and were faced with the cold night air. I didn't think a dark cloak and careful movements would make much difference if the guards were to hear that from atop the ramparts.

So it was that, by all the good fortune I possessed, I made it to the lake unseen, only stopping when I was sure the treeline obscured our presence from above. He'd be safe here, I reassured myself, stroking the child's motionless form. At least for now. I could feel his tiny breaths come and go, but he made no noises of frustration or distress. Instead, he seemed enraptured by his surroundings, tiny eyes wide as he took it all in.

'It's beautiful, isn't it?' I whispered, staring at the moon's reflection in the water. As I did, I was struck by a thought, or a whole host of them, it seemed. The midwife wetting my little brother's brow, stories of pagan goddesses bathing their young charges to make their skin impenetrable, Jesus submerged in the river as John stood over him. There was a power in the water, one recognized long before I came along: the power of life. I only had to harness it.

Laying the baby down gently in the grass so his swaddling

did not come unravelled, I relieved myself of the heavy bag
Morgan had given us and sat down beside him. With both
eyes trained on the child all the while, I stretched out one
cupped hand to dip it beneath the surface of the lake. I felt
its power almost immediately, my connection with this place
so deeply rooted in my soul. The centuries it had seen pass
by, and the centuries it would bear witness to after I was
gone. My palm wetted, I raised my hand above Galahad's
forehead to let a single drop fall on to his skin.

'Let this water give you strength,' I whispered before
re-submerging my hand.

'Let this water give you stability.' And again.

'Let this water give you safety.'

All the while Galahad stared up at me, occasionally
blinking but nothing more, apparently unperturbed by the
impromptu shower. 'There, that'll have to do.' I smiled down
at him and was rewarded by an insufferably adorable hiccup.

Without further ado, I gathered baby and belongings and
took them down into the underwater depths of the palace
I had built, hoping I might get some rest while we waited
for Morgan to join us.

Sleep did not prove easy to come by, however. After
I had tucked the child into his basket as tightly as I dared, I
brought my own quilt from the bed and lay down on the
floor beside him. For hours, I stared intently at the tiny
creature slumbering peacefully before me, none the wiser
to what had befallen him that day. When my own dreams
finally reached me they were fitful and short-lived, broken
what felt like mere minutes later by the wails of a baby who
had awoken ravenous and indignant.

Groggily, I rummaged through my bag until I found the clay feeding pot Morgan had packed and filled it with the equally appreciated goat's milk she had included. The baby supped eagerly at the spout while I held him, occasionally pausing to dribble a little on to himself. He was heavier than I'd expected, not that I had held a baby before, but for a newborn he seemed to be on the bigger side all round. Round pink cheeks, chubby limbs, and dark brown eyes that brought to mind freshly fallen chestnuts. He was the kind of baby who confidently challenged you with every fibre of his being not to fall in love with him.

'Drink up, you're going to need it,' I whispered, thinking of everything that he had already been through in less than a day on this earth; not that he understood any of it. He finished his meal none the wiser and fell almost immediately back to sleep. 'That's right, little one, get some rest.' *Galahad*, I reminded myself, *his name is Galahad*. 'We've got a lot to do if we're to keep you safe, little Galahad.'

I waited like this, swapping between feeding and studying Galahad for the next few hours, until Morgan finally showed up. It was nearly impossible to tell beneath the lake, but I thought it might already be evening again by the time she arrived, based on my rumbling stomach if nothing else. Her arrival was announced by the echo of her footsteps through the empty hallways and the sound of my name on her lips as she pushed open the bedroom door with a bang.

'Shhhh,' I hissed, casting her an angry glare. 'He's asleep.'

Morgan winced. 'Sorry, I didn't think.' More carefully this time, she came to sit down beside me on the bed. 'How has it been?' She wrapped her arm around my shoulders and pulled my body closer to her own. At her touch I immediately softened, letting my head rest on her chest.

'Tiring.' I shrugged. 'But manageable. What about out there?' I didn't want to say the words aloud and, evidently, I didn't have to.

'I buried the body using magic. I wanted to mark the grave but I didn't know what was safest. So I gave her a bed of forget-me-nots.' She shivered and I hugged her more tightly.

'I'm sorry.'

'Yes, well. I brought you some more supplies, and some dinner.'

'Oh, thank God.' I grabbed the bundle from Morgan's outstretched hand and unwrapped the cloth to reveal two thick slices of bread and cheese. 'I'm famished.'

'I can see that,' Morgan chuckled. 'What about the baby? How is he?'

'Better-fed than me.' I smiled between mouthfuls. 'He seems all right though, just content to be fed and kept company, I think.'

'Poor thing.' Morgan stared down at the sleeping Galahad in his basket. *Poor thing indeed.*

'I can't stay down here with him forever,' I pointed out once I had polished off the last of my meal.

'I'm looking into that. There's a king visiting from across the sea who arrives in a day or two. All we need is one sympathetic ear among his retinue. In the meantime, we can take turns hiding out down here and taking care of the child.'

'No, I'll stay with him. Your absence is more likely to be noticed, and if I'm being honest, I don't exactly know how this palace will behave without me in it. You've never been here without me.'

Morgan nodded, chewing on her lip and rubbing her thumb across my knuckles absent-mindedly. 'I'll make your excuses if anyone asks where you are. And I'll get you both more supplies as you need them.'

I leaned into her, letting my head nestle in the crook of her neck, and sighed. 'We can do this.'

She nodded. 'We have to.'

TWENTY

Morgan was as good as her word, stopping by every other day to lavish Galahad and me with food and other supplies. Her visits were a brief but welcome respite from a role I was otherwise supremely underprepared for: motherhood. With what I knew about children I would have struggled to fill a pamphlet, let alone a book, yet there I was, the primary guardian of a newborn baby whose mere existence was a threat to the crown. No pressure. Except with each passing day I struggled with the term newborn.

On the first day I didn't notice anything strange. Nor the second. But by the fifth day I had realized something was wrong. Galahad was sitting in the bundle of blankets I'd made up for him, playing with a small wooden horse. *Sitting.* It shouldn't have been possible. Not at less than a week old. Yet there he was, head held high, a bright smile plastered on his face as he wiggled his chubby limbs. If I hadn't known any better, I would have assumed him a child of at least six months old. But I did know better. I'd been there when he was born, hadn't I?

Morgan, it turned out, was even less familiar with children than I was, and I was surprised when I had to be the one to point out what was 'wrong'. 'Do you notice anything strange about him?' I'd asked after a week and a half had passed, but she'd merely stared nonplussed as Galahad chewed his tiny fist and shrugged.

'He's growing too quickly,' I elaborated.

'What do you mean?'

I rolled my eyes. 'Come on, Morgan, babies can't support their own necks after a week, let alone sit up and play peekaboo.'

'They can't?' Morgan looked genuinely shocked. 'That seems incredibly impractical.' This elicited a bark of laughter from me.

'No, they can't. Not to mention he's twice the size he was four days ago.'

'It is a little strange, I suppose.' Morgan held out a finger to the child and he grabbed hold of it with delight.

'A little.' I snorted. 'I wondered,' and now I hesitated, 'if it was this place? The palace?'

I'd been rolling this theory around my mind for the past couple of days. I couldn't deny there was magic here I didn't fully comprehend. More and more I grew certain I had revealed what was already there rather than building something from scratch. And perhaps I was just spending too much time cooped up with limited company, but occasionally I thought the shadows that floated past our walls were far too big to be ordinary fish.

Morgan seemed to consider the idea, tapping her finger absently against her chin. 'Anything is possible, I suppose, but I've not started turning grey, have I?'

'You've never spent more than a night here at a time. Nor were you brought here within hours of your birth and then spent every waking hour of your life here since.'

'And you?' Morgan asked. 'You've been here as long as he has.' To which I could only shrug.

'It's just a theory.' I scooped Galahad up into my arms and sat him in my lap, returning his discarded toy to his hands. 'Either way, he can't stay here forever.'

'In that regard I might have found a solution.' A grin broke out across Morgan's face.

'Oh?'

'King Ban of Benoic's party arrived a few days ago, and I've since learnt something interesting from the servants.'

'Go on!' I prompted. Morgan had always been far too inclined to dramatic pauses for my liking.

'Well, his queen, Elaine, is desperate for a child but has been unable to conceive. Of course she can't just adopt any old child, but I've been thinking, if she can pass the baby off as Ban's, pretend he had been born during their travels, then the king would gain an heir while the queen would get her son.'

'And the prophecy?' I asked. 'They will surely be able to guess why we wish to hide him.'

Morgan snorted. 'Not everyone is as amenable to Merlin's visions as my brother. Plenty were quietly unhappy when he demanded any children born on May Day be reported to the court. And Ban isn't even from here. I bet I could convince them.'

I nodded. It was the best bet we had in that moment, and we couldn't necessarily wait around for another. 'Just be careful.'

'Of course.' She said it as if I would be mad to think otherwise. I was not.

'You know,' I mused, 'I've been wondering who his father might be.'

Morgan shrugged. 'Clarine wasn't married, and I've never seen her with any of the men around the castle, not that that means much.' She reached out a hand to tickle Galahad's belly, making him squeal happily in my arms and eliciting a chuckle from her own throat. 'You know, I've never wanted children of my own, but I have to admit this one is rather cute, as they go.'

'Just hold on one minute while I check on your milk.'

I handed Galahad the small patchwork sheep I had been holding in front of him a moment before – it turned out those sewing lessons had more uses than I'd realized – and took his delighted squeal as a sign of approval.

It had seemed prudent to keep Galahad in the room we had designated for sleeping while I brewed his tea over the fire in the main chamber. It was a concoction of my own making, warm milk infused with chamomile and lavender, plants that promised both peace and restfulness, and which I hoped might have a similar effect on Galahad. Without an explanation for Galahad's rapid ageing I had no solid solution to offer, but that didn't stop me from trying. Of course, I wouldn't have risked putting anything in his milk if he had truly been a babe of a few weeks old, but by my judgement he had to be considered at least eight months by now. Although, and maybe it was wishful thinking, I thought the drink might be helping.

While my eyes were trained on the cauldron, my ears remained focused on Galahad, listening to his garbled murmurings as they floated through the open doorway. It sounded almost as if he were having a conversation with himself, leaving long pauses in between his non-sentences for someone else to fill. I assumed he'd picked up the habit from our own interactions and smiled to myself.

Wrapping my hand in the scrap of cloth I kept for the purpose, I carefully lifted the cauldron from its tripod. Before I could place it down on the floor, however, I heard something that made my heart stop. Fumbling with the handle, I dropped the cauldron, hot liquid splattering the hem of my dress and burning my bare feet. Not that I felt it. I was too focused on the noise that had emanated from the other room.

Abandoning my brewing, I dashed back to the room in which I had left Galahad only to find everything just as it had been. The baby was laughing away to himself, waving his stuffed animal in the air as if it could fly, none the wiser to the thundering in my chest. Because only seconds ago I could have sworn I'd heard another voice – a woman's voice.

My fear was momentarily allayed when I realized Galahad was unharmed. I swept him up in my arms and hugged him tightly to my chest, causing him to squeal in surprise.

'I'm sorry, wee one,' I whispered, stroking his head while I looked around the room again.

Nothing.

No, not nothing.

The voice was gone but I realized that Galahad wasn't looking at me. No, he had his eyes trained on the wall, where the shadows floated by, waving his sheep in the same direction as if he were showing it off.

I ran.

Later, when I was standing in the damp grass, the sting-ing heat apparent in my left foot, Galahad fussing in my arms as he experienced the chill in the air for the first time since he was born, I would scold myself for my panic. This was my home. I had made it with my magic because, yes, I was a sorceress with the power of earth and water at my fingertips – I was not a frightened, powerless girl, scared of shadows that might not even be there. In the moment, however, that was exactly what I had been. Alone and fright-ened, and I knew the only thing that mattered was keeping Galahad safe.

TWENTY-ONE

I had to return to the palace eventually: it was that or the castle. The nights were too cold and neither Galahad nor I had the necessary provisions to spend a night beneath the stars. So I chose what I deemed the lesser of the two dangers.

And I was either delirious or lucky, because nothing jumped out at me from behind the walls and Galahad gave no indication that we had company I was unaware of. None the wiser to my own distress, he settled into his cot and fell asleep, his little sheep dangling from his fingers. He was the only one who would be getting any sleep. I spent the night circling the rooms, chanting words of protection under my breath. I burnt every plant and twig I had to hand that might offer some sanctuary. I did everything I could think of until the only thing to do was sit in silence, listening for the slightest hint of voices that didn't belong.

None of which relaxed me.

By the time that Morgan came to visit us the following evening, I was both agitated and exhausted. Galahad, meanwhile, either missed his 'friend' or had picked up on my unease, because it was almost impossible to get him to settle after he woke that morning. When I had finally got him to fall asleep, Morgan and I settled down on the bed to drink the soup she had brought. Spills be damned.

It took me three attempts to properly explain why I was in such a state and what I had seen the night before, but eventually we got there.

'I wonder . . .' Morgan hummed between mouthfuls.

'What?' I yawned and put my empty bowl to the side.

But Morgan shook her head. 'It's stupid.'

'Morgan,' I prodded her.

'It's just, you don't suppose it could have been your mother?'

Whatever I had expected, it had not been that. 'What are you talking about?'

'Well, you said yourself she might have been fair folk, a selkie even. Would it be so strange that she might be here, in the water, watching over you?'

The irritation I felt came on me without warning. 'My mother is dead.'

'I know, it's just –'

'Stop.' I held up a hand. 'If my mother were alive she would have shown herself before now. How would you feel if I started speculating that your dead mother was hiding behind a door in Camelot after all these years?' My tone was harsh but I didn't regret my words. I was usually all for Morgan's wild dreams, but this was going too far. She seemed to understand this as well, because she nodded and placed a hand on my knee.

'You're right, I'm sorry, I can only imagine how frightened I would have been.'

'We need to get Galahad out of here.' I redirected the conversation.

'Well, on that note, I have some good news.' Morgan's face broke into a grin. 'Queen Elaine has acquiesced to our plan.'

Morgan, I learnt, had approached the queen in private, hinting that she was aware of Elaine's desires; the conversation had evolved over the subsequent days until they'd come to a formal agreement. Morgan would use magic to deceive the party from Benoic into believing the queen's last pregnancy had not ended early, although the king would remain in the loop. Personally, I wasn't sure if this was wise, but Morgan informed me Elaine would not be swayed. She trusted her husband. We would have to wait another week before they could depart, and a labour would have to be falsified, but it would be done, we just had to believe in it.

In the days that followed, Galahad continued to age at an unearthly pace. Not that he seemed to mind. He was as happy and good-natured a child as I'd ever come across, for which I was immensely grateful. Completely unaware of the turmoil that surrounded his very existence, he spent his days crawling around the palace and giggling at the shadowy fish that swam beyond the walls. He'd never even experienced the feeling of the sun on his skin, yet he seemed completely entranced by the small world he occupied. I couldn't deny I'd developed quite the soft spot for him, spending my days playing silly games and telling him stories as he floated off to sleep. Only when he was dreaming did I let my worries overwhelm me, but even that was plenty.

Morgan, meanwhile, continued to prove indispensable. She showed up almost every day with supplies and gossip, yet whenever she left again I couldn't help but resent her a little. It wasn't that I wanted her to stay with Galahad in my place; it was that I wished she could remain there with us. Generally speaking, I tried not to put this on her shoulders, however, lest I sound ungrateful for all the necessary work she was doing herself. But sometimes it was easier said than done.

'In a few days it should all be over,' Morgan reminded me when I let my frustration get the better of me one afternoon.

'I know,' I groaned, 'I'm sorry.'

'Pfft, don't apologize. Better to have a little moan than let it fester inside.'

Her words made me smile. 'When did you get so wise?' I leaned over the child crawling between us and stroked an errant lock of hair from her face.

'You must be rubbing off on me.' Morgan wiggled her tongue at me. 'I'll be glad when you're free too, and not just because I miss you in my bed. All the secrets are getting hard to keep track of.' She grimaced. 'I think Merlin might suspect something. I've told him you're feeling ill, but no one has seen you for almost three weeks now and I'm not sure he's buying it. He keeps offering to pay you a visit to see if he can do anything to help, but I just keep insisting you don't want any visitors, that you're too embarrassed by how disgusting you are.' Morgan flashed me the hint of a smile.

'You're doing amazingly well,' I assured her, cupping her cheek in my palm. 'And like you said, King Ban's party is leaving in a few days, so we've just got to keep him hidden until then. I can deal with any awkward explanations afterwards.'

'If you insist.'

'I do.'

*

Finally, the day came for Galahad to depart. I hadn't expected it to be as difficult as it was to say goodbye. It had been barely a month, yet the child in my arms could have been a whole year old; and I had fed him, bathed him, and kept him warm that entire time. I had been there for the first smile, the first time he rolled over, and only yesterday he had taken his first tentative steps into my arms. If we had waited another week, I was sure he would speak his first words too. But therein lay the problem. Something about the home I had carved out beneath the water was bad for him, making him age magically fast. He would be an old man within a few years if he were allowed to continue at his current pace. And there was nowhere else in Camelot he would be safe.

Although he no longer looked like a child born on the May Day just gone, there were too many risks to keeping him here. And then there was Merlin . . . I didn't want to believe he would advocate for Galahad's death, but I had also heard how he spoke to Arthur that day. He put his faith in his prophecies and his allegiance was to the throne. Where did my own allegiances lie? I wasn't sure I could truly say any more. But I knew I couldn't let this beautiful little boy come to harm. And that meant handing him over to the Armorican king and queen. They would love and care for him like their own. He would be a prince and never want for aught. I reminded myself of all this and still it hurt to say goodbye.

When the time came, I ascended the palace stairs with Galahad at my side, guiding him as he clumsily took each step for the first and last time. Above the water, the gloaming was upon us and Morgan stood nearby, King Ban at her side. The news had spread throughout the castle: the queen had gone into labour three nights ago and subsequently given birth to a baby boy. No one had been permitted to see her, the king insisting she was well and wished to bond with their child alone. If anyone was suspicious, their concerns were diverted by the same enchantment Morgan had used to convince them all that the queen was pregnant. Tomorrow, however, they would depart and Galahad would be with them.

'It's time to go home.' I sighed and looked down at the small boy whose hand was clasped tightly in mine. 'It's not my job to take care of you any more, little one, but I can still offer you some protection.' Getting to my knees so we were at eye level, I gave him my best attempt at a carefree smile. 'You're going to grow up to be a very special man and therefore you will need a very special shield.'

Indicating he should watch, I lifted up both my hands and submerged them in the dark surface of the lake. I let all the love that had grown inside me over the past month pour from me, as though it were something physical I could shape and mould. My fingers tingled before losing all sensation, but I didn't pull them out. I flexed my hands around the rippling water and moulded it to my will. Slowly but surely, my vision took shape, becoming more solid in my grip until I could draw the entire object from the lake and it held its form. What was once water now looked and felt just like bronze. The circular plate bowed to create a subtle dome that could have hidden Galahad, as he was now, entirely with its size. The design was nothing special, based on what I'd seen on the shields of Arthur and his men at Camelot, but the outer rim was decorated with an endless looping design not unlike the ripples cast by a stone thrown into the water. And, at the centre, lay a rugged piece of purple amethyst I'd managed to pick up along the way.

With my gift complete, I lifted Galahad from the ground and let him straddle my hip, supporting him with one arm while I carried the shield in the other. It was time to join the two figures who waited for us at the edge of the trees.

'King Ban, may I introduce you to your son, Galahad.' Somewhat reluctantly, I offered up the small child clutching at my gown. His gaze was assessing, curious about the stranger that stood before him. After a few seconds, however, he seemed to decide he was pleased, stretching out his hands and allowing the king to lift him into his arms. I tried not to be too offended by his eagerness.

'It is my honour to meet you, little prince.' There was not a hint of uncertainty on Ban's face. He looked as awestruck as any father on the day his child was born. Galahad, meanwhile, simply patted his father's tunic before releasing an almighty burp. And for a split second I worried that Ban might change his mind, but instead he began to laugh, a deep and throaty chortle that elicited a squeal of delight from the child in his arms. And that was that.

TWENTY-TWO

Sleep eluded me that night. I tossed and turned, unable to find peace in the ordinary bed after so many weeks in one made of moss and twigs. My senses were on high alert, and I kept expecting to hear Galahad's gurgles from across the room. The only sounds to interrupt the silence, however, were Morgan's occasional snores.

I should have been thrilled to be reunited after so many nights apart, falling into a mindless slumber, our bodies pressed together. But I couldn't, not yet. Although I was glad we had accomplished our task, I still felt Galahad's loss in a way that Morgan couldn't possibly understand. The combined tension and purpose of the past month didn't just disappear as quickly as that. So I lay beside my friend and lover, watching her sleep and contemplating everything we'd done since we'd last lain here together.

When the faint pinkish hue of dawn broke through the narrow window, I finally gave up on rest. Clambering from the bed, I wrapped myself in a blanket before making my way to peer out at the approaching sunrise. It was going to be a clear day, not a cloud in sight, and despite the early hour there was already a small group gathered in the courtyard readying for travel. As I looked on, one figure in particular turned to open the carriage door, thus revealing his face to me. It was Ban. As the king stood there he smiled down at a much shorter figure, wrapped tightly in heavy layers, an even smaller bundle held in their arms, and gestured for them to step inside. I felt a pang in my chest as I watched Queen Elaine hug Galahad close before taking her husband's hand and ascending the carriage steps, but I knew it was for the best.

'How are you doing this morning?' Morgan's words startled me. I hadn't even heard her get out of bed.

'I'm adjusting.' I leaned into her as she wrapped her arms around my waist and rested her chin on my shoulder.

'I can imagine,' she replied softly, nuzzling my ear. 'It's been a hell of a month.'

I snorted. You could put it that way. 'I'm sorry I'm so wrapped up in my own head. I know the last few weeks must have been exhausting for you.'

'I still think I got the better end of the deal.' Morgan let out a small chuckle. I wasn't sure, though. I don't think I would have traded places with her if I could have gone back and done it all again.

'Plus, my time in the spotlight is up now.' She grinned as she twisted me around so that we were face-to-face. 'You're the one that's going to have to deal with all of the court's sympathies and solicitude now that you're out of bed again.' She wiggled her eyebrows and I let out a groan.

'What have you been telling people, Morgan?'

Based on the sympathetic glances I received from almost everyone I passed in the corridors, as well as the occasional but unsubtle berth I was given by others, I was pretty sure they all thought I'd been struck down by dysentery. I wasn't about to correct them. As long as everyone believed our ruse, I was content. Maybe rumours of a messy, infectious disease in my past would even hurt my marriage prospects. With that rousing thought, I decided it was time to ease myself back into life at Camelot.

For once I wasn't tempted to run to the nearby lake, having spent enough time cooped up underneath its waters for a little while. So, with nothing better to do, I suggested that Morgan and I head for the larger of the castle's two solars, this one located above the main hall. There was no real purpose to the visit, but I thought it might be worth at least showing my face, if just to prove to any lingering inhabitants I was still breathing. The room turned out to be surprisingly deserted, however. In fact, there were only two figures inside: a maid tending to the fire and Guinevere, who sat drinking a mug of steaming tea.

'Guin!' I called out, catching the young queen's attention.

'Viviane!' Discarding her cup, Guinevere rose from her seat and closed the distance between us. For the briefest of moments, she paused to scan me up and down before wrapping me up in an unexpected hug.

'It's good to see you too.' I grinned.

'You've missed so much.' The young queen was practically bouncing on the balls of her feet.

'Yes, I've heard. I'm so sorry I couldn't spend any time with the Queen of Benoic. Although Morgan informs me she gave birth to a baby boy during her stay.'

'Oh yes, it's such a shame – they were away this morning before any of us got a chance to meet him.' Guinevere shook her head. 'But it's not just that, Viviane. You'll never guess what. Arthur has been in contact with Bagdemagus. He has invited us to his castle to discuss a possible alliance.'

That was big news indeed. King Bagdemagus was a notoriously elusive figure. He ruled over the neighbouring kingdom of Gorre, rumoured to straddle the border between the otherworld and our own. I glanced at Morgan, who had come up beside me, and raised my eyebrows, but she just shrugged in response.

'This is the first I'm hearing of it.'

Guinevere smiled demurely, not remotely taking pleasure in knowing something Morgan did not; *that* would be thoroughly unladylike. I stifled a snicker. Some people were never destined to get along. 'We only received his letter yesterday. With Bagdemagus we might finally be able to reclaim the eastern territories.'

I couldn't deny the force of her words. It was well known that Uther and Bagdemagus had shared an uneasy truce, one that involved little more than respecting each other's borders. If Arthur could broker an alliance with the king, it would be a great boon for his reign, well and truly cementing him as not just his father's successor but a man destined to rule in his own right.

'And you're going with him?' I asked.

'I am! I set out within the month, ahead of Arthur,' Guin replied with a surprising level of enthusiasm. 'He has a few things he needs to remain in Camelot for, but we didn't want to keep Bagdemagus waiting. My early arrival will be a sign of good faith and perhaps I can befriend his queen.'

Guin didn't say the words aloud, but based on her giddy

expression I suspected she was rather delighted by the prospect of travelling alone, or without Arthur at least. Meanwhile, an unfamiliar feeling rose in my chest as I took in her rosy cheeks and excited smile. It took me a moment to place but I was surprised to find it was something akin to jealousy. Jealous of Guin? Despite what most of the court believed must be true, I'd rarely had cause to envy the young queen. But nor had I had many opportunities to travel since my journey to Camelot from Dál Riada, which had been, what? More than five years ago now.

I wasn't important enough to accompany Uther or Arthur on their diplomatic visits, yet I wasn't insignificant enough to be given free rein to go wherever I wished unsupervised. The furthest I'd travelled since my arrival was the night away with Merlin, and he'd never offered a repeat trip. I supposed that was another reason why the nearby lake meant so much to me. I knew that if I were being fair, neither Guinevere nor Morgan had any more freedom than I did: less perhaps. But reason and emotion didn't always go hand in hand. Still, I tried to brush the feeling aside and focus on Guin.

'That is very exciting news. You will have to tell us all about it when you return.'

'Of course!' Guin nodded. 'Now, let's get you two some tea and I can fill you in on all the gossip you've missed, Viviane.'

It was a pleasantly relaxing way to spend an afternoon, in conversation with Guin and Morgan, and I even found pleasure in the way Morgan occasionally rolled her eyes at the queen, or Guinevere tsked at something the other woman said. It reminded me of when we were all still children and spent our days together in lessons with Mistress Mae or exploring Camelot with Arthur. Although now it was only the three of us. We feigned shock over the rumours that two different members of the Benoic entourage had been spotted coming and going from the knight Gawain's chambers during their stay; and we giggled as Guin regaled us with Pelleas' embarrassment when he'd spilled wine all over King Ban's severe mother at dinner a few nights before. I didn't even notice the time passing until Guinevere's maid interrupted our blethering.

'Your Highnesses,' the maid curtsied, 'dinner is about to be served.'

'Thank you, Beatrice, we'll be down shortly.'

It was my first public meal since the night Clarine had stumbled into Morgan's chamber, and already the noisy clamouring of diners was overwhelming. As much as I wanted to turn around and head straight back to my room, I knew I needed to reintegrate myself into court. While Guinevere found her place beside Arthur, Morgan and I took seats a little further down the table. I could do this.

As the wine was being poured, however, I felt another body slide into the seat to my left and turned to find it occupied by a not unfamiliar figure. Merlin.

'Why, Viviane, it's good to see you.'

'You too.' I nodded.

'You've been missed.'

I rolled my eyes. 'By who exactly? By you?'

'Would that surprise you?' He gave me a look that I wasn't quite sure how to interpret. 'You look well though, one would hardly know you'd been so ill this past month.'

I didn't suspect for one second that Merlin believed Morgan's story. There was a conspiratorial twinkle to his eye that told me he knew I had a secret and would like nothing better than to know what it was.

'I'm pleased to say I feel fully recovered,' I confirmed, nonetheless determined to maintain the charade.

'So you weren't avoiding me?' His tone was teasing but his expression was surprisingly hard.

'Of course not!'

'I'm glad to hear it. Does this mean I should expect to see you in my chambers this week?'

'I . . . yes, if you'll have me.'

I hadn't really considered whether I'd be visiting the sorcerer in the coming days, but I supposed it was what I would have done before everything else had happened. Still, I couldn't help but feel that a new gulf had opened up between us. This man, who had become such an important part of my life at Camelot, was also the reason I had been in hiding for the past month, whether he knew it or not. He was the reason that Galahad was in danger. Although perhaps that was an unfair conclusion. He did not choose the visions he had, or whether to have them in the first place. It was a gift he had no control over. If gift was even the right word. Morgan may have found his declaration unforgivable, but I knew what it was like to be born with magic whether I wanted it or not. Still, I wondered how I would have handled the knowledge had I been the one who was burdened with it. More than anything else, I realized, it was Merlin's neutrality that truly disturbed me.

'Good,' he replied, 'we have much to catch up on.'

TWENTY-THREE

Something felt different, off, about my time with Merlin now. He was, for one, more aloof than usual, if that was even possible. His insistence on my presence, combined with his reluctance to talk to me when I was there, only convinced me further that he did not believe in the tale of my illness. More than that, though, he seemed resentful of my absence, as if I had done him some great disservice. It was . . . frustrating to say the least. And to add insult to injury, his behaviour, whether intentionally or not, left me experiencing an undercurrent of guilt that didn't seem quite fair yet equally made me increasingly desperate to make amends.

'Are you angry with me?' I eventually blurted out after another afternoon of uninterrupted silence.

'Sorry?' Merlin looked up from his desk.

'It's just, I feel like something isn't right between us. Since I came back.' Was that when it had started?

'You know, Viviane, you're not my first student. There have been others before you.'

I nodded. Of course there had, although I didn't understand the correlation. Was he mentally comparing me with my predecessors and finding me lacking?

'I have been grateful for each of my pupils. Each one

has taught me something. But you and I, I thought our relationship was different. Yet your illness . . .' he paused on the word, waiting to see if I would react. When I did not, he carried on, '. . . has made me think . . . perhaps I have failed you?'

'What?' I started. This was not what I had expected. 'You haven't failed me. It wasn't your fault I was ill.' I cringed inwardly at the layers of lies.

Merlin gave me what passed for a grateful smile. 'Not in that way. But I worry you are holding back from me. Do you feel we have not been exploring your full potential? Maybe I have gone easy on you, thinking you were just a child. You're not a child any more, are you, Viviane?'

'No,' I answered slowly, unsure where his words were going, not able to follow the transition from one thought to another, but beginning to feel the first hints of a guilt I didn't truly understand.

'No,' he nodded, 'you are young, yes, but you are also a woman fully grown.' He pushed back his chair from his desk and turned so his body faced mine, curled in my favourite armchair. 'I asked you once before, but allow me to ask again: why do you wish to be a sorceress, Viviane?'

Where in the world was the conversation heading? Still, my answer came easily enough. 'Freedom,' I breathed.

'And is that what you have?'

I frowned, confused, and slightly uncomfortable. 'I . . .' didn't know what to say.

Merlin gave me a sympathetic smile and stretched out a hand to take my own. 'I think you are a bird, Viviane, trapped in a cage.' He stood and I was forced to stand with him, our hands now interlocked. 'I think you make the most of what you have but you are stifled.'

'I don't understand.' I felt like that a lot, I thought, feeling irritated but not sure with whom.

'I can give you freedom.' To my horror, Merlin brought his free hand to my cheek and trailed a finger along my cheekbone. 'I've watched you for a long time, Viviane, waited for you to be ready. You have such potential and I can help you harness it. Together we could be so powerful. I have seen it.'

I tried to withdraw from him, to lean back and free my arm from his grip, but he moved with me, taking my motion as an opportunity to manoeuvre my body up against the nearby wall.

'What are you doing?'

Merlin chuckled. 'No need to be coy. I know you know the pleasures of the flesh.'

I felt sick. I didn't want this. I didn't want him. 'Morgan and I –' I began to stammer before he interrupted me.

'The naive experiments of young girls,' he scoffed. 'This will be different. Better. Trust me.'

I had trusted him, that was the problem. Yet here he was pushing my back against a wall, his left hand wrapped too tightly around my upper arm while he ran the fingers of his right hand down my trembling shoulder. I wanted to slap him, kick him, spit in his face, and then I remembered it was Merlin and I shrank from the idea. He was my teacher, my mentor; I would, before this moment, maybe even have called him my friend. I should have felt safe in his presence.

Instead of making me feel safe, however, Merlin was

leaning in to me, his whole body pressed uncomfortably against mine, and before I could say anything else he was trailing his lips down my neck.

'No,' my voice came out as barely a whisper, but he was so close he couldn't have failed to hear it. Yet still Merlin ignored me, licking his tongue against my bare skin, sending an unpleasant shiver down my spine. I was frozen. I couldn't wrap my mind around what I needed to do. *What do I do?*

'Viviane?'

It was Morgan. Morgan's voice that broke through the muffled buzzing in my ears; Morgan's voice that brought me back to my body and caused time to speed up once more.

'Morgan,' Merlin had stepped away from me as smoothly as if he'd never been there, and moved towards the other woman, 'I wasn't expecting you.'

Morgan glanced between the sorcerer and me, confusion etched across her face. 'I was looking for . . .'

But I wasn't listening to what she was looking for. Taking advantage of Merlin's retreat I scurried across the room to Morgan's side, refusing to look the sorcerer in the eye. My heart was thundering in my chest and I could barely make sense of my emotions, let alone voice them. All I knew was that I wanted desperately to leave this room and, preferably, never come back.

Morgan glanced between Merlin and me, the expression on her face unreadable.

'I was just about to leave,' I muttered. It was all I could manage before I dashed for the door.

Morgan wasn't far behind. As I hurried down the stairs and into the wide corridor beyond, she slipped her hand in mine, quickly taking the lead. Without objection I allowed her to guide me further down the hallway, away from Merlin's tower, until we reached a small alcove in the wall where we might have some semblance of privacy.

'Morgan?' I whispered, guilt roiling in my stomach over something I knew I shouldn't feel guilty about. The strained expression that met me only heightened my anxiety.

'What was happening in there, Viv, between you and Merlin?' Morgan frowned.

'He . . . I . . . it was nothing, a misunderstanding.' I felt the bile return to my throat. 'He just . . .'

'He just what?' Morgan looked angry now, and instinctively I found myself curling my shoulders inwards as if to shield myself. 'He was touching you, Viv. Did you want him to touch you?'

'No, it's not like that,' I murmured, my eyes turned down and brimming with tears.

Morgan raised both hands to my arms and it took everything in me not to flinch at her touch. 'Viviane. Look at me?' Her voice was filled with anger and something else, a pleading note I did not recognize. Steeling myself, I lifted my gaze to meet hers and saw my own tears mirrored in her eyes.

'I didn't mean to let him think . . . I mean . . . I love you, Morgan.' The tears were streaming down my face now and there was nothing I could do to stop them.

'No, no, no, Viv, no!' Morgan's voice cracked as she looked desperately back at me. 'I don't care about that. What I mean is . . . shit, I'm messing this all up.' She paused for a moment, glancing around the corridor as though she might find the words she sought sewn into the wall hangings. 'Has he done this before?'

'No. I don't know.' I squeezed my eyes shut, trying to block out the feeling of his lips on my skin. 'He's never tried to kiss me.'

'But he has made a pass before.' It wasn't really a question.

'Maybe.' I thought back to the day of Arthur's coronation and felt a cold shiver pass through my limbs. 'I . . . I . . . should have seen it coming, made my feelings clearer –'

'You shouldn't have done anything.' Morgan looked like she wanted to stamp her foot. '*He* shouldn't have done anything! He shouldn't have touched you.'

I collapsed in on her, allowing her to hold me up as silent sobs wracked my body and I buried my head in her shoulder. I clung to her, grateful for the safety and comfort of Morgan's arms as they wrapped around me, holding me against her body. I wanted everything else to fade away, to simply let this moment be the only thing that existed, but it wasn't. No matter how much I craved it, I couldn't dispel the tightness in my chest or the pain in my heart.

'We have to tell Arthur! He can do something, punish him.'

I shook my head, still burrowed in the crook of her neck. 'I can't. Not tonight. I can't face it.'

'Tomorrow then.' Morgan stroked my hair – one, two, three, four – the steady motion calming my very soul. 'I won't let him get away with this, Viviane.'

TWENTY-FOUR

My dreams that night were filled with looming shadows that crawled over me, trapping my body beneath their weight and staring down at me with featureless expanses where their faces should have been. I woke during the first hints of dawn, throat tight and desperate to scream. All I could manage, however, was to take huge gulps of the air my nightmares had denied me, leaving no space for sound to break free.

'Viviane, it's all right, I'm here.' It took me a moment to remember I wasn't alone. That Morgan's comforting presence was there beside me, one arm reaching out to pull me in closer on the bed and stroke my hair. 'You're all right,' she murmured, the repetition helping to calm my desperate breaths.

'I'm sorry,' I eventually croaked, attempting to burrow my head deeper into her chest.

'Never be sorry.' Of course I knew on some level she was right. What did I have to be sorry for, truly? Would I not say the same thing if it were her in my place instead? Yet I couldn't shake the sense of shame that engulfed me. One word continually circled in my mind: weak.

'Are you still with me?'

'Just about.'

'We're telling Arthur, this morning. He'll have to do something.' Morgan's words were spoken with a certainty I couldn't conjure for myself, but in that moment I was happy to let her take the lead.

As we approached the entrance to the keep, we were greeted by a familiar guard. On first sight, Alrec held up his hand to stop us in our tracks, moving his body so that he blocked our path.

'Let us pass.' Morgan waved a dismissive hand.

'The keep is the private residence of the king and queen.' Alrec eyed me suspiciously. I couldn't help but wonder if he'd faced a scolding from Arthur after he had let me through the last time.

'And I am the king's sister,' Morgan huffed. 'Now let me in to see my brother or else I'll turn you into a toad.' Morgan had never been shy about lauding her magic around the castle and it was clear from the expression on Alrec's face that he took her threat very seriously.

'My apologies, Your Highness,' he muttered as he ushered us past.

'Pray, do tell how you intended to turn Alrec into a toad?' I whispered as we headed up the stairs.

'What my understanding of magic cannot do for me, other people's lack of understanding can do instead.'

'You're wicked.' I snorted, a small smile tugging at the corner of my lips.

My levity was temporary, however, as we approached the royal solar and I remembered why we were there. Every muscle in my body was telling me to turn around again and return to my rooms. To not cause trouble. But trouble was Morgan's bread and butter.

'Arthur,' Morgan stormed into the room ahead of me, 'we need to have a word with you.'

'What's going on?' Guinevere looked up in surprise from the book she was reading, reclining on the settle by the fire.

Arthur was perched beside the window, perusing a small pile of correspondence with a cup in his hand. It was a surprisingly domestic picture.

'Indeed, what has brought you storming into our private chambers at this hour, sister? Uninvited, I might add.'

'Merlin,' Morgan growled before glancing back at me. It hadn't been a conscious decision, but while Morgan had stridden into the room without hesitation, I had found myself lingering in the doorway, unable to bring myself to cross the threshold. For a few fraught seconds Morgan stared at me, obviously waiting for me to speak, but when it was clear I couldn't, she simply nodded and turned back to her brother.

'Your sorcerer tried to force himself on Viviane yesterday.'

'Ah, I see.' Arthur sighed, placing his cup down on the table beside him.

'Do you?' Morgan's voice was higher now. 'He would have raped her. He must be punished.' Guinevere gasped, while I flinched at those words. Yet I couldn't deny them.

'I have already spoken with Merlin on this very subject last night.' Arthur kept his own voice low. 'He informed me there had been a misunderstanding between himself and Viviane, that she had taken offence to an offer he had made.'

'A misunderstanding? This was no misunderstanding!' Morgan was yelling now.

'What do you expect me to do, Morgan? I can't punish every man in Camelot who dares to flirt with a woman.' He didn't even look my way.

'I don't believe this. I don't believe you. Your sorcerer attacked her.' Morgan looked genuinely shocked.

Arthur finally met my gaze. 'Did he ruin you?'

Ruin me? *Ruin me?* I wanted to choke on the words. It was clear what they meant, and I wanted to scream at their implication. For whatever reason, however, the fire that raged within me refused to be set free. Perhaps if I had it would have burnt down everything around me.

'No, he did not ruin me,' I murmured, casting my eyes to the ground.

'If your virtue remains intact then I cannot demand he wed you.'

I found my voice came more readily at these words. 'Marry him? You think I'm after his hand in marriage? That that's what this is about? You are a greater fool than I thought.' I was grinding my teeth together as I spoke, I realized. 'I would not marry that man if it would save all of Camelot from burning.'

'Watch your tongue, Lady Viviane.' Arthur's tone was hard and his eyes narrowed at my outburst.

Morgan spat out her next words. 'I thought the king was supposed to protect his people, the women under his care.'

'Merlin is an invaluable asset to this court, to this kingdom.'

'So because he provides a few charms he's more

important than the rest of your subjects, than your family? I could do that!'

'Without Merlin's visions, we would have been ambushed in Linnuis, outnumbered at the Bassas River, and decimated in the Caledonian forest. Tell me, Morgan, can you do that?' When she remained silent, he ploughed on. 'If it weren't for Merlin, I might never even have been born.'

'Maybe that would have been for the best,' she snarled.

'Get out of my sight, both of you, unless you wish to see someone else punished this morning.' Arthur pushed back his chair and rose to his feet, towering over us. 'I mean it.'

I could tell Morgan wanted to keep fighting, but the dark expression that had fallen across Arthur's face unnerved me. It was unlike anything I had seen there before. Deadlier. Donning his father's crown had changed the young king, and that moment did not seem like the time to test exactly how much. Grabbing Morgan's hand in my own, I pulled her away from her brother, forcing her to follow me towards the staircase. On any other day she might have fought me too, but I was grateful when she acquiesced. I think she realized this was my choice to make and I was making it for both of us. Before we could disappear from view entirely, how-ever, Arthur, his tone calmer but still with an edge, called out once more.

'Lady Viviane, just let me know if you would like for transport to be arranged to take you back to Dál Riada, if you'd be more comfortable there. But do know that my sister will not be coming with you.'

My heart twisted in my chest but I ignored the threat,

increasing my pace and gripping Morgan's hand more tightly. We were already passing a bemused Alrec when I heard a third set of footsteps clattering down the stairs behind us.

'Viviane, wait.' Distress was etched across Guinevere's face as I turned to face her. 'I'm so sorry. I believe you – you do know that?' I shrugged, because what was I supposed to say? 'I'll try talking to him again, maybe he'll see reason.'

Morgan snorted at Guin's words and I couldn't help but silently agree. Guinevere's offer was a kind one but I didn't imagine there would be much point in her pursuing it; I'd yet to see the young queen exercise any real sway over her husband. Arthur's allegiance was to the throne, and Merlin was good for the throne. Of course, I didn't say any of this out loud.

'Thank you, Guin.' I placed a hand on her arm and squeezed lightly. Was I comforting her? It didn't matter. In that moment I truly valued her solidarity.

I opted to skip the shared meal that evening and despite my protestations Morgan decided to join me. We sequestered ourselves in her rooms and whiled away the evening nibbling on the cheese and dried fruits Morgan had swiped from the kitchens. Conversation was a struggle, I was so trapped in my own head, so I was grateful when Morgan finally took it upon herself to read to me from a bound copy of *Aesop's Fables*. Most of the words went in one ear and out the other – a patient tortoise, a compassionate mouse, a hungry grasshopper – but the simple gift of her voice was enough to soothe my frantic mind. Only when all the lights had been extinguished and we were curled beside one another in her bed did I let myself speak about what had happened.

'I wish we could leave this place, just run away and start a new life together.'

'And what would this new life look like?' Morgan gazed sleepily up at me.

'Anything. We could build a cottage by the sea, brew remedies for the locals in exchange for bread and cheese. Hell, we could get a cow and learn how to *make* cheese.' Morgan's soft giggles encouraged my daydream. 'We could wake up early at the crack of dawn each day and go swimming in the sea, gather shells to decorate our home, and spend the evenings snuggled up by the fire.'

'You, get up at the crack of dawn each day? You're sure you're not feeling ill?' Morgan pressed the back of her hand to my forehead playfully, but I batted it away.

'Hmmph! It's just a silly fantasy.'

'Why does it have to be a fantasy?'

I scowled, wondering if she was teasing me some more. 'What do you mean?'

Morgan pushed herself up to a seated position so that she was looking down at me. 'I mean, why can't it be a reality?'

'You can't be serious.' I didn't want to take her seriously lest it turn out to be a tease.

'I am always serious, Viviane.' When I raised a sceptical eyebrow, she rolled her eyes. 'I am when it comes to you and me. Let's do it. Let's run away together!'

'You're not teasing me, are you.' It was a statement rather than a question. 'You'd really leave Camelot for me?'

'For us?' She leaned down to gently rub her nose across my cheek, sending a surge of affection through me. We were really going to do this? My brain was struggling to keep up with our conversation, to accept that a life together beyond these stone walls could be a reality. But I had to hope.

TWENTY-FIVE

Hypothetically, I could likely have left Camelot without anyone coming after me. At least at first. If my father were to learn I was missing, it might be a different story. Assuming he still saw me as a useful asset. But by the time it would take for such news to reach him in the North, I'd be long gone. Morgan, on the other hand, was the king's sister. Her unexpected absence would surely be a scandal, even if only for how poorly it reflected on Arthur's dominion. We would need a plan, therefore, if we were to abscond from the castle together, and a good one at that.

Then there was the question of where we would go. Morgan was all for throwing a stone at a map and seeing what happened, but I needed more than that. I wanted to know that wherever we went we would be safe, that we could survive. I was embarrassed to admit that neither of us had developed strong enough bonds with any other nobles to expect them to take us in – especially without Arthur's approval. I certainly wasn't about to turn up on my father's doorstep without warning. But as much as Morgan bristled when I pointed it out, we didn't exactly have a lot of experience of caring for ourselves and living independent lives. In fact, now that we were faced with the possibility of leaving,

I was starting to realize how woefully unprepared the life of a courtly lady had left me.

'We can find a village, grow herbs and trade remedies,' Morgan insisted more than once.

'Maybe.' I shrugged. 'But wouldn't we draw a bit of attention?' Two strange women who lived alone and purveyed potions surely wouldn't pass without notice.

Morgan didn't have an answer for this.

'And what about Merlin?'

My stomach turned whenever I thought of him, which was all too frequently. What was it he had said? *Together we could be so powerful. I have seen it.* Would he really just let us – me – leave, without doing anything about it? Could we even hide from him if he really wanted to find us? Morgan was right on one thing: our craft gave us more freedom than most women might have and for that I was eternally grateful. Yet for all that Merlin might be the reason I was so desperate to leave, he was also the reason I might be able to do so, and I couldn't seem to get past that.

When I voiced these feelings to Morgan, however, she was emphatic in her denial. 'No,' she insisted, 'he's not. You are. We are. We're the ones who honed our craft, who practised our skills; he can't take credit for that!'

'I wish I could believe that.' I sighed. 'But it's easier said than done.'

The Morgan I knew might have continued to fight me in the past, but in that moment I thought she could see how broken I was. How shut off. I didn't want to wrestle with words. I wanted to crawl into a dark space and close myself off from the rest of the world. So, rather than push, she pulled me in, inviting me to nestle against her chest while she stroked my hair.

'One thing's for sure, we should leave when Arthur does, or not long after.' As planned, Guinevere had already departed on their diplomatic visit to Bagdemagus' kingdom; Arthur, however, would not set off until the first signs of spring. 'Court will be distracted,' Morgan continued, 'there's no safer time to slip away without anyone noticing we've left. They might even forget we haven't travelled with him. At least until Arthur and Guin return. But by then we will be long gone.'

'We just need to decide exactly where we're going,' I agreed.

Yet, somehow, the more we planned, the more we colluded and schemed, the less real it seemed. The less possible it felt. Instead, all I felt was trapped. I desperately wanted to get caught up in Morgan's enthusiasm, but it all just seemed so impossible. I had spent my entire life within the walls of castles, under the care of kings and courts. Even the palace I had built for myself had started to feel like just another trap, tainted by my original motivation to build it. Even now, after Merlin had revealed himself so thoroughly, I couldn't bring myself to tell Morgan the true reason I had constructed our underwater hideaway. It wasn't the sorcerer I sought to protect, but the sanctity of what we had down there. I didn't want Merlin to be a part of it, but a bit of me felt he always had been. His omnipresence had forced me down there; his visions and the threat they posed had forced me back. It wasn't that I loved Camelot so much that I was desperate to stay, but there was something bitter about being forced to leave – without a home, without a safety net. All I had was Morgan and myself. I just hoped it would be enough.

The worst part was that while I was the one with reservations, I was also the one with the least to lose. Morgan, for all her criticisms and complaints, loved Camelot. She had found a place here in the years since I had arrived. Servants and residents alike came to her with their ailments, and she was always there with a tincture or potion to ease their ills. She might possess an intimidating air but the people knew they could trust her. She cared about them and she was loyal, always. She wanted what was best for the kingdom, even if that didn't always align with her brother's vision.

I knew it must be exhausting, therefore, to hear me always come up with a reason to shoot down her suggestions. But I couldn't seem to help it. I couldn't find anything else in me. It overwhelmed me. The pain. The doubt. Ever since that afternoon in Merlin's chambers. And for all I loved Morgan, sometimes I just needed to be alone, to feel like less of a dead weight. In these moments, I turned to the only place I could – the palace. Its silence and sanctuary allowed me to wallow in my frustration without feeling a burden to the one I loved.

It was one such morning that I found myself beneath the lake's surface, unable to bear the hustle and bustle of the castle, desperate to escape but feeling completely and entirely helpless to do so, when I gave in to it. Overcome, I let out a wail that reverberated off the glassy walls before slumping to the floor, finally shedding the tears that I had been pushing down for days. There I sat until it hurt to blink and my eyes were dry as uncut stone. My chest felt empty and my limbs heavy, but I wasn't ready to give up. Not yet. There was still a flicker of defiance inside me that I hoped no one could ever extinguish. I just needed to feed it, to accept Morgan's help and believe we could be free.

Slowly, I climbed back on to my feet, the muscles in my shoulders and back groaning as I finally unfurled from my crouched position. Distracted as I was by the pain and stiffness in my body, it took me a few minutes to realize that there was something different about my surroundings. When I turned to the opposite wall, however, it was impossible to miss.

I sucked in a breath. *A door?* A tall, slim door carved into the iridescent planes. Beyond the apparition its surroundings looked exactly the same – the distorted reflection of the sun breaking through the water, the featureless shadows of fish and plant life floating past – but the outline was undeniable, and there to the left of centre, a door handle. I supposed I shouldn't have been entirely surprised. It was magic after all. Yet, since the day I'd built this palace, not a single thing about it had changed. It always appeared exactly the same.

Maybe I should have debated my next move longer. Considered all possible outcomes first. Sought out Morgan to see what she thought. But the pull I felt in that moment was almost a compulsion, my hand reaching out, feeling the magic that travelled between myself and the unexpected doorway.

I opened it and stepped through.

Rather than the watery depths of the lake that part of me had been expecting, the doorway led to a small antechamber with the same high ceilings as the palace I'd grown so familiar with. There was no furniture or anything else to occupy the space – just a spiralling staircase that disappeared into the shadows above. Well, what else could I do? I set my foot on the bottom step.

As I climbed the stairs higher and higher, I began to experience the same sensation as when I came up to the surface of the lake via my usual route; a slight pressure building in my ears as if they were readying to pop. The feeling only spurred my curiosity and I took the final few steps two at a time. When my head finally crested the surface of the water and I stepped out into the full light of day, I was as dry as always, the water seemingly repelled by my skin. My surroundings, however, were less familiar. I may have risen from a lake, but it was not the same body of water I had first entered; that much was immediately obvious.

For one thing, the lake that I was standing at the edge of was significantly smaller than the one at Camelot. I could have swum the breadth of it in under a minute if I really wanted to. The water took on a pinkish hue that had nothing to do with the rich shade of aquamarine that was the sky I could glimpse out of the corner of my eye. Where exactly was I?

So focused on the lake itself, I was unprepared when an unfamiliar voice pierced through my reverie.

'You finally came to visit! I was starting to wonder if you ever would.'

My whole body jerked backwards in surprise and I swivelled on the spot, finally scanning my surroundings properly. A woman – presumably the owner of said voice – stood a few yards to my right, smiling widely. She was not alone, either. The lake, I now realized, was positively thrumming with activity. Various figures were dotted around its shore – a few men, but mainly women. Not all of them looked entirely human. One of the men I could see wore nothing on his upper half, but from the waist down thick fur coated his flanks, the hooves of a goat or sheep where his feet should have been. Meanwhile there were at least two women with horns spiralling out from their temples, and another whose skin had an unusual greenish hue. In contrast the woman who had first spoken to me looked remarkably ordinary. Her dark hair was braided in a crown around her head, decorated only by a simple gold band with a crescent moon in its centre. Her clothes were equally plain: a white tunic, cinched at the waist and falling only as far as her knees. Her feet bare.

'Who . . . what . . .' I stammered.

'It's nice to meet you too, child. My name is Diana.'

TWENTY-SIX

I didn't faint, but I thought I could have. I did, however, take a fumbled step backwards, my feet finding water and causing a tiny purple frog to screech at me in indignation. Meanwhile Diana, as she had identified herself, merely continued to smile over at me.

'Where am I?' I asked, although I had a suspicion I already knew. 'How did I get here?' My eyes darted back and forth between the strange figures and the landscape.

'You hail from the North?' Diana tilted her head to one side, examining me. 'You probably know it as Elphyne.'

The fairy realm. My instincts had been right.

'I don't understand.' I might have stumbled back further if I hadn't known I would fall flat on my backside as soon as I tried. Nor did I want to take my eyes off my host until I knew it was safe to do so – whenever that would be. 'Did you send that door?'

'Oh, no.' Diana's laughter was light as she watched me, an amused curiosity etched across her features. I wished I could feel so at ease. 'You must have summoned it with your own magic.' When I just stared at her dumbfounded, she released another one of those airy chuckles and continued. 'Your palace has always been here, half in our world, half in yours, but we couldn't access it, only catch brief glimpses of you from the water.' I felt my cheeks heat: was nowhere private? 'We've been waiting for you to cross through to our realm ever since you first built it.' Her grin widened. 'Beautiful work, by the way.'

This was too surreal.

'But why now?'

Diana shrugged. 'You must never have tried before.'

But I hadn't tried this time. Or had I? Had I not been looking for a way out? Had I not been desperate for an escape? Perhaps those feelings had translated into magic without my even intending them to.

'Come, sit with us.' Diana stepped forward, taking my hand gently in hers, and I let her lead me towards the figures dotted along the lakeside. I really was throwing caution to the wind today, but what else was I to do? Run screaming back the way I had come? If Diana or her companions intended me ill, they'd simply stop me – I was outnumbered a dozen times. And if they were benevolent . . . what might I miss out on?

It was overwhelming to be guided towards a group of unfamiliar, smiling faces and invited to sit down among them. A few murmured greetings and one ethereal, grey-haired woman even gave me a hug that I was too disorientated to return. Without being asked, I was handed a small cup full of deep red liquid while Diana was given another. I hadn't noticed at first, but as I lowered myself to the ground I realized the grass was different here, a slight metallic sheen coating every blade. Another oddity to add to the list, I supposed.

'And how is the child?' *Galahad?* My surprise must have

shown on my face, because Diana chuckled and carried on. 'I liked him. A few of us used to play games with him through the walls, when you were sleeping. Children are very observant, you know.' You would have thought I was numb to surprises at this point, but I was nevertheless startled by Diana's words.

'He's gone. We found him a family, far away, who will keep him safe.'

'Hmm.' She studied me, her expression pensive. 'He will return, though, I see it.'

'What do you see?' My pulse quickened, thinking of Merlin's prophecy.

'That is all, simply that he will return.'

I frowned. It seemed all those with the gift of prophecy were equally vague. Still, I had to focus on the here and now. Where I was and who I was with. Diana. Although her face meant nothing to me, there was something about that name. Something familiar. And then I realized where I had heard it before.

'Your name, Diana? The same as the Roman goddess?'

Diana clapped her hands together. 'Oh yes, that's me!'

She seemed delighted. I, on the other hand, was stunned. I hadn't really expected her to be *the* Diana. Although why not at this point? I groaned, pressing my empty hand to my forehead and massaging my temples.

'Don't worry, child, the shock is understandable.' Diana had reached out to rub my back and I couldn't decide if it was comforting or distressing. 'Few mortals find themselves in the presence of a deity in their lifetime, and you have spent your entire life in the mortal realm.'

'But I was told you were killed, by Faunus' followers . . .'
I trailed off as I caught Diana rolling her eyes.

'Whoever told you such a thing is a fool. You cannot
kill a goddess – not so easily, at least. We are a part of the
land itself. I was injured, yes; in pain and in pieces, yes. I do
not recommend you let your head be separated from your
body, child. But I was also alive, insofar as my kind can ever
be called alive. Life is such a mortal concept.' She waved
a hand in the air as if to emphasize how insignificant she
found us.

'So, I lay where his followers had thrown me, at the
bottom of this very lake, unable to move, and, for a time,
I thought I might lie there forever. But then the people
of this isle found me, those I believe you call the fair folk.
They took me to their world, which runs parallel to yours,
and cared for me as one of their own. It took a long time,
but eventually I healed from my wounds and became whole
once more. Unfortunately – or not, depending on how you
look at it, I suppose – I could no longer return to the mortal
world.' She sighed, her gaze seeming to stare off into the
middle distance where she might be able to see the past. 'I
lost many of those who worshipped me during that time.
They abandoned me for newer gods. Then again, that has
always been the way. I am happy here. I have made a new
home.'

I frowned, confused by something else now. 'But didn't
you kill Faunus?'

Diana laughed. 'I trapped Faunus, I didn't kill him.
Thanks to me he is forever encased in stone, unable to
plague the world with his presence.'

'Alive?' I hated how I sounded so continually surprised.

Diana nodded. 'While I'm sure something of him remains, he is no longer conscious. But alive? Yes.'

Realization hit me all at once. The story Merlin had told me that night as we lay between the standing stones. Stones that had thrummed with magic, through which Merlin had channelled his powers, and I had been given a glimpse of both past and future. I gasped.

'You think me cruel?' Diana cocked her head to one side, misinterpreting my shock yet seemingly unperturbed by it. Meanwhile, I was tempted to shake my head, but I was almost certain Diana would have seen it for the lie it was. So I decided to be honest. Given her own forthrightness, I thought she'd appreciate candour.

'It is obvious the story I was told is not . . . the whole truth,' I chose my words carefully, 'so I can't help but wonder what really happened all those years ago.'

'Ask away.' Diana took a sip of her wine.

'Well, I was told that you . . .' How could I word this without causing offence? 'That Faunus got his mortal lover pregnant and this was what drew your anger?'

Diana's expression grew dark. 'Lover?' she spat. 'Faunus raped that woman. Adhan. She was one of my followers, one of my favourites actually, and he forced himself on her. I only found out when she was already six months pregnant, but there was no way I could let his betrayal go unpunished.'

I was unsure, based on Diana's words, if she saw Faunus' actions as a betrayal of herself or of Adhan, but I was not about to ask lest I offend this powerful, otherworldly woman.

I wondered about Adhan, however. What had happened to this woman who had been so cruelly mistreated? In that moment I was glad of Faunus' punishment, regardless of Diana's motivations.

'Now it is time to answer me a question, child of the water,' Diana interrupted my musings. 'What brings you here? Why did you finally open the door?'

I considered what I wanted to say carefully. I still wasn't entirely at ease in these strangers' company, and I was feeling more cautious about bestowing my trust since Merlin had turned my world upside down. 'I was feeling trapped . . . looking for somewhere I might feel free.' I didn't mention Merlin.

'You're welcome to stay here, you know.' Her tone was casual, but her expression was surprisingly earnest. 'This is as much your home as it is any of ours.'

I shook my head. 'I have to go back. There's someone waiting for me.'

'Well, stay for a drink at least.' Diana waved at a lithe young man to our left. 'There is no one so skilled on the flute as Fodor here, you must hear him play.'

'Um,' I hesitated, glancing down at my still full cup.

'I promise we're not going to force you to stay, Viviane of Dál Riada.' Diana smiled. 'Drink your wine, relax a moment and then return to your lover with tales of the otherworld you might escape to together.'

That did sound rather appealing, I thought, gazing around at the ethereal surroundings and smiling faces. I supposed I could stay a little while.

*

It was dark beneath the lake as I descended the staircase, the sun long vanished behind the horizon. Diana had been telling the truth when she'd promised there was no intention to keep me against my will. I'd happily stayed another hour or three, listening to Fodor play his instrument and sampling the richest wine I'd ever tasted. I'd been introduced to Diana's companions, many of whose names I had already forgotten, and relaxed as the otherworldly woman regaled us all with tales of Rome.

Now, as I returned to my own world, my mind was abuzz, thinking about what I had seen and what it could mean. Could Morgan and I really abscond to the realm of the fairies? For all the magic in my life, I found the prospect difficult to digest. I needed to talk it over with Morgan.

When I re-entered the palace through the mysterious doorway, the only light in the room emanated from a single candlestick sitting beside the bed. The bed, which to my surprise contained Morgan, curled up on her side atop the sheets. I supposed she'd come looking for me when I hadn't returned for dinner.

I found myself just standing there, smiling at her sleeping form for a few minutes before I finally approached. 'Hey, you,' I whispered as I climbed into bed beside her, the mattress shifting beneath my weight.

'Hmm,' she responded, rolling on to her back. Then, 'Viviane,' she jerked into a seated position 'you're back! Where have you been?'

I chuckled, reaching out to embrace her. 'Why so worried? You saw me only last night, you know.' But Morgan didn't smile back.

'What are you talking about? It's been a month since I last saw you.'

I frowned. Morgan couldn't be serious, yet she seemed genuinely distressed. 'Morgan, that's not funny.'

'Funny? Funny!' Her voice was shrill as her eyes darted across my face, looking for something. 'Do you really not know, Viviane?'

'Know what, Morgan? I left this morning and you'll never guess where I've been. I've got so much to tell you.' I reached out and clasped both her hands in mine.

Morgan stared at me like she couldn't believe I was really here. Before I could say anything else, she tightened her grip around my hand and tugged me from the bed. 'Morgan, what, wait?' I shrieked, but she ignored me, pulling me through the corridors of the palace and back up the stairs we used to enter the watery depths.

When we finally broke through the surface of the water, I was struck by the chill in the air, the hairs on my arms standing to attention beneath my thick woollen dress. The sensation was nothing compared to the sight that met me, however. The grass which had been decorated with crisp, orange leaves when I had first descended beneath the lake that morning was now hidden beneath a thick layer of fluffy white snow. A freak snowstorm? No. Morgan's words were finally settling in.

'Believe me now?'

I nodded, experiencing a sinking sensation in my stomach. *A month?* My plan of fleeing to the otherworld felt like it was slipping from my fingers.

'Now tell me where the hell you've been.'

So I did. I told her everything that had happened over what for me had been the past twelve hours. Of how my desperation had opened the doorway, how I had climbed the staircase only to find myself in an otherworld. I told her about Diana and her companions and how she had ended up there. This, of course, also meant telling Morgan the tale that Merlin had shared with me long ago, one I'd only neglected to narrate to her because it had seemed so insignificant at the time. Thankfully, she didn't care about that: how were either of us to predict this turn of events?

'And don't you see? This might be our way out. We can leave, run away, through the door.' I glanced back to confirm that the entrance to the otherworld remained, and then it struck me. 'But wait, if you saw the door, why didn't you go through it?' I asked, wondering if I was the only one with such little sense. No, I thought, out of the two of us Morgan had always been the most likely to barge ahead, consequences be damned, ready to discover whatever might be waiting out there.

'It wouldn't open for me,' she explained. 'I tried everything I could think of to get through, but not even my magic would do it.'

'I guess it was my spell, even if I didn't intend it. I must have to be there to open it.'

I stared around at the snow-covered ground, wrapping my arms around myself as a shiver travelled down my spine. I had thought I'd found us a solution to our problem, a place to go. But the revelation that during a measly few hours in the otherworld a month had passed here at Camelot was terrifying. Morgan could clearly see my distress as she wrapped one arm around my shoulder.

'I'm glad you're all right, Viviane, but something else has happened.' She withdrew her arm and let it slump to her side. 'Dammit, a part of me thought you might at least be together.' I frowned but let her go on. 'While you were gone, there was news from Gorre. Guin has gone missing.'

TWENTY-SEVEN

If I had been alarmed by my own disappearance, that was nothing to what I felt at Morgan's latest revelation. At least *I* had known where I was.

Morgan nodded. 'We received the news from Bagdemagus two days ago. She never showed up. Arthur has gone with Merlin and his knights in search of her.'

'What about her guards, her driver, her lady's maid? Someone must know where she is?' I wrung my hands, unable to stop the anxious movement.

Morgan shook her head. 'Bagdemagus found her entire entourage along with her carriage not far outside out of his borders, apparently. Everyone was asleep bar one, a guard. He'd been run through. Only Guin was missing.'

'Magic?' It had to be magic.

'Presumably.'

'Then we have to do something. If magic is involved, then magic has to be the solution.' I recognized that Merlin was likely already employed to do what he could for the missing queen, but I trusted Merlin about as far as I could hurl him.

'But what about the door? Diana?'

I had to admit, it was tempting. But regardless of Morgan's relationship with the queen, I considered Guinevere a friend.

'We can't just abandon Guin, not without trying. Maybe after . . . then we can talk about leaving again.'

Morgan nodded. 'What have you got in mind?'

Scrying. It was something I had read about but was yet to attempt myself. Well, there was no time like the present.

You started with a bowl of water, although the best element to use depended on the spell caster (Morgan had suggested soil but I insisted on the water). For clarity, I placed a lit candle atop the liquid, making sure it was the only light in the vicinity, while Morgan sprinkled dried eyebright petals across its surface. Hand in hand, we sat cross-legged on either side of the bowl, focusing on exactly who it was we wished to find.

Come on, Guinevere, where are you?

After a few minutes had passed – the only thing to break the silence the sound of mine and Morgan's breathing – slowly but surely, an image started to emerge. Just as I'd hoped, there was Guinevere, her usually tightly bound hair hanging loose around her shoulders, her face contorted in an angry grimace. It was as though she were there in the room with us, her features were so clear. In that moment, I found a weight I had not wanted to acknowledge was lifted from my shoulders. Guinevere was alive.

Where the queen might be found was far harder to ascertain. All around her was a sort of fog, blurring her surroundings so they were no more than indiscernible shades of brown. No distinguishing markers that might guide those searching for her. Nor was there anything natural about this fog. It moved and warped with Guinevere's movements as she marched back and forth scowling to herself. Wherever Guin was trapped, there was one thing I was sure of: magic was all around, and it was preventing us from seeing any further than the face of the woman we sought.

'Where could she be?' Morgan whispered, staring intently at the water's surface.

'I've no idea.' Slumping backwards, I let Morgan's hands slip from mine, watching as Guinevere vanished, the spell now broken.

That night I couldn't sleep, my mind abuzz. Where could Guinevere possibly be and how could I help her?

While Morgan snored softly beside me, I ran through everything I did and didn't know in my head. When it came to the world of magic, there was still so much to learn. In the past I would have gone to Merlin and posed him my questions, but now the thought filled my throat with bile. Still, in that moment, I couldn't help but wonder if I needed him anyway. No, not the sorcerer himself, but his library. There was nothing I needed from that man now, and perhaps nothing I had ever needed from him. My magic was my own. A gift from my mother that I had nurtured with hard work and passion. What had Merlin really given me but an excuse to break the invisible chains that confined me? The breaking I'd done myself. With that realization I knew what I needed to do. I needed to take the knowledge I required, and to do that I needed to channel a little bit of the woman who had got me into trouble in the first place.

As I climbed those stairs full of trepidation and anticipation, a part of me was sixteen again. This time, however, the excitement was gone, and my fear of Merlin's discovery came from an entirely different place. Yet still I pushed on. I would not be deterred.

He was gone, I reminded myself, somewhere far away in search of Guinevere. If I wanted to access his library, then now was the perfect time. Even with this knowledge, there was only one place in Camelot I believed myself to be beyond his sight, and so I had donned a necklace of black-thorn for protection before slipping from my room.

I had decided not to wake Morgan, who as far as I knew was still sleeping soundly, unaware of my absence. It wasn't my intention to keep my excursion a secret, only that a part of me felt I needed to do this alone, and Morgan surely would have insisted on coming with me.

I was pleased to discover Merlin's room deserted as anticipated, everything where I remembered it to be. Still, I knew better than to delay. I scurried deeper into the chambers and began to rifle through the overflowing bookcases. I wasn't sure what exactly I was searching for – something on summoning, perhaps – but surely if the answers were anywhere, this was the place they would be. By the time I had moved from the first room to the second, I had yet to find anything even remotely relevant to my search, but I wasn't about to give up. I ran my finger down the spine of each book in turn, processing their titles, and occasionally pulling an unmarked volume from its shelf to leaf through the pages, only to discover they concerned woodland fungi or Latin verbs.

Maybe I was being too literal in my search. For all I knew, there was a fungus out there that could conjure up a missing friend. If that were the case, however, where did I begin?

'If you wanted to borrow a book, you only had to ask.'

My stomach lurched and my heart stuttered in my chest. I was no longer alone. It might have been my imagination, but upon hearing that voice the whole room seemed to shift around me. The air grew thicker, stifling my ability to think, to breathe. The walls felt closer, the ceiling lower, and everything around me seemed darker, but then that may just have been my eyes narrowing. I swivelled on the spot, my heart tightening in my chest, and stared at the man who had spoken. Merlin.

'Stay away from me.' The words came out as a growl.

'Why?' For a moment the sorcerer looked genuinely confused, which only made me angrier.

'You know why,' I barked. Was I turning into an animal?

'Ah, I see, you are still angry at me for before.' He was so calm I wanted to scream. No, more than that, I wanted to jump at him and claw the placid expression from his face.

Instead, I continued to stare him down, willing him to let me leave and never look back. To my frustration, however, he did no such thing, simply letting out a deep sigh as he watched me, a look of what I could only describe as disappointment on his face.

'I have kept my distance, as Arthur asked me to.' Arthur had told him to leave me alone? That was news to me. He sighed before carrying on. 'But I had hoped it had been long enough now that we could put the past behind us, talk about it like adults. It seems I was naive.'

'You what?' I was too shocked to really sound angry.

'I understand now I was too hasty, too eager. I should not have expected you to soften to my touch so quickly. I was misled by your eagerness to explore the carnal delights with your little friend. I took you by surprise. I should have spent a little more time in wooing you as a lady likes to be wooed. I admit I am a little rusty in the art of courtly love.' As Merlin spoke he actually had the audacity to release the briefest of laughs.

'You think if you had not pushed me against a wall and left bruises on my skin I would have come to you willingly?' I was, to put it mildly, stunned.

'Eventually.' He shrugged. 'Although I admit I had grown rather impatient.' The smile he gave me was more akin to a leer. 'Our destinies are irrevocably intertwined, little sorceress. One day you will have to accept this.'

'So you say,' I snorted. I no longer trusted a word that came out of his mouth. 'What are you doing here, anyway? Shouldn't you be looking for the queen?'

'And here I thought you knew where she was. You've both been somewhere I cannot see into.' I frowned. Merlin tilted his head and took another step towards me; instinctively, I flinched backwards. He didn't try to touch me, however; he simply looked me up and down, sizing me up. 'I had a dream the night you came to Camelot. I saw you grown. I saw you as you are now. A young woman. A beautiful woman. One full of so much raw potential. I saw us coming together, mind, body and magic – more powerful than either of us could be alone.'

His words did nothing to sway me. If anything, they made me queasy. 'Weren't you the one who told me that a prophecy is ours to embrace or reject?'

Merlin eyed me curiously. 'If that's how you wish it to

be, leave now, Viviane. Play at husband and wife with your little girlfriend. Young love burns fierce and quick. You'll see things my way eventually. I can be patient. Have I not given you time alone to think these past few months, after all?'

'You could give me one hundred years and it would not be enough.'

Although he had given me permission to leave, Merlin did not move and I was forced to push past him to escape. Just another of his little power plays. I felt a surge of humiliation that it had taken me so long to see him for what he was. A power-hungry manipulator. Then again, was that not what he had done to me – manipulate my trust, foster my reliance on him, encourage my isolation – ever since I was barely more than a child? It was all too much to process. The hurt, the grief, the shame, the anger. So much of it pointed inwards despite my lack of control in it all.

I was not a child any more, however. I still had some way to go, in rebuilding myself, in restoring what Merlin had taken from me, but in the meantime I couldn't let the sorcerer drag me down any further. Right now, I had some magic to do – I just hoped my suspicion proved correct.

'Wake up.' I gave Morgan the tiniest shake of the shoulders.

'Huh?' She jerked awake. 'Viviane, what's going on?'

'I've had a thought. What if Guinevere is in the fairy realm? And that's why we can't see where she's being kept?'

'The spell only works on this plane?'

I nodded. 'Doesn't Bagdemagus' kingdom guard a crossing to the fairy realm?'

'That's the rumour.' Morgan sat up fully in the bed.

'Well then, that's how we'll get her out.'

'You want to go back through the door after all?'

'No,' I moved to my dresser and started rummaging through my things. 'The otherworld is too big and we don't know how we'll be affected by the time there. But I thought, maybe . . . ah-hah!' I drew an ornate hairpin from my drawer and turned back to Morgan who was rubbing at her eyes.

'I'm not sure I can be fully awake. Why are you brandishing a hairpin at me?'

'It's Guin's,' I explained, 'she gave it to me.' Returning to the bed, I handed Morgan the carefully carved piece of bone, a tiny bird perched on its head.

'Right . . .' she trailed off, turning the item over in her hand.

'I thought, well, I opened a door to the fairy realm once before, maybe I can do it again? But this time near Guinevere.'

Morgan looked up at me, suddenly more alert. 'And you wanted something of Guin's to direct the magic.' I nodded. 'Well, it's worth a stab.' Morgan grinned, pointing the sharp end of the hairpin at me like one might wield a knife. 'How did you do it last time?'

I blushed. 'That's the thing, I'm not sure. I was just so desperate to escape, for a way out, and then it appeared.'

Morgan hummed as she turned the piece of bone over in her fingers. Thoughtful. 'You're pretty desperate for Guin to return, aren't you?' she said after a few minutes and I nodded. 'Maybe that's all it takes, then? You're connected to the fairy realm, Viv, through your mother. Maybe you just need to want it enough.' She offered up the hairpin again and I took it.

'No pressure,' I murmured, but Morgan just smiled.

'I'm here,' she whispered as she took my free hand in hers.

Closing my eyes, I took a deep breath and felt the magic flicker between us. Tiny pinpricks tickled my skin where our fingers interlinked and I let myself relax into the moment. Rather than the pain and desperation I had felt that morning beneath the lake, I let myself revel in the comfort of loved ones – lovers, friends and sisters. Family. I had Morgan by my side but Guin should be here too. Guin, who might not always understand me but would never abandon me. Guin, whose arms were always open, who would fight her husband on my behalf. Guin who was far, far away, lost to another world.

'It's time to come home,' I murmured so low my lips barely parted.

The tingle that had started in my fingers spread up my arms and down my spine, warming my body from the inside out. A breeze passed across my face that shouldn't have existed and I heard a splash of water that wasn't there. It was all rather pleasant, until my hand seared red-hot.

'What the –' The bone hairpin tumbled from my hand, now scorched black, and hit the stone floor.

'What is it?' Morgan gripped my hand more tightly. 'Did it work?'

'I . . . I don't know.'

TWENTY-EIGHT

I felt like a naive little girl. Had I genuinely expected a door to appear out of thin air? For Guin to come striding out, maybe a little the worse for wear, but safe and unharmed? Instead, all I had to show for my brilliant idea was a scorched hairpin and a cold dose of reality. I was not as powerful as I'd hoped.

'Viviane, stop it.' I looked up from our joined hands to find Morgan glaring at me. 'I can see the self-doubt in your face.' She shook her head. 'And I won't have it. We don't know it hasn't worked. Maybe the time difference between here and there means there will be a delay?'

It was possible, I thought. Inasmuch as anything was possible when it came to unknown magic.

'Maybe we should go to the lake? See if the door there has opened?' I suggested, feeding off Morgan's determination.

'Great idea. Let's get dressed.'

We never did get as far as the lake, however. Just as I was slipping on my second shoe, my ears pricked at the sound of rapid footsteps beyond the door. When I paused, Morgan shot me a confused look, but I simply held up a hand and indicated she should listen closely. Slowly, the footsteps were joined by strings of indistinguishable chatter and even the occasional shout. Whatever was happening, it seemed the whole castle was awake for it and hurrying in one direction.

'Quick.' I grabbed Morgan's hand and made for the door. 'Something's happening.'

Once outside in the bustling corridor, we let the surprisingly large crowd scoop us up and followed it all the way to the main hall. When we arrived, the chamber was already packed and we were forced to take positions at the very back of the crowd. In front of us, Arthur stood before the court and he was not alone. To his right stood Guinevere, slightly bedraggled but alive and well. At the sight of the queen, I couldn't help the wide grin that spread across my face and I gave Morgan a not-so-subtle nudge with my hip.

'Our spell, maybe it did work.'

'Shh,' Morgan silenced me, although I saw she was smiling too.

Meanwhile, to Arthur's left, another figure stood between the king and Gawain, one I did not recognize. This stranger was lithe and tall, taller even than Arthur, with dark skin and black, closely shorn hair. There was nothing particularly notable about his clothing, his long tunic layered over loose trousers with a scabbard belted at his waist. The materials looked fine, so I had to assume he was nobility, but otherwise there was nothing to distinguish him from any other knight or lord. Then he shifted slightly and the shield in his left hand rotated to face the crowd. I had to stifle a small gasp. That shield – I recognized those concentric circles, the lump of amethyst in the middle. But it couldn't be. How was it here and in the possession of this unfamiliar man?

'People of Camelot,' Arthur opened his arms wide and beamed around at the gathered crowd, 'allow me to introduce the newest knight to accept a seat at my Round Table, Sir Lancelot du Lac.'

Cheers broke out amongst the assembly, reassured by Arthur's smile although still rather befuddled.

'Both Queen Guinevere and I are in Sir Lancelot's debt. I am honoured to have him join my court. As you know, our recent journey did not go as planned. My queen was ambushed on the road to Gorre by none other than Bagdemagus' son, Maleagant.' Gasps rang out around the hall and Arthur waited patiently for them to dissipate.

'The prince was acting of his own accord, in the hopes of sabotaging our alliance with his father. In this, I can confirm, he failed and King Bagdemagus has sworn allegiance to Camelot.' This roused another chorus of cheers. 'Your queen, however, was taken hostage by Maleagant. For weeks my knights and I searched the countryside, but to no avail. Until we met Lancelot. To him we owe the queen's safety and the safety of our alliance with Bagdemagus, for he rescued her from captivity.' Arthur reached out and took hold of the new knight's arm by the wrist, lifting it in the air to renewed cheers – the loudest so far.

Once Arthur had finished regaling the court with his story, the crowd erupted into cheers and shouts. Some celebrated the return of Queen Guinevere, others the alliance Arthur had ensured between himself and Bagdemagus, while even more welcomed the latest knight to join Camelot's company.

'Can you wait here for me? I need to talk to Arthur,

to find out what happened.' Morgan waited for my nod before pushing her way through the crowds to join her brother.

I watched Lancelot. At first, he smiled and waved, even shaking the hands of a few courtiers who approached him. Eventually, however, he turned to Guinevere who was standing silently, her expression somewhat removed from the clamour happening around her, and said something I couldn't hear. From the expressions on their faces I thought he might have asked her a question. When she replied, the new knight turned back to the room, scanning the crowds for something. I wondered what he had asked her. Then, to my utmost surprise, his brown eyes landed on me.

Dumbfounded, I glanced around myself, trying to figure out if I'd misinterpreted the direction of his gaze. Maybe he had spotted someone behind me. But there was no one there. And when I looked back in the stranger's direction I realized he was now striding directly towards me, a wide grin plastered across his face. That smile, those sparkling brown eyes. I felt my stomach do another turn and I hoped I wasn't about to faint. I knew those features.

'Lady Viviane?' Lancelot gave me a deferential bow upon his approach. My own voice stuck in my throat, but I managed a brief nod of agreement. 'I hope I'm not being too familiar when I say I'm pleased I found you. We already know each other, you see.'

'Galahad?' I whispered.

'I prefer Lancelot these days,' he smiled.

'Lancelot.' I rolled the name over in my mind. This must have been the name that Ban and Elaine had given him.

'It's really you.' Lancelot took my hand. 'The lady of the lake.'

'What did you call me?' I couldn't help but let out a little bark of laughter at the affectation.

'I remember you, from my childhood. The golden-haired fairy who took care of me beneath the water.'

I shook my head. 'I'm not a fairy.'

'But you are an enchantress? I was told that Camelot was home to three sorcerers. The mighty Merlin and two women who trained with him. I knew one of them must be you. My adoptive father told me that this was where I was born.'

'Yes, but you can't be . . . it can't be . . .' I trailed off because I knew it was him, just by looking into his eyes. 'You kept ageing.'

He nodded, his smile falling. 'With every cycle of the moon I age roughly two years. It seemed briefly when I was a teenager my curse might have ended, but then I shot up as if overnight again. But I also learn faster than anyone else I have met. I was reading Homer by the time I was six months old. I could ride a horse better than my father after two days' practice. I learnt sword techniques that should have taken months in a matter of hours. I am, if anything, more accomplished than any man of twenty has a right to be. But none of it was worth it . . . So last month I decided the time had come. I left home to come here. To find you, in the hopes you could take this curse from me.'

Bile had risen in my throat. 'Curse?' The word sounded heavy on my tongue, but what else could you call it? It certainly sounded like a curse for your life to flash by in the blink of an eye, growing old as those around you barely aged. 'I don't know why this happened. It was never my intention . . .' I trailed off, too many questions swirling through my mind to formulate a proper response.

'I believe you.' His expression was sincere. 'You saved me. But there must be something you can do now? Some magic you can wield, or else I will be an old man in a handful of years.'

I nodded, although I wasn't sure to which part. 'Perhaps Morgan and I –' But Lancelot cut me off before I could complete my sentence.

'You can't tell anyone else.'

'But Morgan –' He shook his head again.

'The more people who know who I am, where I came from, the more danger I'm in.' My eyes swept across the room to settle on Arthur briefly before returning to the man before me. Lancelot seemed to sense my train of thought. 'I don't intend him any harm, I swear it.' He held my gaze. 'You owe me this.'

Finally, I nodded. 'Meet me tonight, in my chambers, when the rest of the castle is asleep.'

All evening I found it impossible to settle. I paced my room back and forth, back and forth for what felt like hours and still I felt restless. Dinner had been stiff and awkward, for me at least. Everyone else was having a whale of a time. The wine flowed and the laughter echoed. A feast in honour of Camelot's newest knight; in honour of the queen's safe return. Yet if anyone had looked as uncomfortable as me, it was Guinevere. She was seated between Arthur and Lancelot, and whenever I'd glanced their way it had seemed as though she was simply studying her food rather than enjoying it. I might have been more curious if my mind hadn't been so consumed by my own problems.

Morgan had tried repeatedly to engage my attention, but when I couldn't tell her what I was really thinking I didn't know what else to say. So I had excused myself at the earliest opportunity, when I was sure my absence would not be noted as strange, and retired to my chambers alone. And here I was, hours later, pacing back and forth while my teeth chewed a little too hard on the inside of my lip. If I continued like this for any longer, part of me worried I might never be able to stop; trapped in a Sisyphean cycle of tramping around this chamber for eternity. It seemed like the worst fate imaginable, until there was a soft tap on my door and I realized there was a possibility still worse.

'Come in,' I called lightly in the hope that my voice would travel no further than the hallway immediately beyond.

At my invitation the door swung open to reveal the visitor I had been anticipating: Lancelot. His expression was unsure and at first he did not move beyond the doorframe. When I gestured for him to come inside, however, he did so, closing the door gently behind him.

'Thank you,' he murmured, bowing his head slightly.

'Don't thank me yet,' I sighed. 'I can't make you any promises.' He simply nodded, apparently waiting for me to take the lead. 'I think it's best you take a seat.' I indicated the rug beside the hearth where a few large cushions were scattered for this very purpose, and I was grateful when he did as I asked without question. I then set about extinguishing the candles dotted around the room. I needed to focus in on this moment, on this man before me. Finally, when the only remaining light emanated from the crackling brazier beside Lancelot, I took my own seat across from him.

'I can't promise I can fix this,' I repeated, desperate for him to understand. 'But I also can't try to fix this without knowing what magic has caused it, and in order to do that I need you to open up to me.'

'I already explained everything to you.' He didn't look annoyed, simply puzzled, and I had to resist rolling my eyes, a little bit of the weight leaving my shoulders.

'Not like that,' I explained. 'I need to understand what's going on inside you, and in order to do that I need you to relax, to be open to my magic.'

'I am at your command, lady of the lake.' He gave me a small smile, one full of trust and, I worried, hope.

Reaching across the rug, I took Lancelot's hands in my own. A large part of me was still struggling to comprehend that these were the same hands that had wrapped around just one of my fingers less than a year ago; that this fully grown man was the same little boy I had nurtured for almost a month of my life. It pained me that so much of his life had already flashed by so quickly, but if there was anything I could do to help him, I would.

Pushing my heartache to one side, I closed my eyes and let my body relax, focusing entirely on the feeling of his skin in mine. He may not have lived the same number of years as most knights, but his hands bore the unmistakable calluses of swordplay. They were also much larger than mine to match his lofty height. Still, they were gentle. He let me take charge, his fingers lying lightly in my grasp, no tensing or fidgeting, just trust. This I was grateful for.

As I held his hands in mine, the rest of the world slipped away and I reached out with my mind. I let the magic trail down my arms and through my fingers to his, as though we were one. And then I felt it. The pace at which the life ran through his veins so unlike my own. On the surface, everything seemed right, a life unfolding as it should, but underneath there was something unnatural, something otherworldly that didn't belong to this man who should still be a boy. It was as though his years trickled through my fingers like water. I thought I might throw up. It was too much for me to handle, and without thinking I dropped his hands from mine. My breaths came hard and fast, something akin to panic welling in my chest as I met Lancelot's eyes across the hearth.

'What is it?' There was more fear in his voice than I'd ever heard before.

'I don't know, I don't know, I don't –' I was blabbering. Scrambling to my feet, I practically sprinted across the room to the water basin in the corner. Ignoring everything else, I submerged my hands in the cool liquid, soaking my sleeves, and proceeded to splash my face with abandon. Nothing I could do would rid me of this feeling, however; the guilt that roiled in my stomach, the tears that threatened to pour forth from my eyes. It was all too much.

'I don't know,' I eventually managed to stammer out. 'Your mind and body seem well, healthy, but it's like they don't understand the passage of time, or where they are.'

'I don't understand, Viviane.' Lancelot rose to his feet.

'Neither do I, not really. I still don't know how this happened, but . . .' I forced myself to meet his eye. 'I think it's my fault. Something to do with those first few weeks.'

'But can you fix it?' Lancelot sounded desperate now and it forced me to remember that this wasn't about me.

I straightened my back. 'I'm going to find a way.'

The last thing I thought before I finally drifted off to sleep that night was that, in the midst of everything else, I'd failed to ask Lancelot what had happened out there, to Guin and him.

TWENTY-NINE

Before our rupture, I might have enlisted the help of Merlin. Not directly, of course – I had promised Lancelot my silence and he would have it – but I would also have had access to the wealth of literature in the sorcerer's library. After breaking in once for a book and being caught in the act, there was no way I was going back if I could avoid it. I didn't want to be alone with Merlin again, not now, not ever. That meant I was on my own. Without even Morgan to help me, because how could I hide what I was trying to do if I were to involve her in my research? I couldn't, that was the answer. I understood Lancelot's caution, I truly did. But I also trusted Morgan and I was sick of keeping secrets from her. But this wasn't my secret to share, and I couldn't deny that Lancelot was right: I owed him.

I must have done something wrong, or else missed something I should have caught. I'd been sure that when Galahad, no, Lancelot, was taken away from the palace beneath the lake, away from Camelot, whatever magic had been causing his rapid ageing would cease to function. Now I knew I had been wrong. The weight of caring for an infant in secret, one in so much danger simply for the crime of existing, had dominated my thoughts. But now I wondered if I should have spent more time trying to figure out why he had aged so quickly in that first month he'd spent with me. I'd been his de facto guardian, and yet I'd allowed an unknown magic to sink its teeth into him before sending him on his merry way.

There was only one way I'd be able to process and move past the guilt I was feeling, and that was to find a cure. Just as I had indicated to Lancelot, however, a cure required a cause. So I tried to reflect on what little I did know. Lancelot's curse – because there was no better word for it – began the day he was born, or at least in the days immediately following. I had seen that for myself. It had begun beneath the lake. Yet it had not ended when he left the water behind. The very rhythm of his soul was out of sync with this world, which made me wonder how he had fared in the other one.

I needed to ask him about it. I needed more details about his life and his journey to Camelot. So that was where I would start. At the break of dawn the very next morning, I decided to seek Lancelot out before doing anything else. Maybe I could even suggest we visit the lake together. To see what he remembered and how he responded to the magic there. I didn't know exactly what that might achieve, but any plan was better than no plan in that moment.

It was still early, and so the first place I thought to look for Lancelot was his recently allocated chambers. On arriving outside the door one of the castle attendants had indicated was his, I gave it a few hard knocks just in case he was still asleep. I didn't have time to waste. If he wasn't up already, he hopefully would be now. After a few seconds passed, however, I received no response. So I knocked again. This time, I leaned in further, my ear practically pressed to the door, and I realized I could hear movement within. Impatient and anxious, I tried one more time, but when no one came to open the door I decided to try the handle myself.

It was unlocked.

'Lancelot,' I called, as the door swung open. 'Are you decent?'

With an air of confidence I strode into the room, only to be met with a sight I could never have prepared for: Lancelot stood in the centre of the room, his arms wrapped round the waist of another person, a woman, whose head of dark hair was buried in his chest. That head of hair was familiar to me. Decorated with a thin band of gold that had been entwined in her tight braids. It was, I knew immediately, Guinevere.

'What the –'

'Viviane!' Guinevere squeaked, having spun around at the sound of my voice.

'What the hell is going on?' I glanced between Lancelot and Guin.

'It's not what you think.' Her eyes grew wide. 'We haven't . . . I haven't cheated on Arthur.'

'It's true.' Lancelot nodded emphatically.

As soon as the words had been spoken aloud, I realized that I couldn't care less if Guin had slept with Lancelot. That wasn't why I felt a hot flare of anger in my chest.

I turned on Lancelot. 'You've not been telling me everything!'

He looked ashamed but that didn't soften me. 'I did, I swear, everything that was relevant.'

I narrowed my eyes. 'And does she know?'

He nodded. 'I've told her everything. There are no secrets between Guinevere and me.'

'Yet you didn't tell me about this, despite asking for my help, despite demanding my secrecy.'

'That's my fault, Viviane. I asked him not to tell you.' Guinevere had stepped forward, both hands stretched out in front of her body in a gesture of placation. 'I didn't want to complicate things further, for either of you.' I supposed there was a grain of truth to that. But I also imagined the danger this secret would have placed them in had played a part as well. Not that I begrudged them their desire for secrecy. I likely would have done the same. I did, however, resent being asked to keep a secret I didn't know the whole truth of – especially from Morgan.

'Well, I'm here now, and you need to tell me everything.'

Lancelot nodded, his gaze fixed on his feet, but said nothing.

'Let me.' Guinevere placed a hand on Lancelot's arm before turning back to me. 'This part is my story to tell.'

Nodding my acquiescence, I allowed Guinevere to guide me to the wooden bench at the end of Lancelot's bed and took a seat beside her while Lancelot remained standing.

'It's a little different from how Arthur represented it.' Guin laughed but it came out sounding more bitter than I was used to. 'It wasn't exactly an ambush. He came in the night, Maleagant, while we were sleeping. I didn't even wake up until we were far, far from camp.' I frowned but

Guinevere simply shrugged. 'He used some sort of magic, I assume.

'Anyway, I didn't realize it at first, but when I awoke I was no longer in the mortal realm. Maleagant had taken me to the otherworld. Although I might not have believed it if it hadn't been for the strangeness in the colours; I don't know how to explain it, but nothing was quite like it is in our world.' Of course, she didn't need to explain it. I knew perfectly well to what she referred.

'I don't know how long I'd been gone before they discovered the carriage,' Guinevere hesitated before carrying on, 'because I know what everyone has been saying, that I was gone only three weeks, but Viviane, I swear I was there for nine months.' Her expression turned a little desperate. 'Arthur doesn't believe me, but you do, don't you? You understand there are things in this world that can't be explained.'

I nodded. I did believe her. I had no reason not to. Guinevere may have experienced a trauma but to imagine that nine months had passed when it had only been three weeks would be a particularly strange response, unless it were true. And while our experiences differed, had I not my own story of missing days and time that did not match up?

Satisfied, Guinevere continued her story. 'It was eerie, you know, quieter even than the forests that lie beyond the castle, but it was also beautiful. I hated that Maleagant had brought me there, yet part of me wished I could stay, Viviane. Is that mad? It was so peaceful.'

'Stay with Maleagant?' I was somewhat surprised, to say the least.

She grimaced. 'Good God, no.' I was even more surprised to hear the pious Guinevere take the Lord's name in vain. 'Not with him.'

'I see.' I didn't see at all.

Guin snorted. 'He was never really interested in me. I was just a convenient way to upset Arthur, and therefore Arthur's alliance with his father. That much was clear almost immediately. Talk about daddy issues.'

I wasn't used to this derisive Guinevere and I wasn't entirely sure what to make of it. 'Um, go on.'

'He locked me up in a tower – a tower! Can you believe it? And he had a guard bring me food twice a day. At first I was terrified, but by the sixth or seventh day I was just angry. I'd been grabbed in the night by a stranger, taken somewhere otherworldly, and no one had even bothered to tell me why. So I started screaming.' A slight blush rose in her cheeks, reminding me more of the Guinevere I knew.

'I screamed and I screamed. In fact, it felt like I was screaming for hours. And when the guards tried to silence me I just told them I'd keep screaming until I spoke to the man who had brought me there. It took most of the day, but finally Maleagant turned up.'

I coughed a little as a small bubble of laughter caught me by surprise. 'You're lucky they didn't hurt you, Guin. That was pretty brazen.'

'Yes, well, I realized that afterwards but it seemed like a good idea at the time. I just couldn't stand it any more.' She chewed her lip. 'Lucky for me his plan didn't seem to involve killing me, or else why keep me at all?

'Anyway, Malageant told me the bare bones of what was

going on, who he was and where we were, and it wasn't exactly difficult to fill in the rest. He told me I would be safe with him if I didn't cause a fuss. He even offered to take me as a mistress, can you believe that?' She let out an indignant snort. 'And when I refused he was off again, leaving me to my stuffy little tower and dry, basic meals.' I laughed again – what a time to be criticizing the cuisine.

'There was a window at least. It was a tight fit but I spent the next few days practically hanging out of the thing, wondering if I could figure out a way to climb down, and how I'd get away if I did. In the end I didn't need to, because that's when Lancelot came. It was he who rescued me. That part at least Arthur got right.' Guinevere glanced over at the knight, a shy smile dancing across her features.

'I met Gawain on the road. He and the rest of Arthur's men had split up in search of Guinevere, and when he explained to me what had happened I offered my assistance,' Lancelot elaborated. 'After a few days of searching I was about ready to give up, until I heard the voice of an angel calling to me through the trees.'

I glanced over at Guin, who was blushing profusely but said nothing.

'I don't know when I crossed over into the fairy realm, but I followed the voice until I came to the clearing in which Guinevere was being held. I saw her, stretching out of the window, calling out for help. I knew then I would do anything for her.'

For a long moment, the knight stared over at Guinevere, an adoring expression on his face, until finally I had to clear my throat to remind him where he was.

257

'It wasn't exactly difficult to stage a rescue mission.' He turned his gaze back to mine. 'I don't think Maleagant had really thought anyone would find his hiding place so there were only three guards on duty. I stormed the tower and knocked them out before retrieving Guinevere from her prison.' There was more than a little pride in his voice, but I supposed he deserved it after what he'd explained.

I was just managing to digest all of this when something occurred to me. 'Guin, you said you were in the other realm for nine months, but Lancelot found you in under one . . .' My question tailed off as Guinevere's cheeks darkened by another shade.

'For the first week after we escaped, we couldn't figure out how to leave. Whatever door Lancelot had used the first time was gone and I had no idea which way I'd come in. So we travelled together for days, searching for a doorway, and oh, Viviane, you have no idea how beautiful it was.' Only I did, but I decided not to interrupt. 'It was so beautiful that after a while I gave up looking for an escape. Lancelot tried at first to convince me,' Guinevere cast the young man a shy smile which he returned tenfold, 'but I was pretty obstinate, if you'd believe it.' She let out a soft chuckle. 'Eventually Lancelot gave in and we focused on our surroundings. We'd set up camp each night, sleep beneath the stars, swim in the hot springs – it was heaven, truly. Until Maleagant found us.' Guinevere winced.

When it was clear from Guinevere's expression that she was uncomfortable with this next part of their tale, Lancelot interceded.

'We duelled. And if it had not been for Guinevere, I would have slain him where he lay.'

'He begged me for his life. Me.' Guinevere wrung her hands for emphasis, the memory evidently a distressing one. 'I know what he did was wrong, but I just couldn't let Lancelot kill him.'

Lancelot lowered himself to one knee and took one of Guinevere's shaking hands in his own. 'You have a kind heart.'

'The door came later, I don't know from where, but I found it while I was bathing. It was strange. I could have sworn I smelt something burning, but when I turned to see what it was there was nothing there but a reflection in the water. A reflection that didn't match our surroundings. So I fetched Lancelot and we realized it showed the same woods where I had first been taken.' A river? I wanted to laugh. Of course, it had been in water. Still, now didn't seem like the moment to brag.

Lancelot meanwhile straightened and looked back at me. 'Then we found Arthur and the rest is as you know.'

It was certainly an exciting tale – more adventure than I would ever have expected from Guinevere. I felt a twinge of guilt for underestimating her. Yet, one thing had stood out to me above all else during their story, and it brought me back to my original reason for being there.

'I need to ask you something.' I waited for Lancelot's nod before proceeding. 'By my calculations, if you were trapped in the otherworld for even two months, you should have aged another three years, four if it was longer.' I gave him a questioning stare.

'It's sometimes more erratic than that, but yes, in principle.' He shrugged, clearly not grasping where I was going.

'Well, did you?' I pushed, although I suspected I already knew the answer.

'I . . .' The moment realization dawned on him, Lancelot's entire demeanour changed; his shoulders slackened and his eyes went wide as he answered me. 'No, I didn't. It was like time slowed down while I was there.'

I nodded. 'I wish I could tell you I have a simple spell that will undo what has been done, but I don't.' I had decided that honesty was the best policy. 'I don't know if my inexperience does you a disservice or if there simply isn't one that would work. Regardless, I think the best lead we have for now is the time you spent in the fairy realm. So what I need to know, Lancelot, is would you consider returning? If it might end your curse?'

Lancelot's reply was immediate. 'I don't want to leave Guinevere.'

I sighed, for I had wondered if this would be the case, but I was saved from lecturing him by Guinevere.

'I trust Viviane, Lancelot. You have to try whatever she suggests, even if that means you have to leave court for a time.' She looked at me. 'Is that what you mean?'

'I'm not sure. Perhaps. First, I need to talk to Morgan, and I need to tell her everything.' Both Guinevere and Lancelot made to object, but I held up my hand to silence them. 'If you want my help, you'll have to let me do it my way, and that means with Morgan. We're partners.'

It was obvious from both their expressions that they weren't pleased, but neither of them argued with me. Instead, they exchanged glances before giving me cautious nods of approval that were more than I might have expected, given the circumstances.

I left them alone after that, with a reminder that not

everyone would be as kind as I had been were they to be found alone together in each other's chambers again, and set off to find my own partner and discuss what came next. I'd be damned if I was going to continue keeping this situation a secret from Morgan. We were a team, and I was going to tell her everything. I still wasn't sure what the future held, for any of us, but one thing was for sure. Right now all signs were pointing in the same direction, and that direction was Diana.

THIRTY

When Morgan wasn't to be found in her chambers, I knew the next best place to look was the castle's solarium. This small room to the back of the kitchens, where the ceiling was constructed from sheets of selenite to allow the sunlight in, was the perfect place for various plants and herbs to flourish, and over the years Morgan had firmly carved out a space for herself in its day-to-day usage.

I was so wrapped up in my thoughts as I made my way through the winding corridors, however, that I didn't notice when another body was right in front of me.

'Sorry,' I mumbled, trying to step around them but finding myself blocked again. Confused, I glanced up to get a proper look at the figure before me only to realize who it was: Merlin.

It was rare for me to run into him like this, although we shared a home, albeit a vast one. Merlin moved of his own accord, often holing up in his chambers for days on end, and sometimes disappearing for weeks to who knew where. It took me aback, therefore, to find myself face to face with the sorcerer when I had least expected it.

'Ah, Viviane, how have you been?'

I ignored his question and tried to manoeuvre myself

past the sorcerer without acknowledging him further, but he moved with me, blocking my route through the narrow passageway and forcing me to take a few steps back.

'I have somewhere to be, if you don't mind.' I lifted my head so I was looking him directly in the eye.

Merlin didn't move. 'A rendezvous with your young knight, perhaps?' What on earth was he on about? My confusion must have shown on my face, because when I didn't respond Merlin just chuckled and carried on. 'No need to be coy. I know that you received a visit from Sir Lancelot last night, alone in your chambers when you thought the rest of the castle was asleep.'

I could feel my cheeks burn red, but it wasn't from embarrassment; it was anger. He was still watching me, still cataloguing my every move. Even now, after I had refused him more than once, he still believed himself entitled to oversee the minutiae of my life. Like he was biding his time, simply waiting for the perfect moment to pounce once again. His words were a reminder of why I was so desperate to leave.

'You are pathetic.' I couldn't care less if Merlin believed me to be sleeping with Lancelot – although, in an ideal world, this might finally have been enough to make him back off completely. This world, however, was not ideal.

Merlin shrugged, that unnerving smile never dropping from his face. 'I hope I will see you at this evening's meal, Viviane. It should be an eventful one.'

Another cryptic pronouncement, perfectly calculated to pique the listener's curiosity. I refused to play his game, however. Merlin only ever told you what he wanted you to know, and I was no longer clamouring to be let in on his secrets. 'Goodbye, Merlin.' Finally, he moved to the side just enough to let me pass but not enough to prevent me from being forced to brush up against his body as I did so. As soon as the sorcerer was behind me I was gone, practically sprinting the rest of the way to where I hoped I would find Morgan waiting.

Sure enough, when I arrived at the slightly dilapidated solarium, there she was, tending to her plants, the picture of contentedness.

'Hi there,' I murmured as I crept up behind her and peered over her shoulder.

'There you are.' Morgan beamed, turning to face me as she wiped dirt from her dress. Something about that smile overwhelmed me. Maybe it was the stress of the past twenty-four hours, or Merlin's appearance in the hallway, but I needed to kiss her, to feel her lips against mine. So I did.

'What was that for?' Morgan chuckled when I relinquished her mouth.

'Me, it was for me.' I grinned back at her.

'Where have you been? I came looking for you this morning but couldn't find you.'

'Sorry, I was trying to work something out.' I entwined my fingers with hers and held them tight.

'Well, I'm glad you're here now.' She briefly pressed her forehead against mine before pulling back to look me in the eye. 'I know we said we'd consider leaving again once Guinevere was back, but I've had a thought. What if Merlin was the one who was forced to leave?'

Morgan's features were alight with an excitement I

couldn't match. For all I'd struggled with the idea of leaving, did I really want to stay? What was there here for me besides Morgan and Guin? The fairy realm, on the other hand . . . it had changed everything. 'I don't see how –' I began but Morgan interrupted me.

'With this.' She grabbed a small vial from the table behind her and held it up for me to see. 'Eyebright and blackthorn.'

'A truth tonic?' Morgan nodded. 'You don't think he'll detect something if you put that in his drink?'

'It's worth a try, surely? We can make him admit to hurting you. Maybe more!' I wasn't sure I agreed. 'Hey, are you all right?' Morgan added and I realized my hands were shaking.

Taking a few deep breaths to try and calm myself, I decided to start with what had happened on my way here. 'I bumped into Merlin in the hallway. He . . . he thinks I'm having an affair with Lancelot.'

I waited for Morgan to frown or curse the sorcerer, but to my surprise she let out a cackle of laughter and let go of my hands.

'Not that I would have been worried, anyway, but I'm pretty sure I know something Merlin does not in that case.'

'What are you talking about?' I frowned. This had not been the direction I had expected this conversation to take.

'Last night, or this morning, I suppose, I was taking a stroll through the castle.' This part did not surprise me. I knew very well Morgan's penchant for late-night roaming. If we had not shared a room the night before I might even have expected her to show up at three or four unannounced. 'And you'll never guess what I saw.'

'What?' I rolled my eyes.

'I saw Guinevere, sneaking into Lancelot's room. I think our perfect paragon of piety and decorum may in fact be indulging in an extramarital affair.' Morgan gave me a wicked grin. 'What do you say to that?'

I winced. Well, I supposed we were going to get to this part of the news eventually. 'I know.'

'You knew?' Morgan looked surprised.

'I only just found out. But Morgan, it's more complicated than it seems. There are some things I need to tell you.'

Morgan nodded, but at that moment a sharp knock came at the solarium door before it was pushed open a second later to reveal Arthur's guard, Alrec.

'My lady,' Alrec gave a deep bow, 'the king has requested that I fetch you for this evening's feast. He says it is important you are on time.'

'I don't know what my brother told you, but I do not need a nursemaid, Alrec.' The guard shifted uncomfortably under Morgan's glare and I felt a twinge of pity.

'It's fine. Come on. I'll tell you about it all later.' I threaded Morgan's arm through mine and gestured for Alrec to lead the way. We were about to find out what had Merlin – and Arthur, it seemed now – so excited about this evening's meal.

There was something in the air that night as we arrived for dinner. Merlin was there, which was unusual enough, but when I approached the table he stood to pull a chair out, gesturing for me to sit. I wanted to decline with every fibre of my being, but I also wanted to avoid a scene. So I took the proffered seat with a curt nod, staring fixedly at my empty plate. Morgan's plan, if you could call it that, already had me on edge, and I flinched when Merlin leaned over my shoulder as he pushed my chair in.

'You are looking quite beautiful this evening, Lady Viviane.' His voice was neither a whisper nor a shout and I glanced around to see if anyone else was looking our way.

Merlin had not been this forward in public since that day in his chambers. He had, as he said, kept his distance, just as Arthur had commanded. And though Arthur had yet to arrive, clearly there was something different about this evening for him to be so forward.

Before I could conjure an appropriate response, however, the sorcerer had taken his own seat and the doors had opened to welcome the king. Arthur entered the hall, not with Guinevere, who had already been seated when Morgan and I had arrived. Instead, it was Lancelot who accompanied him. And while I hadn't known this version of Lancelot long, it seemed to me that he was intentionally evading my gaze, an expression of discomfort marring his handsome features.

If Lancelot *had* caught my eye, I might have missed seeing Morgan surreptitiously pour the tincture she had shown me earlier into her own goblet while everyone was focused on Arthur's entrance. She then proceeded to place it casually back down on the table, on the opposite side to its neighbour, which just so happened to belong to Merlin. *This is reckless*, I wanted to shout, but Morgan would do what Morgan wanted to do.

The sorcerer, however, made no indication he had noticed Morgan's sleight of hand and the meal proceeded as normal, with everyone chattering across their food and laughing over their wine. There was no reason to feel so on edge, I told myself, but as the minutes passed my sense of unease only grew. Morgan and I exchanged a few questioning glances but said nothing aloud – we would find out soon enough why Arthur had been so keen to have Morgan in attendance.

Just as the anticipation was becoming too much, Arthur finally made his move. Rising from his seat, goblet in hand, he waited patiently as the entire room fell silent, all heads turning to look at their king.

'I have an exciting announcement to make.' Arthur beamed at his subjects. 'I am pleased to tell you that, as of this evening, I have given the hand of my sister Morgan to the knight Lancelot.'

THIRTY-ONE

My grip fumbled the cup in my hand, liquid slopping over the rim to marinate my half-eaten meal. Surely I couldn't have heard him right. Lancelot marry Morgan? No. *No!* I shook my head, although I don't think anyone noticed, so focused was everyone's attention on the king and his sister.

'So I hope you will join me in raising a cup to their union.' Arthur held his own wine aloft, pausing as cheers and shouts spread throughout the gathered diners before finally bringing it to his lips and returning to his seat.

Morgan, meanwhile, had been uncommonly silent during this whole display. Her wide eyes fixed on her brother while her lips remained pressed together in a tight, thin line that did nothing to hide her rage. There was no way she had known about this – that much I was sure of.

'I don't think I can have heard you correctly, dear brother.' You could hear the grind of Morgan's teeth through her words. 'Unless this is some sort of practical joke. Me, marry Lancelot? I don't think so. Surely you would have brought something this significant up with me before now, were it truly your intention.'

'It was decided this afternoon. I informed Lancelot before the feast, but we were unable to find you.' Well, that at least explained the obvious discomfort in Lancelot's demeanour. 'If you have any questions about your betrothal, we can discuss them later. Right now, it is time to celebrate. This union will spell great things for our kingdom.'

'We most certainly will not.' Her tone was venomous, and I wondered that Arthur did not baulk. 'If you're going to bring this up now, we're going to talk about it now. You don't expect me to remain silent simply because we have an audience, do you? I thought you knew me better than that.'

And an audience they did have. While those seated furthest down the table appeared genuinely oblivious to the fact that anything was amiss, a number of those who sat closer were casting surreptitious glances in the direction of the royal family before leaning in to whisper to their neighbours.

'Morgan?' I tried to get her attention but she ignored me, not taking her eyes from Arthur for a split second.

'As your brother, and more importantly your king, it is my duty to choose for you a suitable husband.' His expression feigned coolness but I could see his fingers tighten around the goblet in his hand.

'I don't want any husband, suitable or unsuitable!'

Arthur sighed. 'Morgan, be reasonable. As the king's sister, you cannot truly expect to remain unmarried. I have allowed you more freedom than most women are given by their families because I knew that in the end you would do the right thing for Camelot – the kingdom you supposedly care so much about.'

'How the hell is this the right thing for Camelot?' Morgan's voice was the loudest in the room now.

'If you insist on discussing this now, then you may as well know that Merlin was sent a vision. A vision that told him this union would ensure a powerful ally for Camelot during a coming invasion from across the sea.'

Morgan snorted. 'And you believe him?'

Arthur's eyes had narrowed and a flush of anger crept into his cheeks. 'I have no reason not to. His visions have never led us wrong before.'

I looked over at Merlin who was seated on my neighbour's other side and caught a barely perceptible smile pass across his face. What was he playing at? I wanted to grab him and demand an explanation. Shake him until he took his wretched vision back. But I knew any outburst on my part would not help the situation.

'As far as you know,' Morgan snipped back. 'Right, Merlin? Why don't you tell us the truth, what did you really see?' She took a sip from her goblet, leaning back in her chair. Her tone was too smug, her confidence too assured. I wanted to grab her arm and drag her away before things got worse. Assure her there would be no marriage, even if it meant we had to slip away in the night. But I could do nothing but watch on.

'Perhaps, Your Highness, if you'd allow me a moment to speak?' It was as though the sorcerer had read my mind.

'Please, Merlin, maybe you can make my sister see reason.' Arthur wafted a hand in Merlin's direction, his eyes trained on Morgan all the while.

Merlin stood, drawing the attention of the entire room to him. 'Last night I received a vision, spurred on by Sir Lancelot's arrival, I imagine. It revealed a renewed invasion from across the sea. Reinforcements from our Saxon enemies.'

A few scattered whispers passed among the guests. Arthur's reign thus far had been a stable one and the prospect of an increased Saxon threat was naturally unnerving.

'It is not as bleak as it seems,' Merlin continued. 'Sir Lancelot comes to us from Armorica, and if my vision is correct then an alliance between our people and his will strengthen our shores on both sides, ensuring our victory.' He paused, presumably for dramatic effect. 'An alliance through marriage.'

At least half of those around me were nodding their heads, simultaneously unsettled and reassured by Merlin's speech. I didn't buy a word of it. If his vision was correct? Merlin was many things, but modest was not one of them. I had never heard him speak of a vision as he had just done – an undesirable future with a clear solution. No, this so-called vision was at least a partial fabrication, and I was pretty sure Morgan realized it too.

'You're lying. Just like you lied about attacking Viviane.' I gasped. Why would she say that? My heartbeat accelerated as various sets of eyes darted between myself and Morgan. But she didn't pause, instead turning to her brother. 'I don't care what that old fool says he saw; I will not marry Lancelot.' She had pushed her chair back from the table and risen to her feet, so she was towering over the seated Arthur.

'Your Majesty,' Lancelot attempted, but Arthur ignored him.

'No wonder Father found you so exhausting.' Arthur

slammed his cup down on the table, giving up any impression of calm. 'Why do you insist on making my job more difficult?'

'*Father* was a selfish pig.' Morgan's words were growing more erratic. I knew her to be bold and sharp-tongued, but this was something else. It was as though she'd lost all control of her speech.

Arthur meanwhile had also risen to his feet, his face darkening. 'You will do as I say, Morgan, or you will be confined to your rooms until you remember your place.'

That was when it hit me. My eyes darted from Morgan to Arthur and finally Merlin, who continued to gaze lazily over the rim of his cup as he sipped the untainted liquid. But it was too late.

The whisper of a scream escaped the back of Morgan's throat, her eyes settling on Lancelot who sat behind him. 'You would actually marry me off to your wife's lover?'

The sound of Morgan's hand slapping against her mouth seemed to reverberate across the hall.

'I . . . I . . .' she spluttered, shocked by her own words.

'Morgan.' I grabbed her hand, no idea what I should do, only certain she mustn't speak any more.

'What did you just say?' Rather than shout as his sister had done, Arthur's voice had dropped to a barely audible volume. Not that it stopped him being overheard. The hall had fallen utterly silent.

When Morgan only folded her lips inwards, Arthur rounded on Lancelot and Guinevere who had both been seated to his right. 'Is this true?' he spat. If he'd had any sense he might have dismissed the gathered crowd, or else demanded a private room for the conversation that was about to come, but it was clear he was too far gone for that.

Lancelot, meanwhile, should have immediately denied Morgan's words, scoffed at their validity – that would have been my advice – but instead he floundered, locking eyes with Guinevere's, effectively confirming what Arthur feared most.

'Arthur, it's not what you think.' Guin's attempt to soothe the furious king wasn't much better. I didn't think he'd care much that Guinevere and Lancelot had yet to consummate their relationship. In that moment he was humiliated, his whole court there to bear witness. I had never seen Arthur like this, cold fury marring his still youthful face.

'Guards,' he pointed a shaking finger at Lancelot, 'take this man to the dungeon and have my wife confined to her chambers. Do not under any circumstances let her leave.' Arthur spun on his heel to face the rest of the room. 'Everyone, get out, now!'

The next few minutes were a tumult. Courtiers fled the room, unnerved by their usually stoic king's public outburst but not scared enough to prevent them whispering to one another as they moved. Knights swarmed the head of the table, three individual men grabbing hold of Lancelot's arms while Gawain gently ushered a horror-stricken Guinevere from the room.

Amidst it all I was frozen to the spot, only having got as far as getting to my feet. Morgan still had her gaze fixed on her brother, who was refusing even to look at her, and I couldn't figure out what I was supposed to do.

'Well, that didn't go how I expected it to. Who knew

I had missed so much?' It was Merlin. He had come up behind me without my realizing it and now stood looking over my shoulder.

'This is your doing,' I hissed.

'Is it? I don't recall encouraging the queen to start up an affair.' He actually sounded vaguely disappointed. 'I had different plans for tonight, although this was certainly an interesting development.'

Merlin's words finally freed me from my frozen state. Lurching forward, I grabbed Morgan's arm and, ignoring her surprised shout, dragged her behind me, refusing to look back at Merlin even as I felt his stare follow us from the room.

'What have you done?' The words tore from my throat as I stared desperately at Morgan.

After I had dragged her from the chaos of the dining hall, we absconded to her chambers. I had thought once we were in private, just the two of us, we might be able to talk about this calmly. Yet as we sprinted down the corridors, I had only felt the fury and panic swell inside me until they were impossible to suppress.

'Merlin – he must have swapped our drinks back.'

'I told you the tonic wasn't a good idea. That he'd see it coming.' I wanted to grab hold of Morgan and shake her but knew I couldn't let myself give in to my anger. Instead, I wrung my hands while I paced back and forth before her.

'I didn't know!' she screeched. 'I didn't know.' Her voice broke on the second 'know'. 'You have to understand, Viv. All I wanted was to stop the engagement, and the words came out before I could stop them. I didn't want them to force us apart.'

'Why couldn't you have waited till after the feast?' My voice dropped as I finally stopped pacing. 'Why couldn't you give us time to figure this out? We could have stopped this some other way, together. Instead, your recklessness has sentenced both Guinevere and Lancelot to death. Do you understand that?' I thought I might be sick.

Despite its truth, the tone of my accusation set Morgan on the defensive. 'Do you not have any sympathy for me? I know you care for Guinevere, but Lancelot? He's just a stranger. A stranger my brother would have made me marry.'

'But he's not a stranger, Morgan, don't you see? He's Galahad.' I searched her face for recognition, but when nothing changed I barged on. 'Clarine's son. He never stopped ageing.'

'What're you talking about?' Morgan's voice grew even more desperate, if that was possible.

I nodded. 'It's him. He came here for my help, to take away whatever magic runs through his veins.'

'No.'

'Yes! The same child you risked everything to save from Arthur only months ago is the one whose life you've given up so easily this day.'

'Why didn't you tell me?' Morgan wailed, grabbing my arm, but I pulled it back.

'That's what I wanted to tell you this evening, before dinner.' My words were quieter now because I was already wracked with guilt that I had kept this secret from her for even a day. Look what it had led to. 'But what does it matter anyway? Do you really think I would forgive what you've done if he was a stranger?'

'I can undo it. I swear I can.'

'How?'

'We help them escape.' She spoke the words as if it were that simple. That straightforward. There was no sign of doubt on her features; there never was.

'How on earth do you propose we do that?' I wanted to scream, but I wasn't sure if it was directed at Morgan any more.

'I don't know yet, but I know we can, if we do it together.' Morgan took my hand in hers and this time I let her.

'You better be right, Morgan. You better be right.'

THIRTY-TWO

The announcement came the very next day. Queen Guinevere and Sir Lancelot were to be executed in exactly one week's time. Burnt at the same stake, a symbol of their crime. Even those who had been in attendance at the previous night's dinner showed signs of shock – although whether that shock was at the affair itself, or the fate of those involved, was harder to determine. While half of the castle already looked to be in mourning, with their sombre expressions and hushed conversations, the other half seemed almost to be fuelled by the drama, whispering in corners and staring curiously like they were witnesses to a stage tragedy. An execution equalled entertainment, after all.

Lancelot had been imprisoned in the dungeons while Guinevere had been relegated to her private rooms – she was still the queen after all, treason or not. And that was where they would remain until their joint execution, just as the law decreed. The *law*. The king's word was law. Arthur was entitled to change it, but clearly he had decided to live in the shadow of his father's reign forever and embrace the precedent Uther had set. I felt nothing but disgust. Whatever Guin had done, there was nothing that could justify this.

There was no *justice* in the law. So it was up to Morgan and me to make our own law.

Speed would be of the essence if we hoped to rescue Lancelot and Guin. There was no way we could stay the execution, and that left us with only a handful of days to set them free. Where we had to go seemed obvious now. There was no other option than the otherworld. Despite all my reservations, it was the safest way to escape the reach of Camelot. The door was right there. The only question was how to get them there without being stopped. And given there were two of them and two of us, the solution seemed obvious. We'd have to smuggle them out separately.

'I should be the one to get Guinevere.'

Morgan, get Guinevere? I couldn't help the scepticism that this statement elicited from showing on my face.

'I know, all right.' She rolled her eyes. 'But it will be easier to explain my presence in the keep should I be discovered and questioned.' She paused, her eyes falling to her hands. 'I also owe her.'

This I understood. Morgan and Guinevere may never have been friends, but there was nevertheless a degree of mutual respect that they seemed to honour now that we were adults.

'That leaves you to retrieve Lancelot from the gaol, but he'll be guarded, and heavily,' Morgan added, moving the subject along.

'Oh, that won't be a problem.'

Morgan gave me a look of confusion. 'What are you thinking?'

'Do you still have that old door handle?'

*

Time was not on our side. Thus I found myself alone in the dark castle grounds a few hours later, my path barely illuminated by candlelight, long after the rest of Camelot had gone to sleep.

All right, Viviane, I reassured myself, *you can do this. You've broken into the chambers of the most powerful sorcerer in living memory; what's a gaol cell compared to that? Just think of this as another scavenger hunt. No more dangerous than liberating a guard's helmet from the armoury, or a famous sword from the royal solar —* although perhaps that second example was a little *too* on the nose, given where Morgan was supposed to be right now.

Draped in the dark, heavy fabric Morgan and I had enchanted to avert the eye of anyone who might be near, I skirted the outer wall of the castle, praying to any god who might hear me. Finally, when I reached the point in the stonework that I knew separated the dungeon from the outside world, I drew the familiar door handle from inside my cloak, letting the solid weight of the metal reassure me. We could do this. Or else, I supposed, we'd be arrested and tried for treason along with our two would-be rescuees.

Raising the handle to the wall, I imagined the metal fastened to a thick wooden door and just like that, it was.

'That never gets old,' I smirked as I pushed open the door.

Upon entering the dank, musty room beyond, I was greeted by a series of scuffles and thuds as someone jumped to their feet. 'Show yourself.' A man's voice broke through the darkness.

I gripped the small knife I carried in my other hand that little bit tighter. 'Lancelot?'

'Viviane?' A tiny part of me relaxed as he stepped out from the shadows, allowing the sliver of moonlight from the open doorway behind me to illuminate his face.

'Just stopping by for a visit.' I attempted a grin but it felt stiff even to me. Lancelot was a mess. His left eye was bruised blue and purple and there was a nasty cut on his lip that might have become infected. I probably should have expected it, but the sight tugged at my gut nonetheless.

'H-how?' Lancelot stammered.

'I'm a sorceress, remember.'

He let out a strangled laugh. 'How could I forget?'

'Come on. I'm here to get you out.' I reached out my empty hand to him.

'What about Guinevere? I won't leave her!'

'Yeah, we worked that out.' Perhaps the very real danger of our situation had driven me a little out of my wits because I almost chuckled. 'Morgan is fetching her. We're to meet them at the lake. We're going to take you somewhere you'll be safe.'

Lancelot nodded, although his frown did not disappear. Ever the chivalrous knight, he probably hated the idea of leaving his lady's escape to someone else. Nevertheless, that was the position we were in, and so I ushered him forward to the magical escape hatch I had created, and out into the night.

'Quickly,' I whispered. 'They might look in on you at any time.'

Lancelot, however, only snorted as he kept pace behind me. 'Not likely. Arthur's warders are arrogant; they spend more time playing dice than watching prisoners.' He muttered something else underneath his breath that sounded an awful lot like 'My father's warders would never', but I was only half paying attention.

We had continued to skirt the walls outside the castle, retreading my earlier route as it was the shortest way to the lake; unfortunately, it also meant passing beneath the guarded ramparts. I cursed our limited timeframe again; another cloak of concealment would have been handy, but Morgan's stash of herbs had supplied just enough to enchant my own, assuming Morgan wouldn't need to disguise her presence where she was going. I would have to rely on the darkness of night and Lancelot's own stealth to keep us hidden.

As it turned out, that was too much to hope for.

'Stop them!' The unidentifiable voice came from within the walls themselves and stopped Lancelot in his tracks. Before I could demand he continue our journey, however, the cries were joined by the clashing of steel and the unmistakable sound of a woman's scream. Without pause, Lancelot had turned on his heel and made to head in entirely the wrong direction, towards the distressing noises and away from our route to freedom.

'Lancelot,' I hissed, trying to grab hold of his tunic. 'Stop. What are you doing?'

'That's Guinevere,' was his only response, the fabric of his shirt slipping through my hand.

I stood there, staring at the spot where Lancelot had disappeared through the nearest archway, stunned by this turn of events. This had *not* been the plan. With no other option left to me, however, I shook the surprise from my shoulders and chased after him, praying to all the gods and goddesses that might exist that we might yet make it out alive.

Turning the corner that led to a small covered courtyard, I was met by an alarming sight. Arthur, only half dressed, his hair dishevelled, following behind two armed knights – their prey obvious. There in the middle of the scene was Morgan, one hand held out to shield Guinevere, the other gripping an unfamiliar sword.

'Get back!' she shouted, brandishing her weapon in the nearest knight's direction – a knight I now recognized as Accolon. 'I mean it.'

Accolon, however, was not deterred, swinging his sword at Morgan. She met his blade with her own but she clearly felt the shock of the strike as her arm shook and the weapon wobbled in her grasp. Despite her childhood enthusiasm for the subject, Morgan never had learnt how to wield a sword and what she lacked in experience could not be made up for in spirit. Before I was even halfway across the court-yard, Accolon had dashed the sword from Morgan's hand and grabbed Guinevere by the arm, dragging her against his chest while keeping his weapon trained on the now dis-armed Morgan. Arthur, meanwhile, had reached the bottom of the stone steps and pointed at Lancelot who was rushing towards the three figures.

'Stop him.'

The second knight, who I now realized was the young lord Gawain, lunged towards the unarmed man, brandishing his own sword. Lancelot had not been exaggerating when he had recounted his accelerated fighting prowess, how-ever. Sidestepping Gawain's thrust, he sent him sprawling on to the floor, then dove forward, grabbing Gawain's fallen sword and turning on Arthur.

I was frozen, unsure which group to turn to, while Accolon turned his and Guinevere's bodies to face Lancelot, looking to his king for further instruction.

Arthur, however, only laughed.

'You're waving your weapon at the best swordsman in Briton, traitor.' He held out a hand to indicate Accolon should stand down.

'And I'm the Prince of Benoic. You are not my king and your Brittonic arrogance means nothing to me.' With these words Lancelot lunged, brandishing his sword with expert deftness, but Arthur parried him easily.

Undeterred, Lancelot sliced at the young king, forcing him backwards to avoid the blow. Yet Arthur refused to be forced onto the defensive, responding with an equally ferocious attack of his own that narrowly missed his opponent. For a few moments it looked as though the two men might be evenly matched, repeatedly avoiding each other's blows just in the nick of time. Yet I had seen Arthur spar on countless occasions. As I watched on, it became clear that he had the advantage on Lancelot. While each of the king's movements seemed leisurely and precise, the exertion of the duel was written across the latter's face. Arrogant or not, Arthur's earlier declaration looked to be ringing true.

As if to prove me right, in the next second Arthur's blade had made contact with Lancelot's non-dominant arm, slicing through the tunic he wore, the gleam of red undeniable upon his sword.

'Lancelot!'

'Arthur!'

Guinevere and Morgan's cries came in unison, but I was already tuning their voices out. Letting everything but the clash of swords fade to nothing. My eyes honed in on Lancelot's sword, focusing all my attention on its weight, its movements, its purpose. It was relatively easy, the moment so charged with violence even the energy of those around me poured into my spell. I lent my own strength, my magic, to Lancelot's weapon. It wouldn't protect him, but that wasn't the point. In the next instant Arthur's sword met Lancelot's mid-slash, but instead of the parry he had intended, the screech that rang out from the clash of metal was unlike any earthly sound. It reverberated off the surrounding walls and I felt myself flinch as it hit my ears, breaking the chain of magic I had created. No matter: the job was done. For now Arthur's hands were empty, the sword I had watched him pull from its stone what felt like a lifetime ago, now smashed to smithereens at his feet.

Shock and confusion played on Arthur's features as he glanced down at the useless pommel in his hand, too surprised to defend himself against what came next. Seizing on his opponent's distraction, Lancelot thrust forward with his own sword, sliding the blade into flesh. For the briefest of moments, everything around me was silent, and I wasn't sure if it was due to the magic I had exerted. Then, a choking sound wrestled its way from Arthur's throat as Lancelot withdrew his sword as quickly as he had impaled it, a look of horror spreading across his features. The men stumbled back from one another, but while one remained standing,

288

bloody sword in hand, the other fell backwards, sprawled across the ground.

A strangled scream came from somewhere to my left but I wasn't sure if it was Morgan or Guinevere who made the noise. Regardless, it was Morgan who sprang past me in the next second, skidding to a halt at Arthur's slumped form and dropping to the ground beside him.

'Arthur?' she pleaded, moving his hands from his stomach and revealing a leaking wound to all those present. 'Oh gods, Arthur.' Morgan sounded panicked as she brought her own hands to the wound and pressed down, trying to stem the bleeding but only turning her skin scarlet.

'I'm s-sorry,' Lancelot stuttered, clearly horrified by what he'd done.

'Morgan?' I made to move towards her but was intercepted by Accolon, who had up until this point honoured Arthur's instructions not to interfere. As he sprang towards Lancelot, however, Morgan held up a bloody hand and shouted, 'Stop!'

To my surprise, Accolon did as she commanded, freezing in place, his eyes glossing over, and his determined expression fading from his face. 'You need to go, Viviane. Now. More guards will be coming and Accolon won't stay under my spell forever.'

'Morgan, no,' I pleaded, immediately realizing her intentions.

'I have to help him, Viv, he's my brother.' Her voice trembled and her eyes welled with tears.

I wanted to argue, to convince her to come with us. Maybe it was cruel of me, but I found it hard to care about

Arthur's fate after everything that had been said and done. But I recognized that expression on her face. This was my Morgan, the determined woman I knew, who, once her mind was set, could not be told what to do. The Morgan who had stolen from a sorcerer, insisted Merlin teach her magic, refused to be married off no matter what it might cost her, who stood up to kings and lovers alike. If she wanted to stay, she would, no matter what I did or said. We were not the same but I recognized and understood her. So instead of arguing I simply nodded and replied, 'Find me.'

Morgan nodded back.

'Quickly, both of you,' I gestured at Lancelot, who had moved over to Guinevere's side.

I was desperately trying to keep my head as I ushered them from the courtyard, refusing to think further than five minutes ahead. As we turned the corner, however, Guinevere paused, glancing back at Arthur, her face paler than I'd ever seen it before.

'I should –' she started to say but I shook my head.

'No, we need to go.' And I pushed her forward, only glancing back briefly at Morgan who was bent over her brother, hands coated in his blood.

THIRTY-THREE

Lancelot, Guin and I ran. We ran faster than I'd ever run before. It wasn't just Morgan's words; we could hear the castle stirring all around us. Camelot was officially awake.

To my great relief, I still had the enchanted door handle stowed safely in the folds of my cloak and I used it to open a doorway through the castle walls at the first opportunity. From there we continued to sprint across the open grasslands, not heeding our ragged breaths. I took the lead, Guinevere and Lancelot stumbling after me as we passed through the cover of the dense treeline and finally found our way to the lake.

'Come on!' I gestured, wading up to my knees in the water.

'Viviane, what are you doing?' Guinevere sounded panicked but I didn't have time to calm her. We weren't safe until we were beneath the surface, and even then I wasn't sure we'd be truly safe until we'd passed through that final door.

'Do you trust me?' I stretched out a hand and looked from Guin to Lancelot.

'I –' Guinevere stuttered, glancing at Lancelot. The young knight, however, simply straightened his shoulders and nodded, which was enough to decide Guin, it seemed. 'Yes,' she replied in a hushed tone and took hold of my hand.

Together the three of us descended the stairs to my underwater palace. It was strange, I thought, to be bringing anyone other than Morgan down here. Lancelot may have lived here once upon a time, but I still struggled to associate the babe Galahad with the man who now stood beside me. Yet here we all were, inside the home I had built, a piece of my soul stripped bare before them both.

'Viviane,' Guinevere's voice was full of awe, 'what is this place?'

But I didn't get a chance to respond before Lancelot interjected. 'This is where I spent the first few weeks of my life?' He turned in a slow circle, taking it all in. 'I thought my imagination might have been exaggerating.'

'It's beautiful.' Guinevere nodded in agreement and I felt a tiny rush of pride, which I quickly suppressed. There was no time for that.

'Thank you, both, but we're not staying here.'

'What do you mean?' Guinevere looked surprised.

'I'm taking you, us, to the otherworld, where you first met. It's the only place I can think to go that will take us beyond Camelot's reach, and I'm hoping it might also be the best place for Lancelot, given his . . . situation? There's someone there who may be able to help him.'

I had already led them to the main bedroom and brought my hand to the door through which I had first entered the fairy glade. 'Through here.'

'There?' Guinevere frowned and I nodded. 'You never

mentioned . . . when we told you about where we'd been, you never said you'd been there too.'

'Only once.' I gave her an apologetic smile.

'And you're sure it's safe?'

I shook my head. I wasn't trying to deceive anyone. 'No, but I'm sure it's *safer* than Camelot at this very moment.'

'What have we got to lose?' Lancelot shrugged and strode through the open doorway.

'Maybe everything,' Guinevere mumbled, but she nevertheless slid past me, joining Lancelot in the otherwise empty antechamber.

I paused for a split second before following them both, wishing desperately that Morgan were here with us, crossing this threshold just as we'd planned. I couldn't stand there forever, though, waiting, hoping she might be right behind us. We had to go. So I did the only thing I could think of. I took the heavy metal door handle that had proved so trusty thus far and jammed it between the door and its frame, ensuring that even when I let the door go it didn't close entirely behind me; that small crack would have to be enough.

Lancelot and Guinevere were both silent as we ascended the staircase to the fairy realm. Nor did they utter any words of amazement when we broke through the surface of the water and found ourselves in the otherworldly glade. Maybe because this wasn't their first time here, or because there had just been so many surprises already that day. Meanwhile everything was just as I had left it – fair folk included. There they were just as before, lounging by the lakeside (although perhaps pond was a better description in this case), laughing and drinking, none the wiser to what we'd been through just to get here.

'Viviane, you came back! I did wonder if you would.' It was Diana who spotted us first, rising from her cross-legged position on the grass and striding over to us as we exited the lake.

'And Galahad.' Diana held out her arms. 'It's good to see you again.' When Lancelot shook his head, however, the otherworldly woman stuck out her bottom lip in mock disappointment. 'You don't remember me? That's all right. I remember you. Although you're much older than I expected you to be. It's so difficult to keep up with the passage of time in the mortal realm.'

'That's actually one of the things we wanted to talk to you about,' I tried to interject but Diana wasn't listening.

'And who do we have here?' she cried.

I took Guinevere's hand in mine to help ground the young queen. Despite her previous visit to the otherworld, I could tell from her demeanour that she was overwhelmed by her surroundings. 'This is my friend, Guinevere.'

'Guinevere.' Diana rolled the other woman's name across her tongue, assessing it. 'It is a pleasure to meet you. Any friend of Viviane and Galahad's is a friend of mine.'

Lancelot seemed to find his voice in that moment as he finally responded to Diana's words: 'I go by Lancelot these days.'

'How lovely!' Diana clapped her hands together in delight. 'I've changed my own name a few times over the years. In fact, perhaps I'm overdue for a new one.' She grinned over at Lancelot and Guinevere, who both looked equally bemused.

'This is Diana,' I explained, as the otherworldly woman had yet to introduce herself. 'I was hoping she might be able to help us understand what's happening to Lancelot.'

'Happening?' Diana looked intrigued.

She led us over to the same spot I had occupied during my previous visit while we narrated our tale. She and the other fairies listened as Lancelot explained how he'd aged so rapidly since he left Camelot behind, Guinevere recounted her visit to the otherworld, and I summarized what had happened during the dinner that ended it all.

'Are you sure you didn't strike a tithe with a fairy?' one ebony-haired woman asked.

'Maybe he's a changeling!' another suggested, leaning in to get a closer look at Lancelot's features before shaking her head.

'Hush now.' Diana waved the others back so she was face to face with Lancelot and stretched out her hands. 'May I?' Lancelot nodded and took both Diana's hands in his.

For a few moments they simply sat like that, eyes locked, hand in hand, while the rest of us waited with bated breath. I wondered if Diana would see or feel something I had not, or else understand something I had not, with so many more years of magic and life behind her. Gods, I hoped she did.

'How interesting, your mind and body are completely out of sync with the mortal world.' Diana was entirely calm as she pulled her fingers from Lancelot's: curious, but calm. It made me flush at the memory of my own reaction to the magic that affected him.

'Interesting is one way to put it,' grumbled Lancelot.

Diana gave him a soft smile, but when she spoke next her words were directed at me. 'You blessed him?'

'Um, I did. I thought to offer him some protection in the moments after he was born.' I tried not to sound too defensive.

'And what words exactly did you use?'

Exactly? I cast my mind back to the day I had poured the water on Lancelot's brow and murmured desperate words of blessing over him.

'Strength, stability, safety.' I fumbled about in the memory of that chaotic night and found the words. 'I asked the water to give him strength, stability and safety.'

'Well, there's your problem.' Diana laughed and I blinked back at her, none the wiser. 'Your intentions weren't clear enough! Dear Jupiter, who was your teacher? Did they not impress upon you the importance of focus, of honing in on the purpose of your spell?'

'I hadn't really thought of it as a spell,' I mumbled back, beginning to feel more than a little chastised. There had been a lot going on that night, I thought to myself; I had done my best in a situation I could never have predicted. Still, clearly something I had done had not been good enough. And by the sound of it Diana was going to tell me all about it.

'The life that runs through Lancelot's veins is strong, all the strength of a rushing river in fact. It moves with the tides of the ocean, each cycle of the moon a year in any ordinary mortal life.'

My frustration turned to horror at Diana's words. As much as I'd suspected my own magic had a hand in this, a selfish part of me had still hoped there was some other explanation, no matter what that might be.

'But can it be reversed?' Lancelot interrupted our conversation, forcing me to remember who this was really about.

'Oh yes, of course, here.' Diana, to both Lancelot's and my surprise, picked a small translucent stone from the ground at her feet and handed it to the astonished knight. 'A little piece of the earth to ground you, to slow the current of your life. Keep it with you always and you will age as slowly as any mortal.' Diana grinned. 'You might even get a few extra years if you're careful.'

'That's it?' Lancelot looked agog, turning the small piece of rock over in his hands.

'You wouldn't say that if you had seen some of the miracles I was responsible for in the past.' She tilted her chin upwards slightly, a pleased expression on her face.

'Lancelot, I am so, so sorry.' I could feel tears welling in my eyes. 'I did this to you. You lost years because of my mistake.'

'Viviane, no. You might have saved my life as a child, and you definitely saved my life last night.' Lancelot took my hand in his. 'I am forever grateful to you.' He reached out his free arm and wrapped it around Guinevere. 'I have the cure, and a woman to love. I am a happy man.'

He gave Guinevere an energetic kiss on the head, which she returned with a soft smile, although she remained as silent as she had been since we'd sat down.

Diana, meanwhile, gave my shoulder a pat. 'You're young, you'll learn. Until then, no more blessings.' I didn't need to be told twice. 'Well, now that's sorted I think it's time to dine, don't you? Give our guests a proper welcome.'

Without further comment, as though she had simply

plucked a splinter from his finger, Diana looped her arm through Lancelot's and gestured for us to follow them. In the distance there was a table, laden high with dishes I didn't recognize. It wasn't a bad idea to replenish our energy with some food and drink, yet I couldn't get past the fact that Morgan wasn't there. Indicating to the rest of them they should go on without me, I glanced over to the lake, hoping that she might rise up from its surface, having taken advantage of my makeshift doorstop. But there was nothing.

'Viviane?' I turned to find Guin still standing by my side, her expression surprisingly sombre. 'Are you worried about Morgan?'

'She'll catch up,' I said simply. 'But what about you, are you all right?' It seemed an inadequate question, given everything that had happened – but then again, what else was there?

Guinevere shook her head. 'Lancelot will want to travel back to Benoic now, to tell his parents the good news. He mentioned it before, when we discussed his future.'

'But he's asked you to go with him, surely?'

'Not asked,' Guinevere shook her head slowly, 'assumed. He seems very excited about it.'

'But . . . you're not?' Neither Guin's tone nor her words indicated anything close to excitement.

'I . . .' She hesitated, chewing her bottom lip for a split second before carrying on, 'I don't want to go to Armorica. Can you imagine how his parents will look at me? How they'll welcome the woman who made him an enemy of the Britons?'

Before I was given a chance to respond, however,

Lancelot had reappeared by our side, cheeks flushed, a wide grin plastered across his face. 'Come on, ladies, dinner is waiting.'

'Just give us another min—' I began to say before Guinevere interrupted me.

'It's all right, Viviane,' she took one of my hands in hers, 'I need to talk about this.' Lancelot looked confused but he nevertheless waited patiently for Guinevere to continue. 'I . . . I don't know how to say this.' I gave her hand a reassuring squeeze. 'I can't come with you, Lancelot.'

Even in his wildest dreams, I didn't think Lancelot could have been prepared for Guin's declaration. His wide smile vanished as he scanned Guinevere's face. 'What do you mean?'

'If I go with you, I'll simply be following the course of another man's life, just like I was with Arthur.'

'But I'm not like Arthur. I love you, Guin, I'd do anything for you.'

Guinevere smiled kindly. 'I'm sure you would. And I care about you, I do. But love? I'm not convinced either of us truly understand what that means, not that kind of love. We've only known each other for a few months and most of that wasn't even in the real world.'

'A lot can happen in a few months. I should know,' Lancelot insisted.

Guinevere nodded but I could tell she wasn't swayed.

'Is this some sort of self-inflicted punishment, for leaving Arthur?' I frowned.

'No . . . maybe . . . no,' Guin shook her head, 'not a punishment.' She sighed. 'I lived my whole life preparing for marriage. I was raised to be the perfect king's wife. To bear a king's children. Don't misunderstand me – I was content with that. I thought I had a purpose and I was happy to serve it. Yet, when the time came to be a wife, to be a queen, none of it was what I'd hoped for. I no longer felt full of purpose – that had ended when I spoke my vows. I felt aimless, alone, adrift.' Lancelot opened his mouth as if to interrupt her a second time, but Guin held up her hand to silence him. She wasn't done. 'I am grateful for the time we've had together, Lancelot. You are so brave, so honourable, so kind, so . . . so vibrant. I don't regret the connection we shared. But I need to find out who I am without a husband, without any man.'

Lancelot seemed dumbstruck, his expression full of sadness and longing but with not an ounce of anger.

'Then where would you go?' I asked, trying to follow her line of reasoning.

And it seemed Guinevere already had her answer ready. 'A nunnery. The nunnery I lived in before I came to Camelot.'

'You could stay here.' I started. I don't think any of us had noticed that Diana had returned or was listening in. She had pulled a face at the mention of a nunnery, clearly unimpressed. 'We'd be happy to have you.'

'But what about my family? My mother, my father, my brother . . .' Guinevere tailed off and I wondered if she'd been about to count her husband, Arthur, among those she considered family. 'Your world is beautiful. But it is not for me. I don't want to run away from everything I know, everyone I love. I thought, for a moment, that I did, but it was only out of desperation. I just want a chance to be myself. Whoever that is.'

While I could never imagine loving someone as I loved Morgan but choosing not to be with them, I could appreciate Guin's words – had her fate not so nearly been my own? All these years I'd underestimated her, refused to look too deeply. I might have felt shame as her friend if I didn't know how hard Guinevere must have worked to maintain the image of herself that she presented to the outside world.

As I continued to hold her hand, and listen to her words, I felt a cool wind at my back. Strange, I thought. The air in this realm had thus far been almost muggy – dense and solid, nary a breeze to be had. Just as I was about to turn around and examine where the sensation had emanated from, however, I felt something else: a steely grip on my upper arm that didn't belong to any of my companions. Before I knew it, my whole body was pulled backwards, the rock beneath me catching at the fibres in my gown before I fell through the air, the world around me vanishing.

'You didn't think you'd get away so easily, did you, little sorceress?'

THIRTY-FOUR

I was no longer sitting in the otherworld glade surrounded by twisted trees and chattering fair folk; instead, I stood, unsteady and alone, in a bleak landscape, Merlin my only company. The older man's hand was wrapped tightly around my wrist, an irregular half-circle of standing stones set against the midnight sky.

'Let go of me,' I growled, trying and failing to tug my arm free of Merlin's grip. Half of my mind was frantically darting back and forth, trying to figure out how to get away from him, while the other half was still struggling to catch up with my change in circumstances. I could still see the faintest traces of magic shimmering in the air between the two stones closest to us, the place where Merlin must have reached through and pulled me from the otherworld, but what had once been a human-sized doorway was now barely more than the size of a handheld mirror.

'As you wish.' I wasn't prepared for him to let me go, and as soon as he did I stumbled backwards, tripping on my hem and falling, hard, to the ground.

'How the hell did you find me?' My words were a snarl as I clambered back to my feet.

It didn't really matter how the sorcerer had found me,

although I would have liked to know how he had brought me here. But I needed time to figure out what to do next. There was no point in running. I knew very well from our previous visit that there was nothing but sparse treelines and sloping hills for miles.

Merlin snorted. 'You think just because you've been able to hide yourself from me on occasion, I don't know what goes on in my own castle? After I learnt about the queen's adventures, it wasn't hard to figure out where you might have run to.'

'And why, pray tell, have you brought me here?' I wished I could cut him with my disdain.

'I told you,' Merlin gave me the same smile he had always used when I'd asked a particularly simple question in the early days of our lessons, except now it meant much more than just a teacher's amusement. 'You and I, our destinies are intertwined. Your power belongs to me and I have need of it.'

'There is no part of me that belongs to you.'

'So ungrateful.' The sorcerer made a tsk-ing noise and shook his head. 'You would be nothing if it wasn't for me. You'd be an unwanted noblewoman who could breathe underwater. Nothing more. Nothing!' He spat the last word, finally letting the true anger he felt slip through. It took him only a split second to regain his composure, however, plastering that insincere smile back on his face. 'Do you remember the last time we were here?'

I didn't respond, focused on scanning our surroundings, trying to formulate a plan of escape.

'You remember the power you felt when you touched

this stone?' He brought his hand to the nearest monolith, passing his fingers across its surface in a gentle caress. 'That was only a fraction of the magic that resides within. You couldn't even comprehend what truly makes this particular piece of rock so special.'

'Faunus,' I muttered, putting the pieces together and forcing Merlin to retrain his gaze back on me. 'I know the story you told me was full of lies. I met Diana.' This at least seemed to surprise him. He raised both eyebrows at me and let out a tiny huff of breath. 'Why would you care about an irrelevant god?'

'Oh, Viviane,' Merlin laughed, 'Faunus was my father.'

I was stunned.

For a man who'd spent most of the years we'd known each other being evasive and enigmatic, it was as though I was suddenly being beaten over the head with insights I didn't want. Faunus was Merlin's father? I turned this new piece of information over in my head. I knew Merlin was older than he looked, but how old was he really? I had got the impression that Diana's exile had happened more decades ago than one man should live. The fear I felt when I looked in Merlin's eyes increased tenfold. I couldn't let myself be distracted, however; I needed to focus. Wasn't that Merlin's favourite rebuke? The thought almost made me laugh.

'You want to free your father?' That had to be it, I reasoned desperately.

Merlin laughed cruelly. 'Is that what you think I'm trying to do? I couldn't care less if Faunus lives or dies. What I want is his power. Don't you see? It's just lying there, wasted. The power of a god. A power that should be mine.'

'The problem is I can't access it alone. Trust me, I've tried. For years I tried, until I realized the magic that runs in my veins is too close. If Faunus cannot break through this stone, then neither can I. Diana made sure of that.'

'But why me?'

Merlin shrugged. 'For a short while I thought Morgan might be the solution. With her penchant for breaking and entering it was clear she would do anything to learn the craft. Then you came along, so clearly the weaker-willed of the two.'

His words shouldn't have hurt, but they did. 'Go to hell.'

'You were wise to remind me of my own words, Viviane.' When I just stared at him he chuckled. 'It is one of the gifts I did inherit from my father, the ability to see the future. It has been a guiding force much of my life, but sometimes I forget that, even if I like the picture it paints, a different route might be necessary. So, Viviane, if you won't give yourself willingly, I will have to take what I need by force.'

I looked on in horror as Merlin slid his hand into the folds of his robe and withdrew a gleaming dagger. I was going to die. The thought hit me all at once and it was all I could do to keep hold of my senses with it invading my mind. Nothing could have prepared me for this.

'Don't look at me like that, Viviane.' Merlin frowned. 'There's no need for this to hurt more than it has to. If you do as you're told, you might even survive.'

In that moment I would have committed myself to whichever deity would reveal to me even the smallest body of water. But there was nothing, not even a puddle. Water was my element – a place of safety and the friend I knew I could rely on. But there was just grass, and dirt, and stone.

You're a bloody sorceress, Viviane. It was my own thought, but the words sounded an awful lot like Morgan. So much so that I almost laughed; the ridiculousness of which snapped me out of my fear-induced suspension. I was a sorceress, I reminded myself. I still had power.

Merlin meanwhile was casually strolling towards me, not an ounce of doubt in his demeanour. It infuriated me. I wished the ground would just swallow him up. Take him away where I'd never have to see or hear him again. As soon as the idea had come into my mind, I couldn't let it go. Maybe, just maybe, it wasn't an unreasonable wish – if only I could make it true for myself.

I felt it first, and then I saw it, the earth crumbling at Merlin's feet. My anger and determination were travelling through every part of me, down to my feet and through the ground until it shook the soil beneath the sorcerer. *Focus, Viviane.* I felt a surge of excitement when Merlin tripped and stumbled on the uneven ground, his right foot catching on the hole that had opened beneath it and bringing him to one knee. It might just be enough.

At least, that's what I thought until Merlin let out a sharp bark of laughter and slammed his empty hand to the ground, crushing the grass beside his fallen knee. Suddenly my accomplishment seemed minuscule as cracks began to spread out across the earth, radiating from Merlin's touch. The ground beneath me trembled and before I knew it crumbled beneath my feet, sending me flailing backwards on to the upturned soil, a newly exposed, jagged rock tearing through the side of my dress.

Merlin had risen to his feet. 'This is my place,' he laughed cruelly, opening his arms wide to indicate the towering stones that surrounded us.

I tried to scramble backwards, only to realize I had fallen awkwardly, my right leg collapsing at an angle that caused me excruciating pain when I moved.

'Oh, Viviane, what a disappointment you've turned out to be. A few compliments and words of encouragement and you think you're strong enough to take me on. I, who have more decades of magic behind me than you can ever imagine. I, who am the son of a god.' The calm and collected Merlin I was used to was gone – replaced instead by a wild man, inflamed by his own arrogance.

'Morgan won't let you get away with hurting me.'

'Don't be so naive, Viviane. You're not the first woman I have brought here.' He turned slowly, arms outstretched. 'Each of these stones is a reminder of my failure. Their bloodlines did not run strong enough, unfortunately. But we carry on.'

'You mean . . .' I felt acid rising in my throat. 'These stones are the women . . .' I trailed off as Merlin began to laugh.

'Such a vivid imagination. I'm not such a cad as all that. They are gravestones, to mark the spot where each woman fell, to honour her sacrifice.'

Honour her sacrifice? Trapped in stone or buried beneath them, more like. This man felt no remorse for the women he had murdered in his quest for power. We were disposable distractions. Convenient tools. Nothing more. And just when I thought my hatred for Merlin couldn't reach any deeper, it did.

He was upon me now and I tried and failed again to drag myself out of his shadow – only managing to turn on to my belly, the pain it caused my leg forcing a tiny scream from my lips. 'No more,' Merlin hissed above me. 'You will be the last.'

He lowered himself to his knees, bearing his weight down on my injured leg. Blackness flashed in front of my vision. He wrapped his hand around my neck and pushed my face into the sparse grass, muffling my screams. I could feel the soil in my nose, in my eyes, taste it in my mouth as tiny rocks scratched my cheeks. I could barely breathe.

I clawed at the earth, desperate to free myself, but Merlin was too strong.

'It's just a little blood, Viviane, don't make a fuss.' His breath was hot against the back of my neck as I felt the icy touch of his blade against my exposed shoulder.

There was no way I could overpower him physically, so I tried to do the only other thing I could think of: I tried to ignore the weight of his body, the searing pain in my leg and the sharp prick of his dagger, and focus on those threads of magic I was so familiar with. The threads that connected my magic to everything around me. I could feel every grain of dirt as if it were a part of my being. In that moment, I was part of the earth itself. The tiny droplets of moisture collected in the pores of the soil. The worms that burrowed passageways underground. And something else. There was also something else. Someone else. It was them. The women who came before me. I could feel them through the soil – the grief, the anger they had left behind them.

I finally knew what I had to do. Instead of trying to rise

up from the ground, I dug my fingers deeper into the soil, pushing past the hard layers of dirt, ignoring my broken nails, and seeking out my companions. I felt stronger, more powerful than ever before, and it was thanks to them, it was because I wasn't alone. Merlin, on the other hand, most certainly was.

'Viviane? What are you doing, little sorceress?' There was an unfamiliar note of fear in his voice for the first time that night.

'I'm giving you what you want.' My mouth was still full of mud, so I had no idea if he heard me or not, but the next second I felt the weight of his body pulled from me and with a bit of effort I was able to turn on to my back once more, my head swimming.

Meanwhile Merlin was bent over beside me, trying and failing to tug his foot, then his leg, free of the earth that was winding its way up his body.

'You little bitch. You think you can use the magic I have performed here against me.'

'This isn't your story, Merlin,' I spat. 'But if you're so desperate to be closer to your father, allow me to assist.'

My entire body felt broken, blood smearing my hands from where the rock and dirt had bit into them, but it was working. I poured everything I had into the earth, every ounce of magic I could access from myself and the land around me, and directed it towards Merlin. Then I felt a searing pain in my side.

Merlin still had his knife; except now it was buried in my flesh, poking at my ribs and forcing bile to rise up in my throat. I screamed, and for a split second I thought I saw a smile flicker across Merlin's face. A grin I returned as he realized it was too late. It didn't matter if he'd stabbed me straight through the heart; the magic had already overwhelmed him, his whole body turning rigid, the expression of terror on his face the last one anyone would ever see of him.

My head fell back to the ground, a fog encroaching on my vision from all sides. Not that it stopped me from observing what I had done. There, where there had once been fourteen standing stones towering over the landscape, there were now fifteen. The newest addition towering over me, mere centimetres from my feet.

It was all too much. My body didn't feel like my own. In a confused haze, I brought my hand to the knife still protruding from my side and pulled it free. I couldn't keep hold of it though, letting it clatter to the ground beside me just inside the range of my vision, and as I lay there staring at the scarlet-coated weapon, the only thought that flashed through my mind was, *Oh, I'm bleeding.*

THIRTY-FIVE

The sun had begun to rise. Its light broke through the stones and reached out to me across the grass. I was so cold. Maybe, if I stretched my fingers just a little, I might even be able to touch it. It was the only thought I could keep hold of; everything else was a jumble, and when I tried to gather the rest of my thoughts they simply spilled back out and got muddled together in the earth.

I'd been outside too long. Where was I? The soft wind wafted straight through my linen dress and pinched at my skin. Where was my cloak? At least the numbness was setting in, the sharp pain in my side fading to a barely perceptible throb. Thirsty, I thought. I should have been worried, but for some reason I was more concerned about the dryness in my throat than the wound in my side. My kingdom for a cup of water. I smiled but my mouth didn't move.

'Viviane? Viviane? Where are you?'

Was that Morgan? What was Morgan doing here? That was definitely her voice. Yet I didn't have to be able to see beyond my immediate vicinity to know she wasn't standing there beside me. Was this a sign I was dying? I suppose the thought should have crossed my mind earlier, but I was just

so exhausted. Now that it had, however, I frowned internally. I didn't want to die. Not now, not yet.

'Viviane!' The cry came again.

'Morgan?' My voice was barely audible to my own ears
but Morgan must have managed to hear it, as her next words
came quickly.

'Viviane, I can hear you, where are you?'

'I'm here?' Wasn't I? My head was spinning and even the
ground beneath me didn't feel solid.

'Help me find you, Viviane.' Morgan's voice was growing desperate but I couldn't tell where it was coming from.

'Merlin,' I offered up as explanation.

'Is he there with you? Where did he take you?'

'Gone. Alone.' Which was true, in a sense. 'Standing stones.'
Each word was an effort but Morgan's voice gave me something to hold on to, to focus on amid the ever-encroaching fog.

'Viviane, you need to help me.' I was familiar enough
with Morgan's voice to understand she was struggling to
hold back her distress even if I couldn't see her. 'I can't bring
you back unless you reach out.' I knew she wasn't referring
to the physical act of stretching out my hand. She wanted
me to reach out to her with my mind, my magic, and I wasn't
sure I could.

'So tired,' I murmured, my mouth having to work to
form the words.

'Please, Viviane, just do this one thing, then I'll be with
you and you can fall asleep in my arms. I promise.'

That did sound better than falling asleep alone, atop the
dirt and crushed grass, surrounded by memories of Merlin
and dead women. So I focused on the idea of Morgan, her

arms wrapping around me, melting into her warm embrace. I pictured her face on the back of my eyelids, grinning down at me, leaning in for a kiss. I'd opened a door once before. If I could do it again, now was the time. I just needed to focus on where I wanted to be: with Morgan.

My slumber was a disturbed one. Repeatedly fading in and out of consciousness. Occasionally catching snippets of indistinct chatter going on around me. Who the voices belonged to, or where they had brought me, I couldn't be sure, but there was one thing I knew with certainty: Morgan was by my side the entire time. Even when I was unaware of anything else, I could feel her hand in mine, squeezing it tightly like she wanted to be sure I knew she was there. And it kept me fighting.

I'd had some sense of how bad my injuries were when I was lying beneath the standing stones, struggling to stay awake. I had felt the knife slash wildly at my skin, slicing through flesh to the vital organs beneath. But so numb was I from the exertion of my magic, it had almost been as though it was all happening to someone else. Now I knew it had been me. My whole body ached like it had never ached before, and there was a dull throb in my side. Still, I was almost grateful for that pain because it could only mean one thing: I was alive.

'Viviane?' Morgan's voice sounded husky and uncertain. 'You're awake!'

I blinked once, twice, a third time for good luck. 'I think so?' Everything certainly felt fuzzier than usual, a pounding pressure pushing down on my temples, but yes, I was awake.

Morgan threw herself on top of me, only to immediately jerk away again. 'Shit, Viviane, sorry. I need to be more gentle, you're still mending.' She brought a hand to my brow and gently tucked a few errant strands of hair behind my ear.

'Don't be silly, it's all right.' I started to sit up but stopped when I tried to rise too quickly and a sharp pain shot across my forehead. I groaned, lying back down. I definitely still had some mending to do.

Nor was I the only one a little worse for wear. Morgan looked pale and dishevelled beneath the dim light, although thankfully unharmed. Gods, it was good to see her.

'You did so well, love. I couldn't have brought you here alone.' Morgan's smile was soft and adoring.

'Yeah, well, I couldn't have got here alone. Where is *here* exactly?' Morgan used her arms to gently lift me into a seated position and now I could fully take in my surroundings. I didn't recognize the room we occupied, but it was small and luxurious. At first I thought the walls were built from thick logs of wood until I traced them up to the ceiling and realized the tapered branches curled and twined around each other to form a canopy above us, interspersed with verdant foliage – these trees were very much alive.

'Diana's bedroom, I believe . . . she's something else, isn't she?'

I chuckled softly. That was an understatement. 'What about Guin and Lancelot? Where are they? Are they all right?'

'Oh, fine. Guin is set on moving into a nunnery and Lancelot is a little mopey, but what can you expect? He's still planning to head back to Benoic for a while at least, but he wanted to wait until you'd woken up before he left.'

I nodded. 'Good, he'll be safer in Armorica, that was always our intention.' Then I realized who I'd forgotten. 'And Arthur?'

'He's on the mend. Turns out I can be quite useful with a few herbs and a bit of magic.' Morgan shrugged, playing down what she'd accomplished. 'But we're assuming Lancelot was the subject of Merlin's vision.'

'What do you mean?'

'I suppose I've been thinking. Although I think we did the right thing, we can't be sure Lancelot was the baby who would threaten Arthur's reign.'

'He did end his marriage,' I pointed out and Morgan chuckled.

'Still king though, isn't he?' It was my turn to shrug. 'As far as we know, there's another child out there who will one day grow up to come for the throne.'

'So Arthur survives to rule another day.' It was a redundant statement at this point, but I didn't know what else to say.

Morgan smiled. 'He's lucky to have such a wonderful sister.'

I gave a hoarse chuckle. 'I hope he realizes that now.'

Morgan chewed her lip and stared down at me, as if hesitant to speak her next words. 'He's asked me to be his advisor. To take up a seat at his Round Table.'

That I had not been expecting. Not just because there had never been a woman sitting at Uther's table before now. 'Even after everything? Even after we helped Lancelot and Guinevere escape?'

'He's more pragmatic than you give him credit for.'

Morgan grinned down at me, and the expression was so familiar I felt myself soften beneath it. 'He wants to be a good king, he does, he just hasn't always been sure how.' She chewed her bottom lip. 'Maybe he's finally realized I can help.'

I snorted. 'Maybe. What about Merlin?'

'Hmm, I don't think Arthur was particularly impressed when he realized his so-called court sorcerer had abandoned him in his time of need.' Morgan gave me a gentle poke in the side where, the last I could remember, there had been a deep gouge, only now that I was paying attention it seemed it was no longer there. 'I need to ask you about that, actually. It's clear he came after you, but where is he now? Should I expect him to show back up in Camelot any day now?'

I shook my head. 'No, you definitely don't need to worry about that. But I think I need something to drink before I can explain properly, I'm so damn thirsty.'

'Oh, that's been covered.' Morgan gestured to the nearby table, which I now realized was piled high with brightly coloured baskets of food and, to my relief, a gigantic jug of something that looked an awful lot like water.

'Give that here.' I made a grabbing gesture, causing Morgan to laugh. Carefully, she poured the water into a nearby cup and handed it to me.

'Well?' she asked after I'd taken barely two sips.

'Well what?' Morgan narrowed her eyes at me and I felt myself relax further into my (Diana's) bed. 'He's gone. Trapped in stone.'

'You took a leaf out of my book, then?'

Diana really was far too stealthy for her own good. I

turned slightly to my left and found the other woman standing in the archway of branches that functioned as the room's doorway, a bright smile on her face.

'You're finally awake, I see.' She clapped her hands together. 'I was starting to worry. I'd forgotten how fragile even half-mortals were. You've been asleep for three days now.'

Surprised, I glanced over at Morgan, who nodded. 'I'm not sure I could have healed you by myself. Diana did a lot of the heavy lifting.'

'I'm incredibly grateful to both of you.' I squeezed Morgan's hand. 'I'm impressed, really. You could hardly tell I had a gaping hole in my side a few days ago. In fact, I'm feeling better by the minute. What did you put in this water?'

Diana and Morgan both chuckled.

'You'll be up and about in no time.'

I smiled over at Diana. 'And I'm sure you'll be happy to have your bedroom back when we go home.'

For the first time since I'd met the otherworldly woman an expression of genuine concern seemed to pass across her features at my words. An expression which made my stomach drop.

'What is it?' I asked.

'I'm sorry to tell you, child. Like me, you can no longer reside in the mortal realm.'

What?

'What is that supposed to mean?' Morgan's anger was palpable, yet I just felt confused.

'Your wounds should have been fatal, Viviane. In the mortal world they would have been. I did everything I could to help Morgan, but the magic that healed you is tied to this world. You cannot leave it – not for any stretch of time, at least.'

'But –'

'No!' Morgan's exclamation overtook my own.

'If you don't believe me, then see for yourself.'

THIRTY-SIX

Diana led Morgan and me through a doorway neither of us had used thus far and we found ourselves standing on the edge of a grassy cliff overlooking crashing waves below. I had never been to the sea. I'd never had the chance. For all I gravitated towards the water, where I went and where I lived had always been decided for me. And no one had thought it necessary to take me to the coast. My father had met my mother by the coast, that much I knew. Although perhaps found, or taken from, would be a better choice of words. I would probably never know the truth of their marriage. She'd been gone seventeen years now, and I'd long ago accepted this fact. In that moment, however, I felt a closeness with her I'd never known before and it warmed my very soul. I don't know if Diana had guessed this but she smiled over at me kindly as I clutched Morgan's arm and looked out to sea.

'It's beautiful,' I whispered.

'We should have come sooner.' Morgan bent her head to plant a kiss atop my hair.

For a few minutes we simply stood there, wind in our hair, entirely silent as we listened to the gulls call out to one another. Until I felt it. The searing pain I had experienced once before, when Merlin's knife had sliced through my skin, wracked my body, forcing me to double over in surprise. It didn't disappear after a second, however, but almost seemed to get worse. I could no longer hold myself up and the next thing I knew I was on my knees, Morgan's hands clinging to my shoulders.

'Viviane, Viviane!' She screamed my name, but the darkness took me all the same.

For the second time in as many days I found myself swimming back to consciousness beneath the canopy of Diana's bedroom.

'Damn, I've really got to stop doing that.' I rubbed at my throbbing temple with the palm of my hand and looked to my right. Morgan was once again sitting on the edge of the mattress, waiting for me to wake up, and I felt my heart skip a beat at the sight of her.

'It's not funny, Viviane.' That's when I realized she'd been crying. Her voice was hoarse and her eyes red. This time my heart stung like it had been stuck with a thousand tiny needles. It hurt to see Morgan in such pain, and know I was the cause of it.

'I know,' I whispered, stretching out my arms to pull her body into mine. 'None of this is funny. But it's not over either.'

Morgan buried her face in my hair and began to weep once more. Her sobs were hard and fast, her body shaking in my arms. My own tears, meanwhile, fell in silence: tears of acceptance battling tears of outrage.

*

That evening we dined on colourful fruits in shades I didn't know were possible, and sipped on thick honey mead. We listened to Fodor play his flute while an ebony-haired fairy whose name I still did not know sang a song that felt like floating underwater. We listened intently as Diana told us how she had helped her mother birth her own twin brother. It was, by all accounts, magical.

'It's not so bad here, is it?' I nudged Morgan with my shoulder.

'I've been worse places.' The smile she gave me was still full of sadness, however.

The two of us sat slightly apart from the others. The sun now set in the sky, making way for a banquet of twink-ling stars.

'May I join you?' It was Diana.

When I nodded the other woman eased herself to the ground beside me, letting her presence settle upon us before speaking up again.

'I'm sorry it has to be this way, but there is no reason you cannot build a home for yourself here. You've done it once before.'

'What do you mean, before?' I asked, struggling to hide the exhaustion in my voice.

'Your palace exists in this world as well as your own. Morgan could come and go and you would control how the time passed there. That's still an option.'

Permanently make my home beneath the water? Never visit Camelot or any other kingdom again? Should I have been ecstatic? Devastated? I had no idea. But then again, maybe that was the problem. I had spent a lot of time wondering how I *should* feel, and not necessarily figuring out how I *did* feel. So what did I really want?

When I tried to muster up a sense of loss, I found nothing. I couldn't care less about returning to Camelot. The only thing about that place that I'd loved besides Morgan was the lake, and I was pretty sure the otherworld had plenty of those. Nor had I ever really wanted to live in a cottage and make medicines and teas. Those were Morgan's ideas. All I'd ever wanted was to be in charge of my own destiny. Perhaps some would see my current situation as exactly the opposite, but all I could think was I had an opportunity here. An opportunity to live independently for the first time in my life. I had access to a world apart from the one in which I'd grown up. I had a power that kings and queens could only dream of. And all I wanted was to be free.

'Not there.' I shook my head. 'I can't live in the shadow of Camelot forever. I need to build a new home. On my own terms.'

Diana nodded. 'In that case, there's an empty island I think you might like.'

An island? It could be perfect. There was only one thing that concerned me. 'Morgan?' That one word was full of so many questions and I knew she understood. Would she come with me? Would she stay? Would this be something I had to do alone?

While Diana waited patiently, Morgan opened her mouth to respond but no sound came out. She looked lost for words, possibly for the first time since we'd met, and I knew that was my answer.

'It's all right,' I murmured, taking both her hands in my own. 'You don't need to explain. I understand.'

Nevertheless, Morgan shook her head. 'I'm sorry, Viviane, I just can't.' I thought I might even have heard a crack in her voice. 'I'm not ready. I thought I was, but things have changed. Camelot needs me. With Merlin gone, Arthur might actually listen to me. There is so much good I can do in the world yet. I know it.' A single tear slid down her cheek and I stretched across our clasped hands to kiss it away.

I had meant it when I said that I understood, even without her explaining it aloud. And maybe later I would yell and cry some more, but for now I needed Morgan to know that everything was going to be all right.

'Someone has to escort Guin to the nunnery anyway.' Morgan chuckled softly at my words.

'I'll visit though, every chance I get.' She squeezed my fingers tightly in her own. 'Do you trust me?'

'I do.'

'I love you, Viviane.'

'I love you too.'

And I did.

Epilogue

Some time later . . .

She was here. I'd hoped to be waiting on the beach before her boat pulled in, but I'd been too distracted getting everything ready. It was her first visit since I'd made my home on the island and I wanted everything to be perfect.

'It's about time you got here, I've been waiting for what feels like forever.' I ran the final few steps down to the sand and immediately wrapped Morgan up in my arms. 'Welcome to Avalon.' I planted a forceful kiss on her lips, which she returned.

'It's barely been two months.' Morgan grinned back at me when I pulled away.

'Yes, just as I said, forever.'

I leaned in to kiss her again, making this one last longer as I traced her lips with the tip of my tongue before pulling the fuller bottom one into my mouth with my teeth and sucking. Morgan groaned into my mouth, sending a shiver down my spine.

'Maybe you've got a point,' she conceded when I pulled away. 'I'll try not to leave it so long next time.'

'You could always join me here permanently. You know the offer always stands.'

'Maybe one day. For now, Camelot needs me.'

I nodded. I understood. It wasn't my place to push her. All I wanted was to love her. I knew she still thought I'd sacrificed something to come here, but that was the thing. This was exactly where I wanted to be. Really, Morgan and I had never wanted the same things. We simply wanted each other. Now we could have both until one day, in which I saw Morgan growing tired of court and ready to settle down, joining me here in Avalon. In the meantime, we had these moments, these hours and days to look forward to.

'Come on, let me show you around.'

I didn't get a chance to conduct the full tour, however. As soon as we were through the door that led to my bedroom, Morgan had me in her arms again, claiming my mouth in a passionate kiss that left me weak at the knees. Leaning in, I deepened the kiss further while my fingers entwined in the laces of her tunic, tugging them loose. The next moment my own dress was on the floor and I revelled in the sensation of her skin on mine, of the tickle of Morgan's breasts against my own, the pressure of her fingers digging into my waist. Two months was too long. It had made me greedy.

My kisses moved away from her lips and down her neck, tracing along her collarbone with my tongue before dipping lower and taking one nipple in my mouth. I sucked, hard, partly because I knew it would make Morgan's toes curl and partly because I was desperate to make my mark. I wanted Morgan to feel me even when we were apart, because there was going to be a lot of time spent apart in our future. Yet, we could still make the most of the time we did spend together.

Once I was done lavishing both breasts with the appropriate amount of attention, I made to lower myself to my knees before her, but Morgan stopped me. She grabbed me by the elbow, a mischievous smile dancing across her face.

'Wait.'

'What is it?'

'I brought you a present.' To my dismay, Morgan let my arm go and turned away entirely. As I watched on, she headed for her abandoned pack and began rummaging around inside. 'Well, us a present really.' She turned back around, a small jar filled with faintly yellow liquid held in her outstretched hand.

'What is it?' I asked, taking it from her and examining the contents.

'A little bit of this, a little bit of that, some added clove oil for good measure.'

I frowned, removing the stopper and taking a sniff. Cloves was right. 'What's it for?' I doubted it was simply a scented oil.

'Oh Viv, where's your imagination?' It was evidently a rhetorical question as Morgan grabbed the jar with one hand and took my arm with the other, guiding me over to the bed without hesitation.

With a soft but insistent shove, Morgan pushed me on to my back and climbed on top of me, her legs straddling my waist. She was glorious, her raven hair cascading loose around her shoulders, her chest flushed the exact shade of pink she only turned when she was aroused. I stared up at her, enraptured.

'You are beautiful, you know that?'

'Hey, you stole the words right out of my mouth.' I chuckled as I raised a hand and made to tweak one of her nipples just the way she liked it.

Morgan batted my hand away, laughing along with me all the while. 'Focus, Viviane. It'll be worth it. I promise.'

Nodding, I retracted my hand and watched as Morgan dipped one long finger in her mysterious little jar. When she brought the digit away again it glistened with a thick coat of the golden oil. I gazed on as she proceeded to run said finger between the apex of her legs, shivering ever so slightly as she did so. My anticipation building, I waited for her to repeat the motion between my own thighs and was not disappointed. Re-dousing her finger, she trailed the oil through my hair and across my clitoris, lingering at that sensitive spot and drawing repeated circles that made me whimper. As the oil did its work I felt a tingling sensation prickle at my skin and reach inside my core, making the walls of my vagina clench in excitement.

Part of me expected Morgan to tease me with her sharp tongue as I began to wriggle beneath her, but apparently we were done with words. I pushed myself up so I was leaning on my elbows while Morgan shifted her body, lifting her left leg between both of my own. When she lowered herself down so our vulvas came in contact, I fell on to my back and brought my hands to her hips.

I held on tightly as she ground against me, meeting her movements like for like with my own. It was erratic and slightly messy, but I lost myself in the moment, the sensations overwhelming. Our bodies moved together, in desperate tandem, closer in that moment than we'd ever been before, until finally release crashed over us both and I swallowed Morgan's muffled scream with my lips.

Now that was magic.

While I recovered from my own climax, Morgan unhooked our legs and rolled over to flop down beside me.

'Gods, I've missed you.' She sighed contentedly.

'Me too,' I agreed, leaning in to nuzzle her neck. 'So, how has Camelot been in my absence?'

Morgan snorted. 'Oh Viviane, you should hear the rumours.'

'Do I want to know?'

'Well, a lot of people seem to believe that you, Merlin and I got into some sort of sorcerers' altercation' – she wiggled both sets of fingers in the air and I giggled – 'to compete for the position at court, I suppose. A competition which I of course won.'

'Well, naturally.'

'There's even one tale where you're a demoness who bewitched poor, dear Merlin, but I'm pretty sure it was Pelleas who started that one.'

I laughed harder. It was difficult to truly care about gossip when Camelot felt so far away.

'All in all, I think you're beginning to garner quite an air of mystery.'

I snorted. 'I've barely been gone two months.'

'That's gossip for you.' Morgan trailed her hand along my hip . . . comforting.

'He's abolished the death penalty, I thought you might like to know.'

'Arthur, you mean?'

'I think he wanted to grant Guin clemency, but his pride

wouldn't let him. This way he can leave her be without look-ing weak . . . or whatever.'

I nodded. As disappointing as it was that four childhood friends could stray so far from each other, I supposed this was the best outcome for all. And Guin knew, if she ever wanted to, she was welcome to join me here in Avalon: she had my letters as proof. On that note I decided to extricate myself from Morgan's embrace, as difficult as that was, and roll myself from the soft mattress.

'While we're on the topic of Arthur, I've got something for him.' I walked over to the nearby cabinet and withdrew the sword I had stowed within. 'Since I broke his.' I offered the pommel to Morgan.

Morgan accepted the weapon, turning it over in her hands, admiring the weight and slightly uncanny sheen to the metal. 'Did you make this, Viviane?'

'I named it Excalibur.'

'It's beautiful.'

'Thank you.' Outwardly I shrugged, but inside I was beaming with pride. It really was my finest work to date.

'I have to ask though, why? You know you don't owe Arthur anything.'

'What? You don't think I made it out of the kindness of my heart?' I snorted when Morgan raised a sceptical eyebrow. 'Let's just say there's a little magic in it. But it will serve him well, as long as he serves the people of Camelot.'

Morgan gave the sword one last appreciative glance before setting it down carefully on the floor and taking both my hands in hers.

'I'll tell him it's a gift from the lady of the lake.'

Author's Note

Dear Fans of the BBC's *Merlin* (and everyone else),

Please, please don't be mad at me. I too am a big – huge – fan, I swear. I could never have got through writing my master's dissertation without the escapades of Merlin, Arthur and Gwen (even Morgana). But that Merlin has always been pretty far removed from my image of Merlin in the medieval Arthurian romances themselves. That Merlin, who inspired the Merlin in this book, is a complex character, but one of his defining characteristics is the 'seduction' of young women with whom he exchanges magic for sexual favours. Except when I read these episodes it doesn't read like seduction to me; it reads like manipulation, harassment and the abuse of power. In fact, this Merlin reminds me a lot more of another pop-culture figure you might be familiar with: Professor Callahan in *Legally Blonde*. And that's not a Merlin I've often seen represented in modern media. So, that's the Merlin I wrote about here.

But more importantly, this isn't Merlin's story. It's Viviane's – also known as Nymue, Ninianne, and the Lady of the Lake. Viviane is a fascinating character, for she often sits outside of the Arthurian goings-on themselves. She is an observer, an otherworldly woman who turns up when you least expect her, and alternatingly a welcome guest or an interloper. She is not of Camelot, and is therefore not as invested in its business as Arthur or Morgan might seem. But that doesn't make her any less of a significant figure in what we now think of as the Arthurian legends. She is the one who presents Arthur with Excalibur. She is the one who raises Lancelot. She is the one who kills Merlin. And she is also the one who stands beside Morgan le Fay aboard the ship that sails to Avalon. Yet she is, in my mind, woefully overlooked by most modern media.

I contend, however, that the Lady of the Lake, while an elusive character, is a fascinating one, and here I have imagined a version of her story inspired by the medieval Arthurian romances. Of course, this book is fiction and if this subject should come up in a game of Trivial Pursuit there are far better sources to cite in your answer. Still, the tales of King Arthur, Morgan, Merlin, Guinevere, Lancelot and, of course, Viviane have been reimagined for centuries now, and I hope you enjoyed my little rendition. If you'd like to read more of the medieval literature that inspired this tale, might I advise you to check out Sir Thomas Malory's *Le Morte D'Arthur*, Chrétien de Troyes' *Lancelot, the Knight of the Cart* and (although it can be harder to get your hands on) the variously-authored *Vulgate* and *Post-Vulgate Cycles*.

Thanks for reading,

Jean

Acknowledgements

I cannot express how grateful I am to Ruth Atkins and Rebecca Hilsdon at Michael Joseph, as well as my wonderful agent Emily Glenister, for championing me and Viviane from day one. Not to mention their enthusiasm for the sapphic love story between Viv and Morgan. Everything about my experience of writing and editing *The Lady of the Lake* has surpassed the hopes of closeted teenage Jean who dreamed of one day writing novels for someone just like her.

I also have to acknowledge my debt to the 1990s and early 2000s Channel Five weekend line-up – specifically *Xcalibur* (2001–02) and *Xena: Warrior Princess* (1995–2001). This novel would be nothing without you.